HER HUSBAND'S KILLER

An unputdownable psychological thriller
full of breathtaking twists

Please note this book was first published as
Caging the Tiger

MARGARET MURPHY

Revised edition 2020
Joffe Books, London
www.joffebooks.com

**Please join our mailing list for free Kindle
books and new releases.**

www.joffebooks.com

We love to hear from our readers! Please email any
feedback you have to: feedback@joffebooks.com

ISBN 978-1-78931-537-0

For Barbara Melling, whose optimism bolstered me throughout the wilderness years. You are dearly missed, my friend.

O tiger's heart, wrapp'd in a woman's hide!
King Henry VI, Part III, I.iv

CHAPTER 1

He looks peaceful in death. It is as she had imagined it so many times before. His eyes are closed. Once so full of censure, so apt to accuse, at times so piercingly contemptuous. Now, mercifully, all of this is shut out from her, or rather within him, and she will never again feel the heat of his stare. There is no surprise, no fear in the strong muscles of his face, now relaxed, expressionless. So, she had remembered to close his eyes, a practised, gentle stroke of her hand over his face, just as she had released from his grip the sheets, straightening them, folding his hands neatly, one over the other.

Frowning, she puts down her briefcase, eases the bag of shopping onto the bare boards. Something is not right. She studies the scene with detached interest. Afternoon sunlight billows in brief shallow bursts through the open curtain. Spring sunshine, chasing clouds. His body, naked beneath the sheets, lies calm, unmoved by the play of light, peaceful, still warm. His face is tranquil, beautiful as it always had been in repose, his hair, almost black against the white crispness of the sheets seems to catch and flare in the boisterous bursts of sunlight, and she glances anxiously at his face, afraid that the quick movement of light will stir him. She is safe, *for his eyes are closed* — she had not forgotten that. Drained by the

1

effort of concentration, she longs almost to go to the bed and lie beside him but, still frowning, forbids herself. *What is it?*

'Something's not right,' she murmurs.

Ruth will know. She understands the symbolism of dreams, the arcane language. A slight rush of breath — the blood. So much of it. Too much. It has spilled onto the top sheet, red, glistening, not yet congealed. Sunlight flashes onto it with every passing cloud, its coppery smell weights the air. The smell which of late has banished her from the dissection room, a barrier to her presence and another cause for his ill-concealed contempt.

'Helen? What is it?'

The telephone receiver is in her hand. She can't remember how it got there. She is in the hallway and Ruth's voice comes to her again, more urgently, 'Helen, has something happened?'

Helen focuses on three bright drops of crimson spilling onto the floor as clouds part momentarily and sun bursts, sudden and hot, through the stained glass of the front door. 'It's not right,' she repeats, as if that explains everything.

CHAPTER 2

Jack Nelson's amber eyes took in the scene. A little, dark-haired woman sat at the corner of the scrubbed pine kitchen table at the centre of the tableau of three, her head drooping, hair falling onto her face, hiding most of it. She was shaking her head at something the other woman was saying. The second woman bent over her, a tall lean blond, firmly in control, she seemed to be offering advice. She had noticed him come into the room but ignored him and continued talking in a low murmur to the dark-haired woman. A little off to one side a man stood, apparently trying not to listen to what was being said. He straightened up and stepped towards Nelson, introducing himself as DS Hackett. The new guy. An import from Warrington. Tall enough and beefy, but ginger haired. In Nelson's estimation that was a serious impediment; to Nelson, ginger hair was an irrefutable mark of weakness. He nodded to Hackett, barely glancing away from the two women, sliding his eyes over them as if searching for something.

'Mrs Wilkinson?' he said at last, and the smaller woman looked up. Nice eyes. Blue. Not showing much at the moment except bewilderment, but eyes that could betray her, given time.

3

'*Doctor.*'

For a few seconds Nelson let his eyes rest on the professor's wife, on her pretty oval face and small, slightly pouting mouth, then her head drooped again, and she seemed to have forgotten him. He turned slowly to look at the second woman, raising both eyebrows in an ironical twist.

The blonde woman rose to her full height, poised, pausing to notice his wet raincoat and dripping hair before repeating, 'It's *Doctor* Wilkinson.'

'And you are?' Nelson thought he saw a spark of humour kindle around the heavy-lidded eyes. A shade or two lighter than Dr Wilkinson's, they gave out conflicting signals: impatient intelligence and bored indolence.

'Ruth Marks,' she said. Then, '*Doctor* Marks.'

'Detective Inspector Nelson,' he said, showing his warrant card perfunctorily. 'Now we've got the formalities out of the way, perhaps you could tell us what happened, Dr Wilkinson.'

Her head rose and he caught a glimpse of anxiety in her large blue eyes and a flash of white teeth as she prepared to answer.

'Helen isn't well enough to talk.'

Nelson scowled angrily at Dr Marks. 'You're her GP, are you — *Doctor*?'

'I'm her friend, and it doesn't take a medical degree to see that she's in shock.'

He held Dr Marks's gaze for a full half minute, but it seemed the doctor was insusceptible to the smouldering heat of his stare. The wide attractive mouth even curved into the beginnings of a smile, as though, having scrutinized his grizzled features, the rainwater dripping into his eyes and irritating his skin, she had conceived some private joke against him, and Nelson, who was unused to such a level return of his most searing glare, was close to being routed. When the doorbell rang, interrupting their silent tussle, Sergeant Hackett, who had watched the exchange with interest, thought he detected a hint of relief in the inspector's eyes.

The visitor was Dr Wilkinson's GP, Indian or Arab, Nelson guessed, with the unlikely name of Patterson. Ruth Marks had telephoned him. He nodded at the two police officers and then, without asking for permission, led Helen Wilkinson through to a room off the wide hallway. Dr Marks followed them and Nelson, accepting reluctantly that there was nothing he could do until the GP had finished his examination, rounded on Hackett.

'You've let that ruddy woman run the whole show — letting her phone the GP. Allowing her to twitter on to Wilkinson — I don't suppose you know what she said to her? I don't suppose you got any sense out of the wife?'

Hackett eyed his new boss with cool composure. Jack Nelson — nicknamed Jack the Knife — had a reputation which extended far beyond the small patch of Cheshire he had worked since entering the force twenty-five years ago. Some said he had earned the name because he was sharp, clever. Others, who had been at the receiving end of his irascible intolerance of less-than-messianic zeal for the job, said he was called the Knife because he was a back-stabbing bastard who wasn't above giving the blade a final twist after he'd struck it in. Hackett, who had been on the force a good deal longer than his pale, unblemished skin and youthful looks at first indicated, knew that there were reasons for Nelson's behaviour.

'Dr Marks had already made the call when we arrived, sir.' He paused, then added, 'I'm afraid I couldn't get any more sense out of Dr Wilkinson than you did.'

The sergeant's pale green cats' eyes and boy-smooth face showed no outward sign of insolence, but Nelson, who was sensitive to such things, thought he caught a whiff of insubordination. He produced a handkerchief from his pocket and dried his face. 'Talk me through events so far,' he said.

Hackett gave a clear, concise and pointedly unhurried report. 'Dr Marks says she got a call from Dr Wilkinson at four-fifteen. She came straight over. When she found the professor's body, she called us and the GP. We arrived at four forty-five. The police surgeon and SOCOs got here just before you did.'

'Weapon?'

'A knife—'

'I flaming know that, Hackett! There's a few pints of blood spilled over the sheets in the bedroom, and a ruddy great gash in the poor bastard's chest to account for it.'

Nelson had reached the house less than twenty minutes earlier, shaking the water from his raincoat, ill-tempered and breathless from having to walk from the next street where he had been forced to park his car — tourists unwilling to pay the parking fees in the town centre and more bloody tourists booked into the B&Bs which cluttered this end of Chester.

He had stamped dirt onto the mosaic tiling of the vestibule and had tramped more into the threadbare pile of the green-and-blue runner of the hallway. At the bedroom his progress had been halted by the police surgeon and his team. One stab wound. Fatal. Punctured the heart. Fairly recent — one to two hours old. He had been obliged to view the body from the doorway.

'I was about to say,' Hackett resumed, unruffled, still in that warm, measured tone, 'there's a knife missing from the block in the kitchen. A boning knife.'

'How do you know it was a boning knife?'

'Dr Marks told me. The others have been taken away for forensic exam.'

'What time did Dr Wilkinson arrive home?'

'I haven't been able to question her yet, sir.'

Nelson uttered a grunt of disgust. 'I've had enough of this!' He strode through the hallway to the door opposite, through which he had seen Wilkinson and Marks disappear with the GP and was reaching for the handle when the door opened. He gasped, surprised, not by the sudden appearance of the dark-skinned GP, but by the marked contrast between this room and the rest of the house. Even in his foul mood Nelson had been struck by the faded complexion of colour. There was a contrived air of refined dilapidation in the worn blocks of herringbone flooring and the carpets that covered the centre portions of the rooms in miserly, washed-out squares. The walls of the bedroom were painted dove white and there were no paintings. The skirtings were slate-grey — even the curtains were patterned in an indeterminate series of beige and grey stripes. The most vivid colour in the room was the gout of blood splashed immoderately over the fresh white sheets.

The GP stepped back, allowing Nelson into the sitting room. Its colours were vibrant, almost glaring, after the dignified shabbiness of the rest. One wall was hung with a huge abstract in orange, gold and green. Another was decorated with a mural of tropical plants. Bookcases stuffed with books, journals and multicoloured box files ranged from floor to ceiling along one side of the room and a picture window looked out onto a large, walled garden, already thick with primroses and daffodils.

'My patient isn't well enough to answer questions, Inspector,' the doctor said, taking possession of the situation, and with it the woman Nelson needed to interview.

Where have I heard that before? Nelson thought. The doctor looked ill at ease. Nelson guessed this was his first appointment. Young doctor, eager to impress, to establish himself, and since he was already on the university health care listing, he had apparently taken his first few steps up the ladder of professional success. Not a bad placement. He knew about positive discrimination rules and, glancing back at the handsome and athletic GP, wondered if it applied to mixed race.

The professor's wife was lying on her side on a sofa bed set at an angle, facing the picture window. He couldn't tell if her eyes were open, but he sensed from the tension and the careful control of her breathing that she was awake, waiting for him to leave. Well, he wasn't about to make it easy for her.

'We need to talk to Dr Wilkinson as a matter of urgency, Dr Patterson,' he said, with as much civility as he could muster, given the circumstances. From the corner of his eye he could see Ruth Marks watching him, that look of indolent amusement masking an intense scrutiny.

'Tomorrow,' said Patterson. 'You can see she isn't up to questioning just now.'

'Her husband has been murdered. We haven't time to observe social niceties.'

* * *

Dr Patterson looked into the ravaged face of the inspector. His uneven complexion, a barometer of his feelings, had taken on an angry flush. From habit, Patterson made a rapid diagnosis: chronic alcoholism; some degree of liver cirrhosis judging by the slight jaundice, particularly visible around the whites of the eyes; acne rosacea, caused and then exacerbated by the drinking binges — spirits, rather than beer, judging by the gritty edge to Nelson's voice. A more subjective assessment detected a glimmer of incipient madness in the policeman's amber eyes. Patterson was afraid of the inspector and unsure of his ground, but he would not back down. Helen was relying on him. 'I have my patient's welfare to think of,' he said. 'I cannot allow an interview until I have examined her in the morning.'

Nelson glowered from Patterson to Ruth Marks, and Patterson was struck once again by the wild wolf-like tint to the inspector's amber eyes. Then suddenly and unexpectedly, the detective turned and left the room.

* * *

'Has he gone?'

'We're alone now,' Ruth answered. Patterson had followed shortly after the inspector, leaving a prescription, should Helen consent to taking something to help her sleep. Ruth knelt beside her and stroked her hair. Helen watched her silently for some time, deeply troubled; she was struggling with something she wasn't sure she wanted to say and didn't know how to ask. When the words finally came, they sounded somewhere between fear and hope.

'He really is dead, isn't he?'

'Yes,' Ruth said. 'He really is.'

'Oh.' Helen stared past Ruth at the primroses, flattened like tissue paper by the last heavy downpour. 'I thought—'

'What did you think?'

Helen shrugged. What could she tell Ruth? That she had thought this was another of her fantasies, a stage set — her revenge on Edward? Sometimes, as now, she felt a sapping of her energies, as though her mind had limped away from her body, the dissociation of the one from the other acting as a prophylactic, a barrier to the disease she feared was infecting her mind, anaesthetizing the almost physical pain she felt, acting as a balm. Called back to herself, it was often difficult to reassemble the two, to become one again, whole, entire. It was as if her dislocated selves could never quite realign. As a child she'd had an operation to correct a strabismus. For years her mother had taken her on the long trek from Bolton to the children's hospital in Manchester, grinding along on jerky old buses and all, it seemed to her childish perception, to play a game in which she was required to peer through a viewer at two frames; on the left a tiger, fangs bared, on the right a cage. She had to put the tiger in the cage by twisting the knobs on the side of the apparatus. Helen supposed they could tell by the degree of misalignment how much more work needed to be done on her lazy left eye. What had seemed a perfect capture to her might be out by a few centimetres to the normal eye. Was this how she appeared now to Ruth, struggling to superimpose her two disparate selves one on the other, trying to cage the tiger, and failing?

CHAPTER 3

So. It really happened. I really did it, and he really is dead. No dream or illusion. No fantasy. The planning, which had been so pleasurable, such a comfort in its way, had been carried forward, put into effect, just as imagined. The timing was so right! The knife slipping sweetly through the intercostal muscle and into the heart tissue in one smooth, silky motion.

Would I have had the nerve if it weren't for the baby? Nerve? No, that's not the word — it had nothing to do with nerve. Resolution is more like it. Would I have had the resolution to carry the vision through to reality, to take the rehearsal through to finished production? Probably not. But the baby changed everything. I couldn't distance myself anymore.

It was time to act.

CHAPTER 4

The conference room of the department of Zoology and Marine Biology had once been a reading room attached to the chaplaincy. It retained an ecclesiastical aloofness, with its half-panelled walls and mullion windows ornamented by trefoil tracery, but it was not religious respect which curbed the normally confident and assertive spirits of the assembly of academics the morning after Professor Wilkinson's death.

They sat in distinct clusters on the cheap, mustard-yellow foam chairs in the coffee bar. The conference table which occupied the other half of the room, behind fabric-covered screens and potted plants, had been laid with notepads and tumblers; jugs of water had been placed within reach of each setting, but nobody moved to the table, or even glanced in its direction. It was as if it were a source of dread. There was no apparent reason why this should be so: this meeting had been scheduled at the last monthly departmental meeting, but there was a palpable air of anxiety in the room.

The Senate had used the planned gathering to call together the junior departmental members as well as heads of departments, in order to broach the delicate matter of Professor Wilkinson's murder, and the complications it engendered.

David Ainsley had been watching the assembly with the eye of an environmentalist, a role he retreated into when scientific impartiality was less uncomfortable than a more personal involvement. He had seen Tuttle arrive, self-conscious, anxious to hide what was obvious to them all. He had watched the others shuffle from the coffee machine to the chairs, the first establishing a niche for others to colonize. Like attracted like, warning off unwelcome or incompatible approaches with frowns of territorial ferocity. The room smelled of strong coffee and suppressed fear. Mick Tuttle had placed himself next to the coffee machine; it was the nearest chair to the door and also convenient for refills. He did not like attracting attention to himself by making his laborious way from one side of a crowded room to the other. The squelching leather and clinking metallic joints of his callipers embarrassed him as much as they embarrassed others; the noise and the difficulty with which he moved reminded people that he was a cripple — although *cripple* was not a word they would ever use — not to his face. Nevertheless, it was how many of them saw him, and Tuttle didn't want to remind them of his disabilities. He had been among the first to arrive, finding his safe spot, carefully pulling the cuffs of his trousers over the rods and stays on his legs.

'What the bloody hell is *she* doing here?' said Mallory, loud enough for most of the assembly to hear. Mallory was referring to Helen Wilkinson. She had found a seat at the far end of the coffee bar next to Ruth Marks, unaware that her presence had excited such interest. She sipped her coffee from time to time, distracted, staring at the latticework of blurred, buttery-yellow diamonds traced by the play of sunlight through the windows to her left.

* * *

Did he speak? I've been trying to remember — it all happened so fast, slickly, like in a movie — there should have been atmospheric music. I think — I think he smiled, no more, smoothed the white linen, laying

12

one hand palm-down on the still-warm sheet. The air pregnant with
the smell of recent sex. Mouth-drying, faintly repugnant. Irrefutable.

No struggle, no panic. Only a push of breath, hands gripping the sheets, twisting them — shock at the unexpectedness of it. But the knife had been well-honed with every ritualized rehearsal of his carefully planned death, and it pierced dermis, adipose tissue, striated muscle, pericardium, smooth muscle, effortlessly.

Such a small thing, so lightweight, the blade slim, elegant in its way, marked by a thousand tiny striations, sharpened and resharpened in preparation for its work. Strange how one can develop a regard, almost an affection, for one's tools — at least if they give good service.

Like a burst balloon, he seemed to collapse in on himself. A failure of pressure. He was dead in seconds. It was humane, almost painless. The small incision, high in his chest, seeping gouts of bright crimson summoned an image of the crucified Christ.

* * *

David Ainsley turned to look at Mallory. He had the grey skin and bad temper of a convalescent. Tufty eyebrows overhung piercing black eyes and his face wore the jowly folds of a fat man thinned by age and poor digestion. His following had been taken in by his blunt irascibility, they hoped that he would say things which they dared not, and that by association they would be considered forthright and fearless in their opinions. But Mallory seldom thought before he spoke and since his opinions were generally based on malice and prejudice, they were universally ignored. Ainsley despised him.

His questioning Helen Wilkinson's presence had generated a flurry of whispers among his little cohort of malcontents — four zoologists who were more disgruntled than the rest since it seemed likely that the administrative headquarters of the proposed School of Life Sciences would be housed in their comfortable and newly refurbished eighteenth-century buildings, and that those zoologists who survived the reorganization would be moved to the less architecturally pleasing and far noisier red-brick Victorian street frontage. Ainsley eyed the group with undisguised contempt. The junior lecturers fell silent under his disparaging gaze. John Ellis, a postgraduate researcher in the final throes of his doctoral thesis, continued talking; his gesticulations seemed over-elaborate, stagey, to Ainsley's jaundiced eye. Ellis was nervous, he decided. He always talked too much when he was nervous. Feeney, a senior lecturer nearer Dr Mallory's age, sipped his coffee in apparent unconcern, but Ainsley noted the tremor in Feeney's hand, and heard the clatter of his cup on its saucer.

'She should be asked to leave,' Mallory went on.

'Bilious old tosser,' Ainsley murmured through clenched teeth.

Mallory scowled over at him.

'He's probably nervous that Edward discussed his piss-poor performance on the Research Assessment Exercise with wifey,' Julian Rutherford said to Ainsley, stealing a glance at the dreamy profile of Helen Wilkinson. 'It does seem . . . odd, though, Helen being present so soon after—'

'She's as much right to be here as anyone,' said Ainsley, surprising himself as much as the group around him by his defence of Wilkinson's widow. 'Well,' he added, realizing he had sounded too vehement, 'I don't see why people have to mind each other's business.'

'When they have trouble minding their own, you mean?'

Ainsley rounded on Rutherford. 'What's that supposed to mean?'

Rutherford took in the sudden angry flush. Ainsley's fists were clenched, and his clear grey eyes looked somewhat bloodshot this morning. What *had* he been up to last night? Rutherford wondered. 'Only that there are too many busybodies in our caring community,' he said, satisfied that his message had gone home. In the main Rutherford liked Ainsley, but he was prone to a certain smugness which at times he found sickening. He had watched Ainsley analyse the interactions of his colleagues during the past half hour, assessing them as they arrived, evaluating their chances of survival in the reorganization, occasionally flicking his pale-yellow cowlick from his forehead. It wouldn't occur to Ainsley that he, too, may be observed, that his own personal life could be the subject of speculation.

Interesting, isn't it, Rutherford thought, *that Edward, who had all of our lives, or at least our livelihoods in his greasy paw is now gone, the power he wielded so despotically is now meaningless, and what's left of him is already experiencing the destructive force of entropic disorder.*

A movement at the periphery of his vision made Rutherford turn from Ainsley. Smolder stalked across to Mallory and heated words were exchanged, none of which he could hear; Smolder was one of the old school who thought raising one's voice an unforgivable vulgarity. Rutherford glanced over at Helen Wilkinson. She seemed unaware of the argument, which was just as well, since Rutherford suspected that Smolder's attentions would be unwelcome to Dr Wilkinson, no matter how well-meant. Others did notice, however, and there was a sudden pall in the conversation which became a definite silence. A polite cough from the opposite end of the room and all eyes turned to the woman who had appeared from behind the screens near the conference area.

'God,' said Ainsley, 'They've brought in Chambers.' *They* being the Senate, who were now in the uncomfortable position of having to take over the selection (or more accurately, *de*selection) of about a third of the biological sciences staff for redundancy, a distasteful task which they had left, until his untimely demise had made it impossible, to the discretion of Professor Wilkinson.

* * *

Alice Chambers was a woman of indeterminate age. She wore her brown hair in a careless tangle of curls which bounced slightly as she nodded her head when emphasizing a point — something she did frequently and with considerable vigour.

'Now,' she said, leaning forward and balancing on the balls of her feet. 'I know that you will have heard the distressing news of Professor Wilkinson's death—' She nodded on the words *distressing* and *death*. There was a collective intake of breath and Chambers's glance, as comprehensively inclusive as a fish-eye lens, flicked quickly in Helen's direction and then back to the main body of her audience. She took her time, as if taking a mental rollcall. Her eyes protruded slightly, adding to the disconcerting intensity of her stare, and many had difficulty returning it.

'Unfortunately,' she continued, softening the line she had intended to take, in deference to Helen's feelings, 'the Senate has no option but to continue with the schedule as planned. It is by no means an ideal state of affairs, and we would, *of course*' — She nodded once — 'prefer to postpone the selection procedure, but the final staffing matrices *must* be in place before the start of the summer term, so that—' Here she paused and, instead of a nod, gave a little tilt of the head. 'So that everyone is clear as to where they will stand at the new academic year.' She let her eyes rove over the assembly once more. Some became fascinated by the contents of their coffee mugs, others discovered the need to retrieve writing materials from their briefcases. Two people met her gaze directly: Helen Wilkinson, who seemed to be having trouble discerning her meaning, and Ruth Marks, whose expression was a disconcerting mixture of contempt and amusement. 'We have two weeks in which to complete the . . . adjustments,' Chambers concluded.

'If she calls it downsizing or rationalization,' said Ainsley, 'I think I shall do her physical harm.'

Rutherford shot him a look which left him in no doubt that he thought the comment in very bad taste.

Mallory spoke up: 'So you want us to go through with the bloody charade of lectures and seminars?'

Chambers considered. She had not anticipated such a direct involvement so early in the proceedings. She was to have participated directly at the final interview stage, after Professor Wilkinson had made his recommendations. She had left the details to him, and he had told her nothing about lectures and seminars. Would she lose face by openly admitting this, or would openness work in her favour? She chose to repeat the last part of Mallory's question and hope that he would clarify without her really having to admit to her ignorance. 'Lectures and seminars,' she said reflectively.

'If you're worried about time,' said Rutherford, 'We could cut a couple of days by presenting our personal research proposals in a document or paper, to be discussed at the interview stage.'

There was a general murmur of approval.

'Better than having us perform like circus animals for our peers.'

Chambers stared at Mallory, who had made this last statement. She had to admire the man's audacity, drawing attention to himself, after his disastrous showing in the Research Assessment Exercise. Taking her look for disapproval of his criticism of Professor Wilkinson's methods, Mallory stared back with open hostility.

So, Chambers thought, *Wilkinson had expected his colleagues to plead their case before their peers. An exercise in pointless humiliation. Pointless*, she corrected herself, *except for Wilkinson's reputation for vindictiveness.* She glanced over at Helen Wilkinson and wondered, not for the first time, what an intelligent woman had seen in such an overbearing and sadistic man. Helen sighed and took another sip of coffee. It must have been cold by then, but she seemed not to notice, and appeared to be immersed in some internal debate.

* * *

He was flamboyant in his affairs. There was no fun in it without the added piquancy of knowing that those harmed by his casual seductions knew — or at least suspected — what was going on. Edward never passed up an opportunity to humiliate. He went out of his way to engineer encounters, chance meetings, so that he could gloat, fire suspicions, compound the shame.

Well, this was one too many, Edward.

* * *

There was a sudden exclamation from the far side of the room and Miss Chambers drew her gaze reluctantly from the pretty, anguished face. John Ellis had jumped to his feet and skittered off to the coffee dispenser, Helen's eyes following him with the intensity of the distracted. Mallory reached up as he passed, but Ellis shrugged him off. He refilled his coffee cup and turned back to the assembly, who were watching him in silence. They watched, fascinated, as Ellis took two, three steps into the middle of the room and then addressed Helen:

'I don't know why you're looking at *me*,' he hissed. 'Can't you leave me alone?' The academics were divided: the majority were embarrassed by the spectacle, but a few were enjoying themselves hugely and were disappointed when Tuttle stood up from his seat near the machine and laboured over to Ellis. He spoke in a low voice and Ellis blinked fearfully, then fled the room.

His departure triggered a rustling and shuffling as of a starling roost disturbed by a passing owl, then Miss Chambers had their attention once more.

'A fifteen-hundred-word summary of your work, together with ideas for sponsorship or other funding will be quite sufficient,' she said, nodding emphatically and clasping her hands in front of her. 'Shall we say, by the end of the week? In the meantime, heads of departments should, by now, have their accounts and budget requests ready for inspection, so if there are no questions, the rest of you are free to go. HODs or their representatives will convene at the conference table in' — she glanced at her watch — 'ten minutes.'

She stopped on her way to the screened off area. 'I'm so sorry about Edward, Helen.'

Helen looked up, confused. '*Are* you?' she asked. She seemed displaced from what was happening around her. 'Why?'

Alice Chambers blinked, '*Why?* Well, of course,' she said, floundering for the suitable platitudes. 'He was a great scientific mind. He would have headed the new faculty.'

'Oh, of course,' Helen said.

Chambers was rattled; she wasn't sure if Helen was mocking her, but then Helen went on in a tone which expressed the resolution of a genuine bafflement: 'I *see* — it will be difficult to find a replacement at such short notice.'

'No — I didn't mean . . .' What she had meant to do was say a few words of comfort to a woman with whom she had no affinity and even less understanding, about a man she had found deeply unpleasant, and then move on to the business of the day, to fulfil her obligations as an administrator and as a colleague. This bizarre reaction was something she had not expected and did not know how to deal with.

Ruth Marks stepped in to rescue her. 'Helen isn't quite herself this morning, Miss Chambers,' she said. 'She shouldn't really have come.'

'Quite,' said Chambers, with feeling, shaking her curls in disapproval.

'I needed to know what would happen . . . the procedure. If I'm to be made redundant,' Helen said with that dreamy detachment Alice Chambers found so unsettling, 'If I'm to be unemployed I would have to put the house up for sale, look for a new job.'

Miss Chambers's eyebrows shot up. Could the widow really be thinking in terms of her own security of tenure the day after her husband had been murdered? Ruth Marks seemed to read her thoughts. 'You aren't thinking straight, Helen,' she said. 'I'll take you home. Maybe I should call Dr Patterson.'

'Before you do,' Chambers said, remembering the other reason for her detour through to the conference area, 'perhaps you could spare me a few moments.' Her eyes darted around the room.

Ruth tilted her head to one side, looking down at the administrator. 'Okay.' She turned to check on her friends who was frowning at the back of her hand, lost again to reality. Ruth sighed and followed Miss Chambers through to the screened area.

'I'm asking you this because I know I'll get an objective answer.'

'Good opening gambit,' said Ruth, smiling. 'Flattery, wrapped up in a plea for honesty.'

'No flattery, Dr Marks,' said Chambers, unsmiling. 'But, since you are leaving us for pastures new, and would not be involved in the selection procedure, I feel I can rely on you to state things as they are. I assume, from what Dr Mallory said, that Professor Wilkinson had planned to . . . to *require* staff who were seeking re-employment within the new faculty to present their case to the *existing* body of academics?'

Ruth didn't answer immediately. 'How like Edward not to tell you,' she said. 'And how like the Senate not to enquire.' She shot a wicked look at Chambers, who at least had the good grace to seem embarrassed. Ruth shrugged. 'For once in his sorry life, Mallory was right. Distasteful idea, isn't it?' The ambiguity was wasted on Miss Chambers whose only interest was a direct answer to her question. Ruth sighed. 'Edward called everyone in yesterday morning, told them they would have to present a lecture to their colleagues and conduct a plenary session. Full attendance compulsory. A secret vote to follow each presentation. So, our distinguished team of academics were expected to plead for re-employment to the very people they would put out of a job if they were to succeed in their persuasion.'

Miss Chambers' thin lips disappeared to almost nothing. 'You, no doubt, were exempt from these — proceedings.'

Ruth was gratified that the administrator was finding it hard to suppress her feelings of distaste. She smiled tightly. 'But he did give me the right to vote. Between you and me,

I think Ed had already made up his mind exactly what recommendations he would make to the Senate. But Edward liked to rule by division. You'll find few people who actually trust one another in the departments you're seeking to axe, Miss Chambers.' She listened for a few minutes with half an ear to Alice Chambers's explanations of rationalization and projected student numbers, the difficulties of high levels of supervision and equipment costs in practical science subjects, per capita allowances and sponsorship.

'Some of the departments made a very poor showing in the Research Assessment Exercise,' Miss Chambers explained. 'Government funding will be cut by quite significant amounts as a result. We *must* rationalize staff numbers in order to balance the budget as well as looking to the future and ensuring at least a level three ranking at the next assessment.'

'Universities used to be about academic rigour,' Ruth said when she had heard enough. 'Not about balancing budgets. Scientists used to be able to research without having to justify their interests in terms of commercial applications and the need to compile a tick list of recent publications. And what about staff who are excellent teachers? Can't we recognize their contribution?'

Miss Chambers pursed her lips. 'It's heart-warming to see such loyalty, Dr Marks—'

Ruth laughed. 'I hate to disillusion you, Miss Chambers, it's a quaint notion and all that, but I'm not talking about Mallory. He's a lazy, dried-up old prune who thought he could wing it for the next five years till retirement. I'm talking about the poor bastards who have to cram in lectures and tutorials and seminars and marking — and with groups three times the size I taught when I first came into university teaching.'

'*Efficiency*' — Miss Chambers nodded emphatically — 'is considered a dirty word in some quarters.'

'This isn't efficiency. Surely you must see that? Driving people to the edge isn't efficiency. We're not machines. We can't be driven to exhaustion and still be expected to have the creative inspiration to provide the research and the papers required by your criteria for grading. I'd like to know how much weighting you'd give to Dr X, brown-nosing for a research grant, compared with Dr Y, say, coming up with a new perspective on a research area. Knowledge used to be considered a worthy goal. It was our job to ask the profound questions. Corny, isn't it? Embarrassing almost. But no more embarrassing, I can assure you, Miss Chambers, than grubbing for sponsorship, cap — or should I say mortarboard? — in hand. We spend more time grovelling to our sponsors than we do on research or — God forbid — teaching.'

Alice Chambers seemed to think hard before she responded to this. 'I have a certain amount of sympathy with your view, Dr Marks, but we live in the real world.'

'Of academic accountancy—' Ruth broke off. Mallory had arrived. He regarded her with the kind of alarmed concentration her first-year students showed on their first experimentation with electro-stimulation. They knew the animal was dead and couldn't hurt them, but the appearance of life was strangely disturbing, and more were made ill by the twitching of a dead vertebrate limb than by the dissection which preceded it. As her boss, Mallory had good reason to be curious about a junior member of his department — worse, one who no longer had anything to lose — deep in conversation with a senior member of the Senate administration. As an academic approaching sixty who had not published anything of note in five years nor anything *at all* in the last two, he had even greater reason for concern. He had nothing to offer, nothing that would convince the Senate that he should be funded until the next Research Assessment, when he could be safely put out to grass. His reliance of Ellis's crackpot ideas producing anything worthy of submission to the scientific journals proved only how seriously out of touch the man was.

* * *

David Ainsley debated whether to return home and attempt to patch things up with Clara. He had seen Helen Wilkinson leave with the florid, pock-marked policeman and didn't feel up to being questioned himself. He walked out of the zoology buildings and through the gates into the leafy lane at the back. The blustery winds and bursts of sun and showers of the previous day had died down and the morning's brightness had given way to a quiet, sullen greyness. The clouds hung low in opaque folds, unmoving, like fossilized smoke, threatening rain. He turned his collar up and looked first left towards home, then right to his own office in the environmental science building. He decided that he didn't want to patch things up with Clara, just now. He wasn't sure he ever would.

He couldn't pretend to be sorry that Edward was dead; he'd deserved it — David was just sorry that the end had been so quick and clean. And now what? The tabloid press would enjoy finding headlines. It seemed to David there was only one thing they hated more than success, and that was intellectuals. They would find out the sordid details and print them with vulgar relish.

He picked up a few journals and took them to the stacks; they were quiet, most of the first- and second-year students had gone home for the vac, but Ainsley could not concentrate. He found himself in the Horace Shelby coffee bar, a tray in his hand, and a look of slight puzzlement on his face. Renowned across the campus, better by far than the college refectory, although three times as expensive, it served home-baked cakes and biscuits and freshly made sandwiches. Housed in a large basement room of the library, recently refurbished and painted blue and turquoise, it had a light, modern, vaguely Japanese air. The tables were well spaced, and most were vacant, so Ainsley was not in danger of being joined by his colleagues, one or two of whom he could see dotted about the room. He focused with a fierce determination on the chalkboard, scowling ostentatiously as he made his choice. He sat at one of the farthest tables, trying to avoid the eye of any of the academics, but he could not keep his attention from Ruth Marks, who sat with one of her third-year tutees. She seemed to be reading over an essay or some notes. Carelessly slopping her coffee and dropping crumbs over them, she would sit in silence for several minutes at a time, then talk in staccato bursts while the student nodded deferentially, and jotted down notes, darting anxious glances at the rapidly degenerating condition of his precious manuscript.

Ruth happened to look up and smiled over at him. Ainsley looked away, picking up a discarded newspaper as a defensive gesture. The front page bore a picture of Edward Wilkinson, smiling, handsome. He tore the photograph out and carefully shredded it, first into thin strips and then into minuscule bits of dark confetti. He tried telling himself that now he was dead, Edward could not hurt anyone else, but there was no reassurance in the constant repetition. *Edward,* he thought, *would seep like poison into an aquifer, tainting all their lives.*

CHAPTER 5

Ruth found Helen in her office, having spent the last hour looking for her, and being sent from one end of the department to the other by various sightings. She had even sought her friend out at home.

Helen was sitting at her desk, her arms folded, hugging herself. There was a blue tinge to her lips and she had a greyish pallor. Ruth picked up the telephone and dialled through to Patterson's surgery, then she drew up a chair next to Helen and put both hands on her shoulders. Helen flinched, then, looking up at her friend, smiled apologetically.

'I can't stop shaking,' she said.

'I noticed. Where have you *been?*'

Helen glanced anxiously over her shoulder. 'Inspector Nelson—'

'The bastard!' Ruth yelled. Helen jumped and gave a little yelp. 'It's okay,' Ruth reassured her, stroking her shoulder. 'Jesus, he really spooked you, didn't he?'

'I'm sorry. It isn't the police—' Ruth found it difficult to understand Helen because the shaking was so violent her teeth were chattering. 'It's not their fault. It's me.'

Ruth took Helen's hands in hers and stared into the bruised and hollow sockets of her eyes. She hadn't slept much the previous night. Ruth had insisted that Helen stay at her flat, since her own house was still overrun by police; she had woken at five to find Helen in the kitchen, sitting at the table, ghastly pale in the greenish light of the street lamp outside the window, staring at nothing. 'Helen,' she said, 'You kept to our story, didn't you? That we were together most of the afternoon?'

Helen made an effort of concentration. 'I don't know.' She passed a hand over her eyes, pressing at the temples as though it would help her to think straight. 'He kept asking things I — I didn't know what to tell him, Ruth.'

'Oh, Jesus, *no,* Helen!' Ruth grabbed her shoulders tightly and gave her a shake. 'You've got to stop this. You're making them think you did it. It's crazy! You've come through so much and stayed sane. Why let this get to you?'

Helen looked up. 'Let this get to me?' she said. 'My husband has been *murdered.*' Her total bewilderment affected Ruth with unexpected force, a feeling almost of physical pain. How could she have so badly misjudged Helen? Was there more to her reaction than understandable shock?

'Look,' Ruth went on. 'You did *not* kill Edward.' She bent down, trying to make eye contact, but Helen turned her head away and twisted her hands, trying to free herself. Ruth held her fast.

'Let me go, Ruth.'

'Talk to me,' Ruth said. 'Tell me what you're thinking. Tell me what it is that's got you so scared. Better me than that mad-eyed copper.'

Helen continued struggling, but Ruth was strong, and held her.

'All *right!*' she exclaimed, breathlessly, still fighting Ruth, fighting, it seemed, the apathy which had wrapped around her like a straitjacket since she had found Edward. 'Sometimes, I don't just hate Edward for what he did to me. Sometimes I swear I wanted him to suffer like he made me suffer, but not only him—' The effort to control her voice failed entirely and it rose to a scream. 'Sometimes I want to tear the whole *fucking* world apart!'

Ruth moved back, shocked, and Helen gave a short, angry laugh. 'You see it? You see the thing I can't control? It scares you, doesn't it, Ruth? It should do. It should scare you — it scares the hell out of me.' She stopped for a moment, panting. 'It's like I'm two quite different people. One is rational and calm. It takes — took — whatever Edward said or did and barely responded. The other . . .' She paused, thinking. 'The other is murderously *furious* with him. And the really scary thing is that I *wanted* to be the murderer. I have fantasized about it and planned it and done it so many times in my head that I didn't want anyone else to get there first.' There were tears in her eyes now, she was pleading for understanding. 'Do you see, Ruth? Do you see what I'm trying to tell you?'

'And I thought *I* hated the bastard,' Ruth said, lightly, but Helen did not return her smile, and she nodded, dipping her head apologetically. 'All right. I watched him use you, brainwash you, indoctrinate you — Pavlovian conditioning — he rang the bell and you came bounding out of your cage drooling guilt. *There goes the bell — oops! Must be my fault.* Your mother started the job, your religion consolidated it, and Edward, good son-in-law that he was, finished it. If you didn't have anything to blame yourself for, you'd accuse yourself of the sin of pride. I have to say, Jewish guilt never had much of a hold on me — maybe my mother should have tried Catholicism — maybe I wouldn't have turned out so wicked.'

* * *

Inspector Nelson, Helen remembered, had been far less convinced than Ruth of her innocence. He asked questions after question, many of which she missed or could not remember answering. He and the sergeant — Hackett — had set up in Mallory's office. She didn't know where Mallory was, but became preoccupied with the idea that he may return suddenly and demand to know what they were doing. Such inconsequential thoughts had obsessed her since January, and she had often found herself incapable of directing her thoughts to important matters. She caught herself looking around the room, trying to discover evidence that Mallory had been working on his presentation to the interview panel. She supposed there would have to be a panel, now that Edward . . . Her thoughts had trailed off at this point and she had come around a few minutes later to find that Hackett was trying to persuade the inspector to let her go home. She remembered raised voices, but the argument had rumbled like thunder over her head and she had been content to let it.

Hackett had arranged for a patrol car to drop her off at home. The police and crime scene specialists had left and the house was quiet. It seemed somehow bereft in the icy chill of the sullen spring morning. She had stood on the doorstep in the cold, looking up at the window of the bedroom where she had found Edward, and had seen herself, opening the front door, finding him in bed, smelling of another woman's perfume. He had smiled at her and she had gone to him, bent over him, smelling the freshness of the linen she had changed only that morning, and the perfume that was not hers and the spicy smell of his body overlaid with recent sex. She had kissed him, sliding her tongue into his mouth, probing the soft inner surface of his upper lip taking care to avoid his sharp, scrubbed teeth as she slid the knife between his ribs. No more than a flicker, a tease, and then out, and it was done.

She couldn't remember returning to the university, but there, in her own room, she had become aware, gradually, of her surroundings. Of colour and light. A grey, unforgiving light. Rain had begun to spatter the windows and she had watched for some time the random streams of water formed by one droplet merging with another, on and on down the window until it trickled onto the ledge. It was strangely soothing, and she discovered a calmness which was quite unlike the numb feeling of the past day. She turned back to the cosy clutter of her books and notes, the laptop computer standing open next to the PC on her desk. She had been working on her own presentation the previous day; Edward had made it clear that there would be no special concessions for her. She had picked up her notes, not meaning to read them, not having any clear intention in mind. Perhaps it was a simple attempt to connect with something tangible, something comprehensible and safe. Her submission was to be a development of her work on murine leukaemia. Of course, she could not deal with the mice, with their sometimes unpleasant deaths — death of any kind had become too distressing for her — but her cell cultures had brought in some interesting data and several pharmaceutical firms had shown an interest. She was confident she would get sponsorship. Even Edward wouldn't have been able to argue with that. Abruptly, and with a violence which made her drop the typed sheets, she had begun to shake.

'I stood on the pathway under our bedroom window and I remembered it,' Helen said. 'Exactly how I did it, precisely how I felt.'

'You're in shock, Helen,' Ruth said, getting up to answer a knock at the door. 'Tell her, Sanjay.' she said, not bothering with greetings or explanations. 'Tell her she's in shock.'

Sanjay Patterson crossed the room in three strides and knelt beside Helen. 'I'll give you my opinion when I've examined you,' he said, talking directly to Helen. 'You were supposed to be at home. Sergeant Hackett telephoned me. He said he'd sent you home in a police car. He was worried about you.'

'That man's just too *nice* to be a policeman,' Ruth said, flopping into a chair. 'Charming, well-bred, a positive paragon of old-fashioned courtesy. Now, what's your opinion, Doc?'

'BP low, pulse rate up. When did the shaking start?'

'Right after that pustular policeman, Nelson, dragged her in for questioning.'

Patterson shot Ruth a look, silencing her at least momentarily, and said, 'Helen?'

Helen closed her eyes. 'I've had it off and on ever since . . . For the last two months . . . But not as bad as this.'

Patterson took her hand. 'Either,' he said gently, 'you go home, take two of the pills I prescribed and get some sleep, or I book you into the Countess of Chester overnight.'

Helen stared at him in horror. 'I won't go to the hospital,' she said.

He squeezed her hand. 'Then *go home*. You have to remember that you've been through a lot. Not just this, but . . .' Helen looked away and he stopped. He turned to Ruth. 'Will you supervise?'

'Sure, I've one or two things to do in the lab, but it'll only take a few minutes, then I'll drive you home,' Ruth said, 'if that's where you want to go.' She raised both hands to quell Dr Patterson's objections. 'I'm simply suggesting my flat as an alternative.'

Helen sighed. 'I should go home I suppose.' She shook her head to displace the image that was beginning to form of Edward lying on the bed, blood spilling onto the sheets, the knife, made heavy by the weight of guilt, bloody in her hands. 'I don't know what happens next. I mean, will they let me start arranging the funeral?'

Patterson shook his head. 'They're not likely to release the body just yet—'

'Oh God!' Helen's hands flew to her face. 'My parents! If they've heard about this, they'll be frantic.'

'I spoke to them last night,' Ruth said. 'They phoned while you were . . . out of it. Your mother wanted to come over.'

'She can't see me like this!' Helen was suddenly tearful. 'You didn't tell her she should come?'

Ruth and Patterson exchanged a look. 'Helen,' said Ruth, 'Your mother won't expect you to be on top form when your husband has just been murdered.'

Patterson rolled his eyes at the bluntness of the statement.

'Ruth, I can't . . .' Helen looked into Ruth's face and saw that she understood.

'Yeah, yes. Don't worry,' Ruth said. 'I put her off, okay? She said she'd wait until she heard from you today.'

Helen slumped in her chair, hugely relieved. 'I'll phone her when I get home,' she said. Then, to placate Patterson: 'And then I'll take your bloody pills and a few hours of oblivion.'

* * *

The argument between Nelson and Hackett had continued for some time after Helen had left. What enraged Nelson more than anything was the reason he had given way to the sergeant.

Hackett had been restless from the moment he had called Dr Wilkinson into the office they had requisitioned from the head of the zoology department. He had become increasingly tense, kept glancing from the woman to Nelson, then he stood up and paced from the window to the desk and back. Mallory's office was not large; it reminded Nelson of a film set in a black and white B-movie of the nineteen-fifties, cluttered as it was with the kind of artefacts generally used as a visual shorthand for sinister scientific types. An array of rodent skulls of increasing size were lined up along the edge of the shelf opposite the desk, all turned so that the empty eye sockets stared beadily down on the occupant. There were cabinets which seemed to comprise mahogany trays with glass tops. Nelson had taken a glimpse at the top drawer — a carefully pinned out display of different species of a large black beetle; different stages in the life cycle, some with the wing cases splayed open exposing crinkled wings that reminded Nelson incongruously of plastic rain hats his mother used to wear when he was a child. He found the proximity of the shiny black creatures with their hooked legs and huge antennae unnerving. A live tarantula occupied a glass case next to the computer. No doubt it kept Mallory company as he typed up his reports. A human skull sat on the desk — it looked real — with a cigarette clamped between its teeth: evidence of a heavy-handed humour.

The small, airless room was not made for men of Hackett's size and bulk; he stirred the air with his pacing, and Nelson flared his nostrils at the mixed odour of chemical preservatives and dust, the warm, new, plastic smell of the computer and an older, mustier smell, of mouldy books and animal decay.

He had glowered at Hackett, but his sergeant wasn't paying attention, at least not to him. He had asked a few questions of his own, speaking in that imposing bass voice of his. In the confines of this dusty office, it seemed to boom even when he spoke quietly. After a while he had passed a note across the big, buff ink blotter. Nelson had glanced at the note, not really believing the sergeant would have anything helpful to suggest, but willing to give the new boy a fair chance.

You have to let her go, it read. Nelson had screwed the slip into a ball and tossed it into the bin. Hackett had then asked to speak with him in private. He had refused. Hackett had insisted. Nelson had stood up, glaring into the sergeant's pallid face. Strange, how he found those eyes disconcerting. He imagined it was similar to the effect his own amber irises had on people, not realizing that while Hackett's stare was calm, speculative, his own had a frenetic intensity which was truly frightening. He had warned Hackett that he was interfering in the interrogation of a suspect.

'If she's a suspect, take her in, and interview her in compliance with PACE regs. She should have an appropriate adult present.' Hackett added in a whisper, 'She's not making *sense.*'

Dr Wilkinson had retreated into her private world. She had seemed unaware of the row going on over her head. 'She's sick or in shock, or mentally unstable. Surely you can see that?' The emphasis on the *you* was almost indiscernible. Nelson wasn't sure, half an hour later that he hadn't imagined it. *Surely you — you of all people — you who should be an expert in the diagnosis of mental instability.* He had folded. Crumpled. Given in without another word. All on a probably imagined implication. And having let her go, he was now furious.

He had launched himself into a face-saving tirade almost as Helen Wilkinson left, but the sergeant was proving remarkably resilient. If Hackett's skin appeared practically translucent, appearances were deceptive: the man had the hide of an elephant.

'If you ever interfere with my interviewing a suspect again, I'll have your lily-white arse out of here. I'll have you out on the streets knocking on doors and keeping back the sightseers.' Hackett looked like he was considering the advantages of this proposal. 'You're not indispensable, Sergeant. Get that into your thick skull, will you? I won't be undermined by junior ranks.'

'No, sir.' But the look on Hackett's face said he'd do it again. And again. Those bloody eyes! They reminded Nelson of a ginger tom his wife had taken in as a stray. He had booted it off the settee once when he'd caught it licking its backside and dropping fur and spreading God-alone-knew-what diseases all over the place. He never caught it after that one time, but there were always ginger hairs on the Dralon and the sodding cat would be staring down at him from the top of the bookcase, tail twitching, out of reach, out of danger. He was tempted to tell Hackett to piss off back to Warrington or wherever he'd come from. Then he'd seek out a nice, tractable DC, preferably female, who wouldn't mind making the odd brew and typing up his notes for him. But reality asserted itself: they hadn't made 'em that way since the seventies. Nelson grunted in disgust.

'We need to interview some of these lecturers,' he said. 'We're wasting time here.' Everyone not directly involved in the heads of department meeting had scattered when Alice Chambers had dismissed them.

'I could have a chat with Prof Wilkinson's secretary,' Hackett suggested. 'She may know the likely bolt-holes. And I could ask her about this reorganization that's going on.'

'She might also have some background on Wilkinson and his associates,' said Nelson, conceding to the idea reluctantly. 'And talking of background — how's Wright doing with that check on Dr Wilkinson?'

'Nothing on the computer,' Hackett said, 'but I've suggested they do a paper check as well — their computer records only go back as far as nineteen eighty-eight.'

* * *

Mrs Roberts's office was an ante-room to Professor Wilkinson's; a plasterboard wall and a door through to the larger room of which it had once formed part. She was a generous woman, both physically and by disposition, and the cramped quarters in which she found herself seemed all the more stingy when measured against the cloth of her unstinting good nature. She was not tall — five feet seven or so, but her iron-grey hair was extravagantly coiffed into a creation which gave her a couple of extra inches, and she had the kind of padding which takes years of maternity to acquire. She was a solid, comfortable, substantial woman whose generosity extended even to Edward Wilkinson, although Hackett had already developed the conviction that the professor was less than deserving of her loyalty.

'The Research Assessment Exercise — RAE,' Mrs Roberts explained to him in her fruity, rather masculine voice, 'was completed at the end of the last academic year; the reorganization of departments into an umbrella faculty is a result of the assessment.'

'How does the RAE work?' Hackett asked.

'Each department sends in a sheet of information for each member of staff, listing the best four papers they've submitted for publication over the previous five years. Also, details of grants or other funding they've brought in — a very important factor in these lean times, Sergeant.'

'They're given some kind of grading, I take it?'

She nodded. 'By an independent body of specialists, eminent in the relevant field. Each academic is given a rating of one

34

to three — three being the highest and denoting academic work of international importance. The assessors work out an average grade for the department, then compare it across all of the biology departments, so that a ranking may be given, from one to five. Most would feel content with an overall ranking of three.'

'How *content* were the various departments here?' Hackett asked.

Mrs Roberts glanced over his shoulder towards the open door. 'I'd have to check with the Senate before giving out that sort of information,' she said. 'But the result is the proposed merger of several departments and the institution of a "parent" faculty.'

'Which will mean job losses . . .'

She raised both shoulders. 'Inevitable, I'm afraid.'

Hackett asked her to describe Professor Wilkinson's elimination procedure. At first he refused, on the grounds of confidentiality. But he persuaded her that it was defunct, as Miss Chambers's new process had superseded it — something they knew from their latest interviews with staff.

She outlined the professor's requirement that staff present a lecture and research proposals to their peers — all of whom would be fighting to keep their jobs.

'I could see that would make him a few enemies,' Hackett commented. He often found oblique comments far more productive in provoking unguarded responses than direct questions, and Mrs Roberts obliged.

'I hope you're not suggesting that any of the staff would have wished him harm, Sergeant,' she said. 'No matter what Professor Wilkinson was, I'm sure nobody here could ever do such a thing.'

Hackett picked up on the term '*what* the professor was'.

'You didn't approve of his methods?' he asked, hoping to surprise an honest answer from her. He succeeded only in putting her back on her guard.

'I imagine Professor Wilkinson thought it was the best way. Universities are far more competitive than they used to be.'

'Yes, but from what you say these people have been worrying about job security, grants for research and so on for over a year now; that must have a terrible effect on morale.'

'Certainly, this *performance* didn't help.'

Hackett felt he was back on track now, noting the disapproval in her voice — which this time was not aimed at him.

'They must have been dreadfully upset—'

'Well of course—'

'Angry, even.'

'Wouldn't you be? Asked to justify your job, your funding, your research to members of the fraternity who have a vested interest in depriving you of that position, divesting you of your funding and rubbishing your research? Not because the staff here are mean spirited — they are not, I assure you.'

She paused for breath, held it a moment, then, as if deciding honesty was the best policy, she resumed. 'The professor cultivated a climate of interdepartmental competition so fierce that it made even the mildest people desperate.' She stopped and put a hand over her mouth in a curiously childlike gesture. 'I did *not* mean that the way it sounded, Sergeant Hackett,' she said.

He smiled and she narrowed her eyes at him, clearly angry with herself that she had allowed him to lead her into an indiscreet response.

'I'm sorry, Mrs Roberts,' he said. 'I have to ask these questions.' He hesitated, then decided he couldn't descend any lower in her estimation and asked, 'Was anyone more upset — more desperate — than the rest?'

Mrs Roberts's benevolent blue eyes were piercingly cold. 'I do not eavesdrop on the professor's conversations,' she said, letting her tenses slip for the first time.

'I'm not suggesting that you did, but people would have to've made appointments with the professor through you. I suppose they would have to wait in here if they wanted to avoid standing around in the corridor. And you seem to me to be the sort of woman people would confide in.'

'If they did — and I am speaking purely hypothetically — I should certainly not be at liberty to discuss such confidences.'

Hackett sighed. 'Mrs Roberts, I understand your position, really. You are obviously a woman of integrity. But the fact remains that a man has been murdered — your boss, a respected academic — and we need to know anything, *anything at all* which might help us find his killer.'

Mrs Roberts was not a vain woman; she did not respond to his flattery, but he saw doubt flicker over her face and guessed that she was torn between public duty and private allegiance. She fiddled with the notepad on her desk, straightening the coils of the spiral. 'Isn't it more likely that Professor Wilkinson disturbed a burglar or something?' she ventured. 'One reads of people on drugs, schizophrenics and the like—' She murmured something about care in the community.

Hackett was glad Nelson wasn't around to hear that one. He measured the situation carefully and came to a decision. 'There were no signs of a break-in, no indication of a struggle.' He watched Mrs Roberts's reaction carefully. 'I'm telling you this because I want you to understand how important it is that you tell me what you know. And I think you know a good deal more than you've told me. I think Professor Wilkinson knew his attacker.'

Mrs Roberts seemed shaken. She didn't answer immediately but rearranged the writing materials on her desk as though each represented some aspect of what she was about to reveal to him. Hackett waited, suppressing the excitement he always felt when he had hooked an important witness. But Mrs Roberts was not so easily won over.

'They were all upset, Sergeant,' she said, having organized her thoughts. 'You have to appreciate that Professor Wilkinson was . . .' She hesitated, apparently regretting the appearance of disloyalty, but resolving to be perfectly honest, at least in this. 'Edward was a difficult man. He really rather enjoyed having people at his mercy. If I were to give you a list, I should have to say that fifteen of the twenty people he saw in his office yesterday left in tears or furious — or both.'

'Dr Helen Wilkinson,' said Hackett, trying a different tack, 'Did she have to go through the same process as all the rest?'

Mrs Roberts nodded. 'But even if he had exempted her, I think she would have insisted on taking part. Helen wouldn't like anyone to think she had been guaranteed a place next year just because her husband had been appointed to the chair of the new department.'

'That was confirmed, was it? His new status, I mean.'

She blushed a little. 'Not officially, but Professor Wilkinson had told me in confidence that it was merely a matter of administrative protocol.'

'Dr Wilkinson is younger than the professor?' Hackett asked, taking advantage even of this slight imbalance in her equilibrium.

'By ten years.'

'How did they meet?'

'What are you implying?'

Hackett shrugged. 'I'm not implying anything. What did you infer?'

Mrs Roberts raised her eyebrows — the snob in her surprised that a policeman could make the distinction.

'He taught Helen as an undergraduate, but they hadn't seen each other for years. In fact, he didn't recognize her at first. I remember the staff gathering at the start of term—'

'So, he had nothing to do with her appointment here?'

Mrs Roberts threw up her plump hands in a gesture of resignation, then let them fall into her lap. 'You're evidently determined to make nepotism an issue here, Sergeant,' she said.

He dipped his head. 'I'm simply exploring possibilities.'

'Well I don't see what relevance it has to poor Edward's death.'

Hackett raised his eyebrows. *Poor* Edward? What happened to the difficult man who relished the chance to make his subordinates squirm? Was she saying *poor Edward* because she wanted to say poor Helen, but didn't want him to think that Wilkinson's wife had sufficient grievance to murder her husband?

Mrs Roberts rose to her feet, quivering with rage. 'Helen has been through a lot, and I am not about to add to her problems,' she said, apparently reading his thoughts. 'Now, if you'll excuse me, I have an appointment at the Senate offices to discuss my own security of tenure, and I don't want to be late.'

Hackett didn't move immediately. He wasn't quite sure what had caused this sudden and startling flare of anger. Was it his implication that Wilkinson may have known Helen before she came to the university? If he had, then they would be looking at a relationship between lecturer and student. Very improper. And if the professor had done it once, he could do it again.

'What's the matter, Sergeant Hackett?' Mrs Roberts sounded suddenly bitter, too sharp. 'Are you wondering whether *I* had a motive? Well, if it's of any interest, I'm more likely to be put out to grass now than if Edward had become head of the new faculty.' She laughed, an unattractive, dry rattle, like windswept winter leaves, and Hackett was further taken aback. 'Not that he had any special affection for me, but I am used — *was used* — to his little ways, and the idiosyncrasies of his filing system.'

'You should play that to your advantage,' said Hackett, matching her bitterness with sarcasm. 'The new professor will need an interpreter. Someone reliable and sympathetic.'

She stared at him, brimming with dislike. For a moment her resolve held, then he saw, fleetingly, and with regret, hurt in the crystalline blue of Mrs Roberts's eyes.

CHAPTER 6

It's strange how memory works. Ask me to recall an event and my picture of the day is likely to be sketchy; ask me to recall a feeling, and I may be unable to remember even the name of the emotion I might have experienced at a particular time. Emotions are particularly slippery for me — they're . . . I don't know — untrustworthy. Love and hatred have always seemed to me to be so closely allied — it's almost impossible to resolve the two — at least that's what I've found. And memories, like emotions, are so coloured by the mood of the moment. What might have seemed enjoyable, exciting — thrilling perhaps, the day before — becomes tedious, boring, irritatingly dull the next morning when the sheen of newness has gone off it, the exhilaration of noise and laughter no more than an echo in the mind and, let's be honest, sobriety exerts its influence. Of course, the converse is true — awful events can develop a kind of nostalgic charm given time and if a mellow mood takes me. But once in a while something happens which triggers a flashback that is so close to the real thing it's like time travel — like being transported back through time to the exact moment and setting it has evoked — except in these semi-hallucinations I am the age I was when it first happened. Whatever 'it' happens to be. Maybe only a gang of kids playing tick in the street, their voices rupturing the night air, their shouts making puffs of vapour, like Indian smoke signals, and me in the background, watching, disdainful. The trigger depends on the memory. Sometimes it's a tune, an old song, 10cc, The Police — one of the old bands; or it may be a particular tone or quality of light. More often it's a smell. I can never quite get over the evocative power of smells.

I found a beetle in my bathroom this morning — nothing exotic, only a carabid. It wasn't even a particularly interesting specimen. Rather small and with a dull greenish tinge — commonplace. It was trying to climb up the sides of the bath. It would find a scratch in which it could momentarily gain purchase, then it would slip, scrabbling hopelessly back into the well of the bath. I was transfixed for a time, watching it. Struggle, climb, slip, grip. Struggle, climb, slip, grip.

Something about the way the sun dazzled, honeyed, warm through the glass and a faint whiff of new growth which came in through the open window made me recall a day . . . It must have been a holiday, summer maybe, but the way the light sparkled both silver and gold makes me think that it must have been one of those rare spring days which is almost too hot to bear and you begin to believe that the rest of spring and all through summer will be warm, temperate, golden. I can't have been more than nine years old; all gap teeth and scabby knees. I was playing alone, as was my preference, squatting in the dust at the kerb-side, winding molten tar onto a stick, building a stock which I planned to hide and burn later, and make believe I was a medieval knight.

I was in the lane that ran across the top of the street. Prospect Street stood alone, fields bordering one end and a pitted, pot-holed lane the other. My mother had sent me out to play because I was getting under her feet — an expression I scorned, for it gave the impression that I was a clingy child and although I liked to watch her, I had no real need of her. She was an interesting behavioural model, no more. So, she sent me to play; not with the other children — she had long given up on that idea — just out. Away from her. So that I couldn't watch her with my clever, observant eyes. I was distracted from my torch-making by a movement on the periphery of my vision — a giant black beetle.

The image in my mind's eye was so sharp it made me gasp. I had forgotten it — not just its appearance, but the very fact of its existence and now, standing in my bathroom so many years later, I see it with such clarity I might almost be there. The edges of its thorax and wing cases shimmering violet in the heat haze, a multi-layered metallic sheen of green and black and shades of blue — I see it so clearly. It's at least

41

three centimetres long. Its waxy, articulated limbs make tiny scratchy sounds on the ruined tarmac. I bend down, put my ear to the roadway to hear. Scratch, scratch, scratch. The heat from the tarmac is searing but I keep my face close to the ground, testing my endurance while watching the beetle lumbering on like a clockwork toy, its belly raised on its spindly legs, a fraction above the damaging heat. It moves in a straight line, purposefully, as if it has somewhere to go, reminding me of the hard lads who stalked the high street in town, swinging their arms, with their fists clenched. I watch the beetle's meaningless journey from my giant's perspective, and it stares back with its blank red multifaceted eyes, as plump as berries.

I will it to see me, but it carries on, its ridiculous, inefficient, barbed feet scraping the tarmac. Suddenly I want it to notice me with an urgency that borders on hunger. It continues, clawing forward, as if I don't matter, even though I could do anything I want to it and it couldn't do a thing to stop me.

I purse my lips and blow a sharp puff of wind. It freezes momentarily. Road dust lifts like powder, I can taste the grit on my teeth. The beetle waves its antennae and then the maddening paddling motions begin again. It is too much. I pick it up. It feels like one of those fake insects — joke toys — the kind of plastic they use for spiders and bats and bluebottles in the joke shops. For a moment I wondered whether it was a practical joke. I half expect to hear muffled laughter from the field behind the hedge. I turn it over, looking for the groove where the key fits to wind it up. I look around me while the beetle keeps up its incessant paddling motion, trapped between my thumb and forefinger, a fixed diagonal pattern, like rowers with bad timing. I scream into its mute face:

LOOK AT ME!

It appears to quiver, but then it carries on, as though convinced the pointless movements will eventually set it right. I am close to tears with frustration. I want to crush it, to hear the crack of is outer armour and the wet squelch of its soft inner pulp, but that would be too swift: with the impotent rage of a child I want it to know the power I have; I want it to feel my presence and I want to make it suffer. I take it to the side of the road and build a ring of stones. Then I put the violet-purple beetle in the centre. The stones are big and for a time it circles, probing with its antennae, then it starts climbing, but I had chosen smooth pebbly stones, constructed into a sheer wall, and it keeps slipping back.

The heat is baking, and I sit a small distance away, in the shade of the hawthorn hedge already in leaf and speckled with clustered tumescences of flower buds. It takes half an hour for the beetle to reach the top of the stones.

Do beetles feel triumph?

Smiling, I flicked it lightly with one fingernail and it tumbles into the centre of the arena, onto its back.

Do beetles feel despair?

It kept climbing up and I kept flicking it back.

The sun is like a solid mass, battering down, relentless, fierce, pitiless. I feel like the sun, its power is vested in me.

The big black beetle must have been slowly cooking in its own juices. I remember wondering how long it would go on until it collapsed from exhaustion. After an hour or so I got bored. I thought, why doesn't it just fly away? I knew beetles could fly, so why didn't it just take off? How could I know then that there were beetles as earthbound as humans?

I make an obstacle course for it out of broken bits of hawthorn and blackthorn twigs. The blackthorn I make into a kind of barbed wire perimeter, but the beetle doesn't seem to mind the thorns; in fact, it makes the climbing easier. I am hot and thirsty by now and the game hadn't gone as I had planned. I am angry — furious — with the beetle. I hate it for its brutish stupidity, for its barbed black legs, for its inability to fly, and most of all for its refusal to notice me. I pick it up and impale it on a vicious spike of the blackthorn, finding the soft tissue between its thorax and abdomen.

It minded that all right. It noticed that. I felt weak and strong at the same time. I was trembling, breathless, but the punishment of the beetle had given me power; I had broken through a barrier which had, until that point, prevented me from being what I could be. Even as a nine-year-old, I understood the portentousness of that moment. The beetle's legs flailed, and its antennae waved blindly in a futile attempt to find escape. Avoiding its pincer-like jaws, I broke off each antenna near the head. Strange, I had expected it to scream, but it didn't make a sound. I stuck the twig in the centre of the circle of stones and left the hated creature twitching on its spike, its mechanical legs winding down to eventual stillness.

I went back the next day, but it had gone. The arena was still there but the twig and the beetle had vanished.

I don't know how long I stood watching the beetle in the bath, but when I came to the sun had tracked beyond the corner of the house so that the little beetle now toiled ineffectually in the shadow of the bath rim and only a faint gilding of light remained on the naked tips of the shrubs at the back of the house. It was a small creature, unlike the other I had found. Insignificant.

I picked the bleach bottle up from the windowsill, but it was empty. I reached for the hot tap, but something made me pause and, on impulse, I bent and cupped my hands, scooping up the beetle and releasing it through the window, fanning my fingers like a conjurer releasing a dove. At the instant of release its name flashed into my mind: Carabus nemoralis.

CHAPTER 7

The smell of food and the noise of conversation hit them like a solid mass. Helen actually took a step back.

'God,' Ruth muttered, misinterpreting the action, 'Half the faculty's here.'

Helen stood blinking for a moment. The artificially high pitch of the voices above the clatter of cutlery on plates invoked a vivid recollection of meals in her old high school canteen. 'Cabbage,' she said.

'With custard by the smell,' Ruth said, her nostrils flaring involuntarily. 'Sure you don't want to eat in town?'

'I might be recognized,' said Helen. 'And I've had reporters trailing round after me whenever I set foot outside the house — or the university walls.'

They had come to the college refectory because Helen had declared a sudden ravenous hunger and her fridge at home had been empty. 'A gleaming example of minimalism,' Ruth had commented, dryly, lifting the one solitary yoghurt tub from its lonely position on the middle shelf and checking the date on the lid suspiciously. 'I can't say I approve of your standards of housekeeping.'

'I haven't felt much like eating recently.'

Helen had remembered that she had done some shopping on her way home the previous day but, when Ruth checked, she found the carrier bag of spoiled food on the bedroom floor, where Helen had left it.

'You'd've thought the police would have the sense to pack a few bits of shopping away—' Ruth stopped. 'What?'

Helen was laughing. Real laughter. No hysteria, she just found the whole thing hilariously funny. Ruth was torn between annoyance and relief. 'I'm sorry,' Helen said, making an effort — and failing — to compose herself. 'I just had this image of Inspector Nelson packing away my perishables.' She went back to giggling.

Ruth smirked. She had to admit, the idea of the mad-eyed policeman fussing over Helen's supermarket shopping did create a farcical picture. She reached into the carrier bag, which she still held in her hand. 'Can you account, *Mrs Wilkinson*,' she said, imitating the rasp in Nelson's voice, 'for the bloody kitchen roll in this bag?' She lifted out a dripping twin pack and dropped it into the kitchen bin. The pork joint Helen had bought had thawed and leaked over the entire contents of the bag. Helen paled, but Ruth had found the character of Inspector Nelson, the cadence of his voice, the manner of speech. 'I mean, can you assure me that this pork was outdoor reared? That it was treated with respect, allowed to roam free, to roll in shit? (Green, naturally.) Has it feasted on swill? Organic, of course — and was it humanely *laid to rest*?' She stopped as Helen bolted for the door and tore upstairs to the bathroom. Ruth listened to her retching painfully for some minutes, then she followed her.

'You okay?' she asked, leaning against the door jamb.

Helen pulled herself to her feet, using the bathroom sink for support. 'Great,' she said tightly, flushing the toilet, and then running a sink full of cold water and rinsing her face.

Ruth handed her a towel. 'Sorry,' she mumbled. 'I wasn't thinking. I shouldn't have mentioned the blood.'

'Leave it, will you?' Helen sighed into the silence that followed. 'It doesn't help to talk about it, Ruth.'

46

'How would you know? You've never tried.'

'I'll phone Mum and Dad and then we'll go to the canteen.'

Ruth had been sufficiently chastened to forget to correct Helen. The *refectory* — for this was the only permissible term amongst the established members of the faculty — was hot and the combined smells of boiled mince and over-boiled vegetables, chip fat and sweet puddings, were overpowering. Helen asked for vegetable soup and a bread roll. Ruth's selection took a little longer, and consisted of high fat, high carbohydrate, low-fibre fillers.

'I don't know how you eat so much junk and stay so slim,' Helen remarked.

'Bulimia.'

It was said with no hesitation and in such a matter-of-fact tone that Helen turned, slopping a little of her soup onto the tray. 'You *are* joking?' she asked, unable to read her friend's expression.

'You don't think it's funny?'

'No, I don't.'

Another guilty pang: Ruth more than anyone, knew that for the past three months eating even enough to sustain herself had been an effort of will for Helen.

She turned down the corners of her mouth and raised her shoulders. 'Sorry,' she said, and meant it.

They moved on, edging between tables, looking for a quiet corner. The college rented out the undergraduate accommodation to foreign students during the vacations, and they were all here today, practising their English on each other with an assiduousness that was at once touching and amusing. A few of Helen's third-year students, in to continue their honours project work, smiled up at her as she passed, embarrassed, unsure how to greet her, but anxious to convey their sympathy.

They ended up sharing a table with Mallory and his entourage. Ainsley sat at a table for two, looking so morose that even the foreign students didn't venture to ask if the unoccupied seat was free.

'Either DA isn't getting his nooky or his wife is getting hers away from home,' Ruth said, grinning wickedly, as they took their places.

Mallory gave her a sour look, then turned at a forty-five-degree angle so that she was presented with his shoulder and half his back. Ruth rolled her eyes at Helen. She reached past Mallory for the salt cellar and began shaking the container intemperately over her plate of chips. Grains fell in a flurry on her food, the plate rim, her tray, the table, a few even dusted the cuff of Mallory's ancient tweed jacket. Mallory glared at her over his shoulder and she smiled back sweetly. She ate rapidly, spearing four or five chips on her fork and jamming them into her mouth. While she chewed, she smeared her bread roll liberally with the contents of several of the tiny tubs she had picked up from the dish by the cash register, then she made a sandwich with the remainder of the chips.

Such anger, Helen thought, as she sipped at her soup, trying not to think of it as food, because any acknowledgement at a conscious level would summon the nausea she had suffered since January. Surely Ruth hadn't meant what she said about being bulimic? But you never could tell with Ruth. Anger and hunger were, in a way, synonymous in Ruth's mind. Anger at being delayed in her inevitable progression to the top of the academic tree — and it was inevitable, for Ruth was one of those rare people who can, without hesitation, be called brilliant — and who hunger for the opportunities academic success would provide. Ruth had never been interested in material gain. What she wanted was acclaim, a chance to air her views and expound her theories before an audience of academics who would see her as a scientist, rather than a woman; to research under circumstances of generous funding, using state-of-the-art technology, rather than the five-year-old computer programs and hardware which represented the best St Werburgh's could provide. Helen saw her established as a *grande dame* of science, the sort of woman the media would love to consult because of her unguarded

48

comments, her passion for her subject — and her Oxbridge-sculpted English accent.

Helen admired Ruth for her clearness of purpose, her vision, and was grateful to her as a reliable friend. Although Ruth had despised Edward, he had held a grudging respect for Ruth, a sneaking admiration for her intellectual ability and research skills.

Helen nodded to herself, smiling a little to think that her only friend of whom Edward had approved, had been a woman. This was both ironic and predictable: ironic because Edward believed women intellectually inferior to men; predictable, because he routinely flirted with Helen's women friends. Of all of them, Ruth was the only one who had not been taken in by him. 'Passive immunization,' she had said. 'I saw what happened to you and the others when he got bored. They say a standing prick has no conscience; well you could add that a flattered fanny shows no judgement. I've a natural distrust of flattery — and I've never yet been proved wrong.'

Stirring the cooling soup with her spoon, Helen resolved to try another mouthful, but this was a task to be approached crab-wise, and as a distraction she concentrated on her surroundings. The big, low-ceilinged basement room was clad in tongue-and-groove pine, in a style popular in the sixties. It had oxidized to an almost chestnut orange-red and was overlaid with nicotine and vaporized cooking fat. The university had introduced a no smoking policy eighteen months previously and efforts had been made to remove the stench of cigarettes, but it had seeped into the wood, and on warm days it exhaled into the refectory air. The floor — chequered black-and-white tiles — had its usual grubby tint.

Helen looked around at the faces, familiar and unfamiliar, and felt that strange detachment which had become almost a part of her since the New Year. New Year. Time of hope. New resolutions. She frowned. And what have I resolved? she wondered. Rutherford was there, talking in his studied, courteous manner to a postgraduate researcher — Helen couldn't remember his name — looking like a prep school master instructing an acolyte in the art of conversation. Helen liked Rutherford, but Edward had dismissed him as 'a Cambridge queen'. Mallory and his group buzzed like angry wasps to her left, she studied Mallory's profile for a few minutes, wondering how he came to be so embittered with life. She knew he had little chance of retaining his post in the reorganization — Edward had told her as much — dismissing Mallory as 'lax, lazy, incompetent and entirely without ideas'. In this instance, though she hated to admit it, Edward had probably been right: Mallory had not published anything in the past few years, he was pinning everything on John Ellis, and it was unfortunate for both of them that the PhD student had taken Mallory as a role model. She had not examined Ellis's research closely, of course, since it was not her field, but Edward had shown an ominous interest in his work in the last month, and she knew they had argued on the day Edward had been murdered. Ellis was a skinny, rangy young man, no match physically for Edward, but Edward himself had proved that strength was not needed to wound the heart, only a sharp blade and a steady hand.

Ellis avoided her eye, as all the others did, and Helen, pitying him in a way that perhaps he did not deserve, turned her attention away from the gathering at the table, to the rest of the room. Ainsley, poor David, sat diagonally opposite, hunched over his food like a dangerous animal, barely concealing his desolation. Edward had taken his scalpel to quite another part of David's anatomy than the heart, and now, Helen knew, the entire community, and even the wider world, would get to hear about his emasculation. Did David know about this before Edward's death? Did *she* know about it? If she was honest, she did. She knew about all of them. There was a stage between ignorance and suspicion, a point on the continuum, and she thought David had reached that some time ago. Would he have done anything about it? That depended very much upon what Edward had said to him on Monday morning.

Edward had made so many people miserable, seemed to delight in it, that she had thought that his death would bring, if not happiness, then at least a kind of relief, but the fear that had become so entrenched among the biology staff remained; if anything it seemed heightened by his absence. It was as if they felt safer with Edward because they knew what he would do, and it wasn't always the worst he *could* do, but Alice Chambers and the policemen who had rudely elbowed their way into the academic circle which had until now been a haven for them, these were exotic creatures, capable of objectivity, willing to judge actions and draw conclusions which might prove uncomfortable for some. Edward, on the other hand, was at least predictable in his vindictiveness, and they had known that if they had anything to offer him, then he might be prepared to haggle — though not with money: Edward's was strictly a barter system, based on favours owed and repaid; less traceable than money, but often extremely lucrative. Some staff had appealed directly to her, misunderstanding her influence with her husband, but these individuals were few. Nevertheless, she was tainted by her association with Edward, and generally she felt her colleagues did not trust her.

They were, all of them, aware of her, all strenuously avoiding making their awareness apparent, even to the extent of constraining their vision to parts of the dining hall where she was not. There was a pointedness to their looking away, as one avoids the eyes of a beggar or someone who is disfigured. Helen supposed that was how she must appear to them — disfigured by two tragedies, two bloody deaths.

Blood and screaming, and later, a feverish memory, vivid, like the dreams of delirium — a tiny, lifeless form in her own small hands. Unbearably perfect.

She shook her head, clearing her mind of the memory. Her colleagues could not know that the first loss, the lesser in their minds of the two, had left deeper scars.

Helen returned to the other possibility: that one of these people, these seemingly gentle, unworldly academics could not bring himself to meet her gaze because he had murdered her husband. Helen considered how she felt about this prospect and decided that she bore the killer no ill-will. Her mother would call this wickedness, and of course she would be right.

Helen sighed and she looked up. An involuntary exclamation escaped her. Isaac Smolder had seated himself a couple of tables away and was staring at her. He let his gaze drop to his plate, which was piled with plain salad, and began cutting the lettuce into thin strips, attaching it with meticulous care to his fork, chewing slowly, as if counting the number of mastications before each swallow, eating without enjoyment, as though it was a task which must be performed, tedious, but necessary. Helen studied him trying to establish some tangible reason for her abhorrence of him. A small man, Smolder did not carry a physical threat. He was neatly dressed, as always, in shirt and bow tie. His hair was carefully combed. His hands, which manipulated his knife and fork as though dissecting an interesting specimen, were clean, and the nails were evenly clipped. It was these hands, and the fastidious precision with which he used them, that Helen noticed most particularly. The polished nails and smooth, slightly yellow skin, which was barely wrinkled, even at the knuckles, so tightly was it stretched over the bones. She was struck by an overpowering sense of parsimoniousness, as if Smolder rationed out his ectodermis because he couldn't afford to waste it and had nothing to spare.

She looked away sharply when he caught her eye a second time. Ruth was teasing Mallory and she made an effort to listen.

'It must be a bit of a drag, being booted out of your office by the filth,' she drawled, deliberately choosing terms that Mallory would abhor.

'I volunteered the use of my study,' he answered with sniffy dignity.

'Of course,' Ruth said, pursing her lips, 'It's going to hamper your preparations for the written submission—'

Mallory looked at each of his allies, but each, in turn, looked away. He focused on his soup bowl. 'It's all in hand,' he said, stirring the sludgy brownish liquid.

She smirked and muttered, 'Whose?' Then, in mock sympathy she added, 'Even so, the thought of nasty, brutish coppers polluting your air with all those dropped aitches and glottal stops . . .' The smile broadened to a grin, but Mallory, who refused to meet her eye, did not see it. Then, as if a sudden thought had occurred to her: 'Perhaps the Senate will give you an extension, since you're unable to gain access to your notes—'

Mallory flung down his spoon violently and spat into his napkin. 'I bloody knew it!' he shouted, spluttering, red in the face. 'There's ham in this vegetable soup.' He picked up his bowl and stalked off to the cook who stared blandly at him as he blustered and raged. Heads turned.

'That was uncalled for.' John Ellis, the postgraduate student, who had left the meeting so hurriedly the previous day, had spoken. 'I mean, wasn't it?' he added, suddenly appalled at his own audacity in speaking so plainly.

'Let me guess,' said Ruth, leaning on one hand, and using a slightly flaccid chip as a pointer. 'Since he can't do any useful work on his own submission until the police have finished with his room, and since he has such a breadth of experience in these matters and would *really* like to help you out, and anyway, he's your supervisor and there simply *hasn't* been enough time to talk through exactly what it is you've been doing for the past six months, Dr Mallory thought today might be a good time to go through your thesis with you, right?'

Ellis blushed.

'Trust me. Mallory wouldn't give a shit if you couldn't tell a littoral zone from an erogenous zone.'

'I don't know what you're trying to say—'

Ruth smiled slowly and leaned in to whisper, 'I'll give you a clue: the latter gives far more pleasure than the former.'

The flush spread from Ellis's face, down his neck and up to the roots of his hair.

Ruth jerked back in her chair and took a bite out of the chip, grinning. 'But of course, marine biology isn't your *thing*, is it John? *Drosophila melanogaster* is more your line. And what exactly *have* you been doing? I mean we've all heard the hoo-ha about your theory, if you can call that.' She shrugged. 'It's rather like calling Gaia a hypothesis. Earth as superorganism is a pretty concept, comforting, even. But isn't it more an analogy? A metaphor? And analogies aren't testable; metaphors, no matter how beguiling, are, by definition, literally false.'

'There's a growing body of evidence for co-evolution,' Ellis began, but he was not a natural orator and did not have sufficient knowledge of his subject to provide a confident rebuttal to the counterarguments.

'Co-evolution — that's where the Earth is supposed to be evolving to keep us snug in our little niches, isn't it? Well what about global warming, mass extinction, holes in the ozone layer, the depletion of oceanic fish stocks? Are we supposed to let the great god Gaia sort it all out for us? She doesn't seem to be getting very far — that's the trouble with Gaia — no sense of urgency.'

Feeney, apparently caught between sympathy for Ellis and exasperation at his inability to argue his case, chipped in with, 'The Gaian theorists have a lot in common with conventional science. Their ideas and ours do converge at certain points.'

'There you go again — calling it a theory,' Ruth said, clearly enjoying the debate.

Helen was aware from the general hush from the tables around them that they were drawing an audience.

'The *convergence* you talk about can be explained in terms of good, old-fashioned, testable science — biological and physiological feedback, physical and chemical fact,' Ruth went on. 'Of *course* organisms have an enormous impact on the abiotic environment — climate, soil conditions, recycling of minerals — and, yes, there *are* homeostatic features in the system, but it is not new, Feeney. Gaian protagonists are just tearing off bits of the old ideas that fit their models and Pritt-sticking them to their — their *cause*. I'm afraid I can't call it a theory.'

'Lovelock's models—'

Ruth threw back her head and laughed. 'Models!'

Ellis muttered something about the models giving the right answers, and Ruth went on more kindly: 'Look, it's not that I'm against models — they're useful in their place, and I have to say your mathematical model is *elegant*, John, but does it *mean* anything? In terms of actual biological systems, that is.'

Ellis pulled himself together enough to say with pompous self-importance, 'I'll be publishing an interim report in *Nature*, next month, you'll have to read that.'

'Oh, well!' Ruth exclaimed. 'Mallory will be impressed. Or should I say relieved?' She leaned in again and Ellis looked somewhat alarmed. Lowering her voice to a stage whisper, Ruth went on: 'You know they'll want to see some actual stats, a bit of field data, dope, facts and figures — lab work — that sort of thing. Boring details, but even geniuses have to justify their theories.'

'I've got the data,' Ellis said, affronted. 'Dr Mallory thinks—'

Ruth snorted. 'Dr Mallory *thinks*? — I'd be surprised,' she said. 'Look, I've got nothing against you, John. You may be shamefully naive, but that's hardly a crime.'

Ellis's colour deepened and Helen wanted to rescue him: he was such a boy — inoffensive, eager to please, and rather gawky — she saw that Ruth's comments had really shaken him. He was now blushing so hard his ears had turned red and she could almost feel the heat from him.

'Ruth—' she began, but if her friend was already talking again:

'Look, we've all been there,' Ruth said. 'We know all about supervisors who couldn't give a shit about you, who couldn't even tell you the title of your dissertation or thesis, but they want their name right up there on any published material.'

She looked around the table for acknowledgement, but Helen wasn't about to support her in this. Instead, she focused on the escalating row between the cook and Mallory.

'I'm not incapable, you know,' Ellis said, sounding sulky and upset.

'Nobody's saying you *are*,' Ruth said. 'All I'm suggesting is that you be circumspect in what you claim for your research. You have to get a sense of proportion — you have to adopt a realistic perspective. There's nothing worse than being routed by academics. I know. It's happened to me more than once.'

Helen switched her attention back to the group at her table, relieved that Ruth had moderated her tone. Ellis was looking at her friend as though seeing her for the first time. Some of the colour had begun to fade from his face and he was listening intently. The others around the table had fallen silent and were listening too, and Helen realized that in letting Ruth Marks go, the university was losing not only a brilliant academic, but a galvanising force the faculty.

* * *

Perspective. Now you may have something there. I dreamed, once, of giants crossing a causeway — huge, stilt-legged monsters striding jerkily across a vast expanse of sand and silty water. Blue sky above, mud and puddles of captured sky below.

As I awoke, I remember thinking 'It's all a question of perspective.' It was one of those rare revelatory moments in which a small but significant piece of the jigsaw fits into place with a satisfying click, and it's as if you had always possessed this little bit of wisdom.

Just as figures on the horizon seem taller, elongated by mirage and their relative position in the landscape, my rank must seem vast, monumental to those of lower status, so Edward must have seen me, from his vantage point, as bearer of an important title, his accepted superiority magnifying his tiny intellect, fooling even Edward himself into thinking that he held monstrous power in his hands. Looking down, he considered me small, insignificant, dispensable.

* * *

56

Smolder stood up and carried his tray back to the trolley. 'Your cynicism does you no credit,' he told Ruth quietly, then, without allowing her chance to reply, he left the refectory.

Feeney coughed. 'Yes?' Ruth waited, but Feeney fell to picking up crumbs from the Formica tabletop with the pads of his fingers and rubbing them onto his plate.

'A lot of people are going to be seriously pissed off if you don't deliver, John,' she told Ellis. 'Not just Mallory, not just the Dean of Faculty — there's a whole raft of New Age pot-heads desperate to make your results fit their faith. Publishing contracts hang in the balance, waiting for your results before they can be signed, and advances paid. You hold entire *careers* in your sweaty palm.' She eyed him thoughtfully. 'But you already knew that, didn't you?'

'I think,' said Ellis with stiff dignity, 'my results will satisfy both the academic community *and* the Gaians.'

Ruth laughed. 'Naivety, I can tolerate, but pomposity,' she shook her head, 'that's unforgivable.'

CHAPTER 8

'Are you here for the night, or is this a fleeting visit?' Sheila was standing at the kitchen table, peeling potatoes. Her tone was strained, her blond hair tousled and windblown, and she looked flushed and out of sorts.

'Somewhere between the two.' Terry Hackett knew better than to rush in.

'Well, if you've time, you can pick Lisa up from her play rehearsal. I've only just got started on dinner. Your mother phoned — she said it was urgent. Thought someone was following her after she'd picked up her pension from the post office.'

Hackett felt a sudden stab of fear. 'I'll fetch Lisa and call in on my way back.'

'No need. I went round. I think she was just lonely.'

Before his father's death, six months earlier, Hackett's mother had been an independent, bossy, argumentative, infuriating and loveable woman; now, she was lonely, depressed and anxious, a burden to her family and herself. Without Terry senior to argue with and order about, she seemed to lose interest in life, beyond a morbid taste for real-life crime programmes and a belief that, as a widow, she had become a natural target for every type of villain: burglar, confidence trickster, rapist, drug fiend (she called them this, in preference to the more vulgar expression, 'druggy'), or mugger — it didn't matter — she was afraid of them all.

'I'm sorry, love.'

'She can't help it. But you'll have to get something sorted, Terry. At least she could have her money paid direct into her bank account. We can't go on like this.' She moved her head sharply as he reached to touch her hair.

It was unlike Sheila to be so irritable. What she meant was *I* can't go on like this, since it generally was Sheila who ended up doing the looking after, the running around, the calming down and setting right.

He moved closer and kissed her gently on the forehead. 'It's this bloody murder investigation, else I'd be home more.'

She lifted her shoulder and bent her head, capturing his hand briefly and pressing it to her cheek. 'We haven't even had chance to talk about your new job,' she said. 'What's your boss like?'

'Angry.'

Sheila smiled. Terry was fond of summing people up in a word, on short acquaintance. He wasn't often wrong. 'Best watch him, then.'

'Eyes in the back of my head.' He kissed her on the lips this time, and she returned it, holding her arms wide to protect his clothing from the potato she had been peeling.

'Good-looking bloke, that professor,' she said, gently extricating herself and continuing with the work.

'The boss has taken a dislike to his wife,' Hackett said. 'Thinks she had a hand in it.'

'She wouldn't be the first . . .'

'No.' Hackett picked up the kettle and shook it, then carried it to the sink and added enough water for a brew. 'There's a lad — a DC — bit of a whiz on the computer: Jem Tact. Peculiar name. Funny bloke come to think of it. But he knows his stuff, does Jem. He was sifting through the junk in Prof Wilkinson's office and decided to check the files on his networked PC. Took a bit of doing, but the computer services department eventually came up with the right passwords and such. He started with the most recently updated files. Wilkinson had one called Apocalypse.'

Sheila glanced over her shoulder in question.

'There's a lot of staff expected to lose their jobs in some sort of reshuffle,' Hackett explained. 'The file lists everyone he interviewed on the morning before he was killed.'

'Religious, was he?'

'Not as far as I know, but it looks like he fancied himself for the god-slot. Apocalypse is the bit of the Bible where everyone gets their come-uppance, right?'

'Day of Reckoning,' Sheila agreed. 'Four Horsemen. That sort of thing.'

Hackett threw a couple of teabags into the pot and filled it with boiling water, then stirred the brew thoughtfully.

'So, who's for the chop?' Sheila asked, with her usual perspicacity.

'Suspiciously few,' Hackett said dryly. 'There are fifteen entries and it reads like a fairy tale — everyone lives happily ever after.' Rutherford and Ainsley, whom they had already interviewed, both safe. The faithful Mrs Roberts confirmed to continue as his secretary. Mick Tuttle to have his contract renewed. Helen Wilkinson was listed as 'query promotion', Feeney recommended to continue until retirement in a year and a half, two lab technicians cleared for renewal of contract, ditto the departmental librarian, a group of junior lecturers and a couple of researchers.

'Looks like he was a benign sort of deity, then.'

'Inquiries so far suggest Professor Wilkinson was not a philanthropist.'

'Not *all* inquiries, surely, love,' Sheila corrected.

'Excluding the computer files,' Hackett conceded. He had, by now, poured them both a mug of tea and he sipped from his own, sitting at the kitchen table, dunking a biscuit into the hot brew before continuing. 'The only two we had any doubts about were a Dr Mallory who is definitely out on his ear, and a PhD student called Ellis. There was just one word written under his entry—'

'Which was?'

'SHOP.'

'Oh, dear.'

'That's what we thought, until someone told us it stands for Senate House Overview of Progress. It's a panel the PhD students are referred to periodically. A matter of routine.'

'So, Mr Ellis can breathe a sigh of relief. But what about this other chap?'

'Dr Mallory. Bit embarrassing, really. He's loaned us his office for interviews. Then young Jem discovered the file had last been modified on Tuesday at two p.m., the day *after* Wilkinson was murdered.'

'You need to find out either who changed the file, or what the original entry was,' Sheila said. 'Anyone who gets a better deal on the new version is suspect. Be interesting to see if Dr Mallory's entry has been changed.'

Hackett grinned. Sheila had been a CID officer before she had retired to bring up the kids.

'Don't you give me that indulgent smile, Terence Hackett, I'm not one of your trainees. I take it you've checked his office for backups of the original file?'

Terry made an attempt at seriousness, but he could see that the strain of Sheila's afternoon was wearing off with the intellectual challenge of the puzzle he had set her. 'There weren't any,' he said.

'What about home?'

The smile returned, but only briefly as Sheila threatened him with the wet end of a peeled potato. 'DC Tact has been despatched to search the professor's study. I'm meeting him back at HQ at seven. Speaking of which' — he checked his watch — 'I'd best get off, if I'm to fetch Lisa.'

* * *

Lisa took a few steps at a run when she saw him, then stopped, throwing a furtive glance at her school friends. She turned her back on him and stood in a huddle for a few minutes, engaged in excited chatter and over-loud laughter with the three other girls. Lisa was twelve years old and couldn't wait to be grown up. She had coerced her mother into letting her have her ears pierced on her twelfth birthday, and insisted on wearing large, brightly coloured earrings which flashed in her hair. She had inherited his hair colour and she let it cascade gloriously over her shoulders. She fiddled with it constantly, a kind of preening gesture, and Hackett was uncomfortably aware of the attention it drew from boys her own age and older.

She finished her conversation and sauntered up to him. 'Hi, Dad.'

He bent swiftly and kissed her on the cheek before she had time to react and she scowled up at him. 'You did that deliberately.'

He grinned back. 'It was an accident, your honour.'

'Very funny.' She sulked for a bit in the car, but soon forgot that she was supposed to be cross with him, when he asked her how the rehearsals were going. 'Miss Armitage said the boys'll have to overcome their self-consciousness if they're to be at all convincing. Chris was practically *monotonal* in the balcony scene.'

'Monotonal' was a new word she had learned from her drama teacher, and she had been using every opportunity to try it out over the last few days.

'I mean *totally* crap!'

'There's no need for language like that, young lady.'

Lisa rolled her eyes. 'Oh, Dad, crap isn't a swear word.'

'It's not very nice, either.'

'Not *ladylike* enough for you?'

This was an old theme: expectations of girls and boys being different, double standards. 'It's not a question of you being a girl, I just don't like my children using bad language.'

'You should hear what Daniel says.' She slid him a sideways glance.

Hackett realized suddenly that he hadn't seen Daniel at home. 'Where is he tonight?' he asked.

'How should I know?' She flicked a hank of hair over her shoulder. 'Miss Armitage said I was a natural. She said I carried the scene, but Chris couldn't rely on that on the night. Everyone's got to pull their weight. She said Gita's the best Nurse she's seen in years — a real comic talent, she said. Dad, can Gita stay over tomorrow night, after the rehearsal?'

'No.' He knew Gita and liked her. A big, robust, slightly blowsy girl who was inclined to raucousness and insomnia. 'Not during the week, Lisa. You've homework to do.'

'You let Daniel do whatever he wants, but I can't even invite my friends over.' From ennui to enthusiasm, poise to petulance in seconds, this had become the pattern for Lisa since reaching her twelfth birthday.

'Daniel does not have friends over during the week. You know that.'

'Yeah,' she said, 'But you don't know where he is, do you?'

This was said out of spite, he knew, but it made him uneasy. Daniel had become secretive of late. *Normal*, he told himself. *Entirely normal*. The majority of boys Daniel's age went through a phase of not wanting their parents to interfere, but in a way, he preferred the blatant flouting of his authority that had been the norm for a time, the succession of trendy causes on the periphery of what Hackett was willing to allow as 'normal', or even legal. Just after his fifteenth birthday, they had had to fetch Daniel from a demo against a new housing estate which was due to be constructed on green belt land near their home. It hadn't got as far as an arrest, and Daniel hadn't even got his picture in the local rag; it was embarrassing, but at least they had known where to find him. The more subtle bending of rules, the evasiveness of recent weeks had been more difficult to deal with; he had warned himself against overreaction but could not help running through a mental checklist of Signs and Symptoms.

'Do you know where he is?'

'Per-*lease*, Dad, don't do the Detective Sergeant on me.' She looked out of the passenger window and started humming to herself, a sure sign she was hiding something.

It was almost a relief to return to work. Hackett couldn't take Sheila's easy-going approach to their children's bids for independence, and he thought it was probably just as well that she dealt with them more often than he did. Coward's way out, his conscience told him, but at least this way they got some peace at home, uneasy though it might be at times.

* * *

Jem Tact was a curious combination of intense, nervous energy and other-worldly dreaminess. He had a sensitive, kindly face and was softly spoken, and Hackett suspected that if it weren't for his basketball player height and rugby player breadth, he would have been a target for canteen barracking.

He wasn't strong on details, so Hackett had spent the first five minutes of their meeting bombarding him with questions which Tact seemed to view as a minor irritation, and a diversion from the main item on the agenda, namely, the results of his search. Hackett's questions drew out the following facts: Dr Wilkinson hadn't been keen on a second invasion by the police; she was even less keen on the removal of the disks but had accepted Tact's properly made out receipt with bad grace, and only after an argument. Tact had offered to make a copy of the disk for the good doctor, but she had refused.

'Odd thing, to make all that fuss and then refuse a copy.'

'Mm.' Tact was loading the disk files into the computer on Hackett's desk, and was not really attending to the sergeant's questions.

'Have you seen this already?'

Tact gave him a sideways grin; his eyes remained fixed on the monitor. 'Had to,' he said, then, adopting the manner of a man explaining quantum physics to a two-year-old: 'That disk represents about point oh-oh-one per cent of the total bank of floppies Prof W had at home. That's about a thousand disks,' he added helpfully.

'Thank you, Jem.'

'That's okay.' In his intense mode, Jem was immune to irony. 'Luckily, he had a good filing system.'

'Did—' Hackett found himself talking over Tact's lecture. 'Sorry to interrupt, but did Dr Wilkinson see what's on the disk?'

'Of *course* not. I shut the door.'

Consider yourself dismissed, Hackett thought. 'I hope you were, um, subtle about it,' he said, floundering for the appropriate adjective.

'By name and nature,' Tact had apparently learned, even at his tender age, that it was always best to get the name jokes in yourself. Hackett chuckled obligingly. He'd had enough of 'Terry looks a bit *Hackett* off,' type jibes in the early days to sympathize with the lad.

'These're the alterations,' Tact said, indicating the screen. He'd highlighted the changed items of information by in blue font.

Mrs Roberts had been mistaken — or perhaps she had lied to them –Prof Wilkinson had intended to offer her early retirement. David Ainsley's contract was recommended *not* to be renewed. Mick Tuttle was to be referred to the equal opportunities panel — the recommendation being non-renewal of contract. Feeney was down for early retirement, and Rutherford was a borderline case.

'When was this file last updated?' he asked.

Tact grabbed the mouse and clicked in the file menu, too fast for Hackett to follow exactly what he did. A grey box opened on the screen. Hackett skipped down the list: File name . . . Created . . . Last saved . . .

'That's last Sunday, isn't it?' He leaned over Tact's shoulder, a feat which was only possible because Tact habitually slumped in his chair with his size thirteens sticking out the other side of the desk for people to trip over.

'Yup. Last saved at nine forty-five p.m. on Sunday,' Tact confirmed. 'No revisions. He really wasn't a very nice man, was he Sarge?'

Hackett looked hard at the constable, then deciding that this was Tact's brand of irony, replied, 'Wilkinson had already made up his mind what he was going to do — who he'd recommended they keep and who to sack, and he was going to put them through the interviews, the presentations, the seminars, all that crap — I'd say he was an out and out bastard, Jem.'

* * *

Helen looked out, through the pupil of her own eye and beyond it, saw the slightly blurred aureole of iris and pupil of another, distinct eye. Unexceptional, but for the fact that she was viewing it from within, the spokes of radial muscle curved outward, concave, rather than convex, and their colour was the mud brown of muscles, fibres, blood vessels.

She remembered, as clearly as only dreamers can, of that other time when the tiger had slipped free of its prison and her other self had sought out the man under the streetlight. A flash of silver, orange light reflected on tarry black. His look of terror; his mouth opening to scream, the impact that stopped it.

She woke with a start and lay still for some moments, realizing that she had fallen asleep on the sofa in her front room. Had she killed Edward? She had wanted to, though she realized that didn't necessarily amount to the same thing — and she couldn't always remember what her other self had done in those moments when despair, or blind rage took over.

Helen glanced up. There was a face at the window! A man peering in, his hands cupped to the glass. She screamed and leapt from the sofa to draw the curtains, shouting at the man to go away. Her scream, or the subsequent shouting seemed to trigger a burst of noise at the front of the house and Helen whirled, disorientated by the furious knocking and rattling at the letterbox. Half a dozen — maybe more — voices raised, calling for her to come to the door, cajoling, asking questions, wheedling for just one picture. The pills Sanjay Patterson had given her were still working their sluggish way through her system and she felt adrift, out of touch.

Alone in the house, her instinct was to call Ruth. She edged slowly to the doorway of her sitting room and slipped silently into the hallway, keeping close to the wall, inching towards the telephone. She had slept at home the previous night and Ruth had asked:

'You're not afraid?'

'What's there to be afraid of?'

She had sensed Ruth's smile rather than seen it. 'Nothing,' Ruth had said, 'Nothing at all.'

But they had reckoned without the press.

Ruth arrived ten minutes later, striding up the path as though it were empty. She rang the bell, then whirled suddenly on the unruly flock of reporters crowding behind her. They took a joint step back, cameras still ready, pocket-sized tape recorders thrust forward. She scanned the group and picked on a fresh-faced youth with red hair — a photographer, by the look of his gear; he had the dishevelled look of a boy student, first time away from home. She hooked a finger through the straps of his satchel which hung from his shoulder and drew him closer.

'Now, you know you're getting old,' she said, inviting the collusion of the others, 'when they start sending schoolboys to cover murders.' She gave the lad a friendly shove and turned away from them, enjoying their good-humoured laughter.

Helen let her in, hiding behind the front door from the curious faces. The babble of shouting followed them through the kitchen, where Helen had pulled down the blind. 'What the hell started all of this up again?' she asked.

Ruth dragged a folded copy of the *Chester Recorder* from her coat pocket. A black smudge marked the tan wool of her jacket. 'This,' she said, opening the paper and holding it up for Helen to read.

It was a good picture, almost contemplative in its detached serenity. At first Helen did not recognize the subject: a small woman, bundled up in a dark overcoat, evidently slight; there was an ethereal, almost fey quality about her. Her head was tilted upwards and she seemed to be staring at one of the upstairs windows of the house which formed the backdrop of the photograph. Her hair fell away in one silky sheet from her face, revealing a pretty, rather pale young woman. She seemed to see something beyond the glass, beyond the closed curtains of the upper room.

* * *

Jeff Townley, editor of the *Chester Recorder*, had been more than pleased with the photograph. He had previously been agonizing over a choice between using a blurry snapshot of Helen Wilkinson on a field trip with some students, taken several years previously, her face practically obscured by mizzly rain and the hood of her waterproof jacket, and a formal portrait of her in cap and gown after receiving her doctorate.

'What you got there?' Dermot Molyneux had arrived from Dublin nine months ago and had been on the staff of the *Chester Recorder* for three weeks. He had freelanced for the paper for six months prior to that and Townley still couldn't work out how Molyneux had talked him into signing him up and paying him a salary.

Townley squinted aggressively at the photographer — a habit he'd developed when smoking was the norm, and the norm for him was to have one fag permanently in his mouth and another burning to nothing in the ashtray in his office.

Molyneux edged between Townley and Rick Lazenby, his news editor, a practised, insinuating movement, born of years of filching pictures that his elders and betters had spent hours setting up, and Townley found himself nose to curls with Dermot's auburn mop. 'I know her,' Molyneux said, picking up the studio photograph of Helen in cap and gown.

'You damn well ought to — you were sent to get a picture of her yesterday. Oh — but I'm forgetting myself,' Townley said, ladling on the sarcasm. 'An artist such as yourself needs the right lighting, the ambience, the setting.'

'Well you're right about the ambience,' Molyneux said, refusing to be ruffled. 'But finding the subject was the hard bit, in this case. No — what I mean is I've *seen* her — in the flesh, so to speak. Only I didn't know it was her at the time. She's not much like these shots, you know.' He stopped, listening to the silence, relishing it. For a few seconds the only sound in the room was the gentle rasp of Townley's breathing, then Townley, bracing himself for disappointment he said, 'Tell me you got a picture.'

Dermot Molyneux suppressed a sigh of pleasure, allowing himself — just — the tiniest of smirks. 'I'll tell you anything you like, boss,' he said, 'just so long as it makes you happy.'

Townley looked ready to do murder and Molyneux decided it would be safer to play straight. 'Didn't I look everywhere for the good doctor yesterday, and wasn't she nowhere to be found?'

'Do me a favour and cut the professional Paddy crap,' Townley said. 'What's the bottom line?'

'To tell you the truth, boss, I didn't know it was her. I'd given up on finding her at the university and I was too shitscared to come back with nothing, so I thought I'd do a few spooky shots of the house—'

'I saw them,' Townley interrupted. 'Hackneyed.'

Molyneux shrugged. 'Yeah, well.' His ego didn't bruise easily. 'Wait till you see what else I got.' He rummaged in a battered, brown leather satchel which looked like it had seen service during his school days. He placed three A5-sized black-and-white photographs side by side on the desk.

'Fuck me,' Townley said softly, his tone so caressingly gentle that Molyneux couldn't stop the reply tumbling out of his mouth:

'Well that's an interesting suggestion. Perhaps some other time. And what do you think of the photos?' Townley's stare put him in a spin. He'd gone too far. Blushing, he added, 'I mean, sir, Mr Townley, boss. Oh, feck.'

Lazenby laughed, setting the room reverberating with his barrel-chested ho-ho-hos, and Townley, startled by this sudden reminder that he and Molyneux were not the only people in his office, forgot his annoyance with the Irishman.

'It's a pearl of a picture,' he said, picking up the centre photograph as Molyneux had hoped he would. 'Haunting.'

'Now that's what I thought,' Molyneux said, swivelling his eyes in Townley's direction to gauge his reaction. 'At first, I thought she was just another ghoul, come to see the house, but there was . . . I don't know, there was something about her. That face — it — it's . . . What would you call it?'

'Let your camera do the talking, Dermot, lad.' Townley laughed. 'You're no orator.'

'I'll have you know I've kissed the Blarney Stone,' said Dermot.

'Well it's done your mouth no good, but what an eye! Your pictures could persuade the proverbial simians from the arboretum.' Townley examined them at close quarters. 'It's like one of those holograms — look at it from a different angle and you see something else. What the hell is she thinking?'

Dermot grinned. It was just the impression he'd had when he'd taken the shot. It was the very expressionlessness of her face that made it so compelling; was it sadness, or fear, or a dull rage, or cold contempt? It all depended upon the perspective of the observer.

'We'll have to choose the caption carefully,' Townley said, the same thought having occurred to him.

* * *

Helen took the paper from Ruth and read the caption: '*Dr Wilkinson returns to House of Death.*'

'I didn't even notice him — the photographer,' she said.

'You've been pretty much out of it since it happened,' said Ruth. 'Nice to have you back.'

'Oh, *no!*' Helen had begun to read the article under her picture. There were names, details, more than she had known herself. 'Who gave them this? Can they say these things and get away with it?'

Ruth shrugged. 'Don't they say you can't libel the dead? Anyway, it's true, isn't it? I'd say they've a fairly restrained and dignified style — wait till the tabloids really get their teeth into it — the *Herald* is running a story on Don Juan, the Casanova of St Werburgh's. I think they've rather mixed their analogies, but that's the *Herald* for you. And as for who, take your pick — Edward made enemies like I make jam sandwiches: with flair, with panache, and with the compulsiveness of an addict.'

Helen read on. 'Poor David!'

Ruth snorted. 'David Ainsley can take care of himself. The good thing is it's given the police a few more suspects to keep them busy. Don't look at me like that, Helen,' seeing her disparaging look. 'You were out of your skull for a couple of days. You more or less confessed to the murder of your husband. If it weren't for that nice Sergeant Hackett, Inspector Nelson would have you banged up by now. You should be grateful the press have given him a few more names to think about.'

'And if I *did* do it?' Helen asked, thinking uneasily of her dream.

Ruth groaned. 'If? If? What if Gazza becomes cultural attaché to the European Community? What if I'm awarded the Nobel Prize for my contributions to scientific advancement? Hey, anything's possible — it might happen.'

'Now you're being preposterous,' Helen said angrily.

'Because it *is* preposterous,' Ruth argued. 'The notion of you killing — is beyond ludicrous. You can't bring yourself to cross the threshold into the dissection room because the sight and smell of death appals you. You can't even do the research you used to because you can't face the corpses. You haven't eaten properly in months. You're nauseated by the smell of animal flesh — and you're asking me to believe you stuck a knife in him? Watched him bleed to death?' She shook her head. 'You haven't got it in you. Whoops!' She caught Helen as she buckled at the knees and helped her to a chair.

'I'm sick of this,' said Helen, pale, but rallying. 'I'm sick of feeling so weak. So . . .'

'So eat!' said Ruth, imitating her Jewish mother. 'It's no wonder you're passing out all over the place. All I've seen you eat in two days is a bowl of soup and a bread roll.'

Helen stared at her feet, trying to stave off a cold wave of faintness. 'It still seems — so plausible. Why *shouldn't* I have killed him? He deserved it.'

'Why indeed? But you didn't kill him. Someone else did and then left him for you to find. That wasn't very nice of them.'

Helen stared. 'Not very *nice*?' she echoed. 'You don't object to Edward's murder, but you think it was *impolite* to leave his body for me to find?'

Ruth stared back. 'Do I really need to tell you what a shit your husband had been? I could enumerate his many and varied faults but is that really necessary?'

Helen knew that her husband had been a bully, a serial adulterer and a vicious, social-climbing snob whose ambition far outweighed his talent. Helen didn't need anyone to tell her that most of his acquaintance hated, feared and despised Edward.

They were startled by the telephone ringing. Ruth went to answer it, returning a few moments later, subdued.

'Who was it?'

'One of the tabloids, wanting a comment.'

'How did they get this number?'

'Being ex-directory is scant protection against those jackals.' Ruth sighed. 'You'd best stay at my place for a few days.'

She picked up the newspaper which Helen had discarded on the kitchen table and jammed it back into her pocket. 'Come on, I'll take you there now.'

Helen shook her head. 'I'm staying here,' she said firmly. 'I'm not going to let them drive me from my home.'

Ruth's cool blue eyes searched her friend's face. A trace of amusement flickered at the corners of her mouth. 'Attagirl,' she murmured.

CHAPTER 9

The front door slammed, and the baby jerked awake, instantly screaming. Clara Ainsley groaned. Her eyes were red rimmed from lack of sleep and from crying, her hair, normally so sleek and well groomed, was caught carelessly in a scrunchy and pulled back into a ponytail. It had not been washed in two days and she couldn't bear it on her face. She carried the baby through to the narrow hallway; he was overheated and cranky — he smelled of curdled milk and warm talcum powder. He had thrown up on the clean babygro she'd put on him not half an hour earlier and she was damned if she would change him again. He had kept up an incessant keening for the day and a half that David had been missing; that constant, penetrating baby cry that will not be ignored, as though he knew there was something wrong. It had set her teeth on edge until she had fled to the upper rooms of the house, but his howls had spiralled up the stairwell, and even when she played a CD blaring rock music she imagined she could hear him. She had stood at the head of his cot, screaming back at him but that only made him worse, so finally she had gone out of the house — left him — because she feared that if she went to him she would hurl him from the nursery window to the concrete path below. She even imagined it

— the flight, the sudden, soft thud, the silence. The blessed, longed-for silence.

She had walked to the river and for a while she watched the ducks bobbing frantically on the wind-whipped water. It was bitterly cold, and she had left the house without an overcoat, but she could not go back, could not trust herself near him yet. On the flimsy footbridge over the river she saw a young couple kiss, as she and Edward had kissed so often, but never so publicly. Once, they had found a quiet spot in the park on the other side of the bridge half afraid and half excited by the thrill of indiscretion, the risk of discovery. They had talked, whispered, shared their food and drink, sipping from the same glass, feeding each other morsels, laughing, touching, kissing like teenaged lovers. He had slept, briefly, stretched out on the tartan rug that her mother had given her as a wedding present, and she had teased him, kissing him awake. He had feigned sleep until she had been ready to lose patience and then he had grabbed her and tumbled her to the rug and returned her kiss with all the passion that David had once felt for her. She and Edward had shared something special, precious, to be cherished, and he had wasted it. Whenever she began to regret her actions on that awful day, she only had to think of what he had thrown away . . . She could not have allowed him to treat her as he had treated the others.

She had returned an hour later, calmer, able to pick up the still-screaming baby, able to resist the compulsion to shake him. She shushed him, holding him in the crook of her arm as, one-handed, she mixed him another bottle of milk. He refused it of course, forcing the teat out of his mouth with his tongue in ill-tempered self-spite and arching his hot little body until her arm ached. She walked. Miles and miles of carpet-wearing, back-breaking walking, trying him with the bottle until finally, exhausted, he began to suck and within minutes had fallen asleep. And then the front door had slammed.

David Ainsley looked both haggard and sullen. He was unshaven and his suit and overcoat were badly rumpled.

Clara and David eyed each other, the baby carriage forming a barrier between them. It was an old-fashioned Silver Cross pram in the grand style, too big for the house; soon it would be too small for the baby, but Clara had wanted it and as usual he had given way to her.

'Satisfied?' she asked.

'Far from it.'

'Where've you been?'

'What the hell do you care?'

'I was worried.' The baby had screamed without taking breath since the front door had slammed and she patted his back, thinking *if he doesn't stop soon, he'll choke*, then, with a rush of venom — *I hope he bloody does, then David will see what I've been through these last two days.*

'Thought you'd lost both your men, did you?' David asked.

'For God's sake, David!'

'Sorry — I'm not being terribly *adult* about this, am I?'

Clara thought of Edward, so unlike David, both in appearance and in temperament. David's anger — and she supposed he had a right to be angry — seemed like childish petulance. She could not remember, nor even imagine, Edward being anything less than impressive. His anger had been daunting, his criticism crushing, his arguments bruising to the ego. She wondered again why she had ever married David. The notion of love, or even affection seemed outrageous — this sulking, flop-haired child? She made a conscious effort to imagine how Edward would have handled the situation, to frame the words he would have spoken.

'You can't help yourself, can you?'

'Me? I haven't been carrying on a shabby little affair—'

'There wasn't anything shabby about it!' Clara interrupted, flushing, telling herself it was anger rather than shame; but all the same, remembering their meetings at a motel near Heswall — far enough beyond the Cheshire boundary to remove some of the danger, but not too far for her to make the journey by bus, anonymous enough to be safe, hygienic enough to seem wholesome, even guiltless in its laundered sterility.

He was watching her. 'It was beautiful, then, was it? With him?'

She eyed him coldly. 'Strange you've said nothing until now. You must have known — even you aren't quite so dense.'

'How *dare* you!' he growled. 'Of course I didn't know.'

She snuffed air through her nose, despising his dishonesty. He might not admit it to himself, but he had known, and had let the affair go on, suppressing his uncertainties, his niggling doubts about the excuses she'd made.

'Don't play the wronged husband with me, David, I know you better,' she said.

'Are you going to tell me you did it for us, Clara? Tell me you shagged the boss to keep me in a *job*?' His voice rose to a screech and the baby's cries became frightened, a persistent, staccato bleat.

Clara curled her lip in contempt, looking over the baby's shoulder at him, reminding herself to pat rather than hit. 'Don't sully what we had with your sordid interpretation. It wasn't like that,' she said.

'You'd call it something different, would you? What euphemism would you come up with — "love"? Please don't ask me to believe you were in *love* with that shit!'

'Edward cared about me!' They competed with the rising volume of the baby's screams.

'Like he cared for all of them,' he sneered, 'his students who got themselves laid because it would help their grades or because they were flattered by the attention; the junior lecturers and the secretaries and the technicians.' He looked her up and down. 'The sad succession of women who fell for his good looks and questionable charm.'

He must have seen the sudden awful pang of doubt that shot through her, because he added with a spark of triumph: 'You were only there to bolster his ego when it felt a little flaccid—' He laughed harshly. 'And for anything else that needed a female hand to firm it up.'

'You disgust me,' she hissed. The baby hiccupped, took another lungful of air and began again.

'Yeah? Well that makes us even.'

'And what about you, and men like you, hanging onto his coat tails, turning a blind eye to Edward's little transgressions? What does that make you, David?'

He ignored the jibe. 'You think he cared for you? He was about to get rid of you.'

'You're talking rubbish. You didn't even know him.'

'Types are easy to read,' he said. 'And Edward Wilkinson was a type: a walking phallus, a supreme ego. He called us all into his office the day he was murdered.' He felt a cruel spurt of joy seeing Clara flinch at the word.

'He saved me until last. Told me he didn't think my research into dog whelks was *de rigueur*. "Been done to death," he said. "Molluscs are the province of the great Steve Jones, and he does it *so* much better. Find yourself another niche." He did like his little puns. But then, you'd know that, wouldn't you, darling? He suggested that one of the new City Universities might be grateful for someone like me, who would bring a bit of old-style traditional research. "Gives them credibility. A sense of cultural identity." I wish I'd smashed my fist into his self-satisfied, smirking mouth!'

Clara stared at him round-eyed.

'What's the matter, darling? Am I getting through? Are you *finally* making the connection? If Edward intended getting rid of *me*, that means *you* were on the way out.' He grinned, showing his teeth. 'Don't look so hurt, Clara. After all, mumsy, milky, women wafting baby puke, talcum powder and *Eau de merde* weren't exactly '*de rigueur*' with old Ed. He went in for younger, racier models. Who do you think he had spent the afternoon with?'

Clara held the baby too tightly and he squirmed in her arms, fighting for breath. 'How should I know?'

David laughed and she shuddered at the harshness of the sound.

'My God, Clara, was it you? The papers say he was found naked in bed. If it was *you* he was humping, then you're what the police call a prime suspect—' He raised his eyebrows, hugely amused by the idea.

Clara stood gaping but as he stamped up the stairs to their bedroom, she followed him, releasing her grip on the baby enough for him to let out a furious bellow.

'Of course it wasn't me,' she said.

'Not exactly an instantaneous reaction, my love — the denial of an outraged innocent.' David fetched down a suitcase and a few grey balls of dust from the top of the wardrobe.

'David, how can you think—'

'That my wife would do such a thing? Well, I have to admit, it took a while for me to accept that you could be unfaithful. Even longer to entertain — entirely the wrong word — the thought that you were shagging that bloody Priapus. Now . . .' He paused, gave a small shake of his head. 'Now, I'd believe you capable of just about anything, Clara.'

He felt her staring at him as he packed, and for some reason her passivity enraged him even more. The baby's crying had abated somewhat and although he whimpered and complained, snuffling unhappily, he seemed calmer.

David slammed shirts and socks, underwear and trousers into the case at random.

Gradually realization seemed to dawn on her. 'What are you—?'

David threw her a burning, bloodshot look and then continued with his packing.

'You're not going,' she shouted. 'You can't go!' She grabbed his arm, but he shook her off, raising his hand to strike her, then horrified, he lowered his arm.

'You see what you make of me?' he said hoarsely. He was shaking uncontrollably. 'Well I won't let you do it.' He shut his eyes for a moment and drew a breath, then he continued with his packing.

'You can't! You can't leave me!' she screamed. 'What about the baby! Your son?'

'*My* son?'

'You bastard,' she whispered.

He clicked the clasps of the suitcase closed, fixing her with a shrivelling look. 'Are you talking to me or the child?'

She swung at him with the open palm of her free hand, but he caught her wrist and pulled her to him, ignoring the grizzling cries of the baby. 'Read that,' he snarled, fumbling a copy of the *Herald* from his coat pocket. '*Don Juan*, they're calling him — like the pun? Subtle, isn't it? It doesn't name you, but there isn't anyone else it could be. How long was it going on for, Clara? A year? More? How many people knew about it? How many lies did you tell me? Did you let him fuck you here? In this house? In our bed? That would really amuse Edward.' He let go of her and ran downstairs with the suitcase. She flew after him, stumbling with her burden, her screams rising above the baby's.

'You bloody spineless shit, David! You weren't so particular when the affair was clean and confidential, secret, behind closed doors. You were more concerned about keeping your second-rate job than holding our marriage together. You're just another of those little men who tried to get what they could from Edward. Leeches. Parasites — petty, small-minded people with no ideas and no talent of their own. And now everyone is going to know it because the press have got hold of the story and they're going to describe it as it is: Edward took what he wanted and you let him, because you were afraid not to. That's what really makes you angry — facing up to what you *really are*.'

He flung open the door and barged headlong into Sergeant Hackett.

The detective took a step back, looking past Ainsley to his wife and the screaming child. 'Dr Ainsley,' he said mildly. 'We've been trying to track you down all morning.'

CHAPTER 10

It's laughable. The Jehovah's Witnesses say we're different from other animals because we have the power of reason, and a divinity bestowed on us by God. They must never have met story-hungry journalists. I wonder what the collective noun for sharks is — a feeding frenzy? Mindless bunch of pricks! Feed them a line and they swallow the bait, the hook the line, every clichéd word — they'll even fight over it. Give them a good, stiff scandal and they'll print every scurrilous detail: names, dates, hotel rooms, the lot. All I have to do now is wait for the police to pick up on it. They seem to favour the tabloids. Nice to know they keep abreast of current affairs. Well, if it keeps the bastards from focusing on the real target, who cares?

* * *

Helen Wilkinson looked up from her work. She resisted the compulsion to stand and pull out a chair for Mick Tuttle. He smiled, hovering in the doorway, embarrassed, she knew, by the last conversation they'd had.

'I came to, um—'

'Offer your condolences . . .' Helen hesitated. 'I'm not sure that's entirely appropriate. You know how things were between us.'

Tuttle dipped his head, neither accepting nor denying the truth of what she said. There was a silence in which he seemed to be considering, then he came into the room, closing the door behind him. He leaned with his back to the door for a few moments, whether for support or to give himself time to gather his thoughts was unclear, then he walked to her desk — a few steps only, but the effort it took him seemed a deliberate letting down of the barriers and in a momentary revelation, Helen realized that this was a physical manifestation of trust. For Mick was hypersensitive to the impression his arduous, creaking, leg-swinging movements made on others. He caught the rug with his foot and Helen made an involuntary movement.

He smiled, bending to straighten the rucked edge.

'Nice rug,' he said.

'I brought it in from home,' Helen said. 'I couldn't stand the institutional drabness of the place.'

Tuttle nodded.

'The apricots and blues are a little out of keeping with all this mahogany and oak,' she said, filling the silence as he laboured into the room with babble, unable to stop the words from tumbling out of her mouth. 'But at least it's cheery.'

She clamped her mouth shut just as he reached the chair by her desk and lowered himself into it.

'I should have come earlier,' he said, 'but—' He seemed at a loss for something to say, and Helen couldn't trust herself not to launch into a new tirade of meaningless prattle, so she lifted her chin in acknowledgement and said nothing.

He looked out of the window behind her and then nodded at her computer monitor.

'Working on your research proposal?'

'I was lucky to be given an extension,' Helen said in answer. 'I thought I'd finished it. But I'd prepared it as a presentation for the seminar.' That seemed better. Calm and to the point.

'How's it going?'

She glanced at the text onscreen. 'I've had to cut a lot of the good stuff out — the explanatory, the background. I think it weakens the argument, but I think I can convince the selection committee.'

A frown creased his brow for a second and she recognized it as confusion that she was discussing her research proposal quite coolly, and had expressed surprise at being granted an extension — even though the reason was the death of her husband.

'Emphasize commercial sponsorship — they'll go for it,' Tuttle said, filling what was becoming a difficult silence. 'If you want me to look at it—' He stopped.

Did he think that she might distrust the offer?

'I'll do a print-out now.' Helen said, turning away and focusing on the screen. She clicked on the print icon and then, conscious of his close attention to her profile as she worked, she turned back, catching him staring. Tuttle looked away and she pretended not to have noticed. 'It was just as well you didn't come earlier,' she said. 'Ruth says I've been out of my mind.'

'Understandable.'

His eyes dark, almost black, searched hers. There were depths of meaning in that look Helen was not yet ready to fathom.

'I also came to apologize,' Tuttle went on. 'What I said that day — it must have sounded like whining self-pity.'

Helen's mind switched to the morning of their previous encounter. Monday morning. The day Edward had died. It was something over which she had no control, this instant replay: virtual reality. She watched it as a bystander as it played in her mind:

* * *

'I've just had my interview.'

Helen takes a breath. She can imagine how Edward had treated him. 'I'm sorry.' The words are a reflex, a reaction to his evident distress, and they so inadequately convey her feelings that she blushes.

He runs his fingers through his hair and Helen notices with too-rapt attention how thick and dark it is. Mick is deep-chested, handsome — in some ways like Edward. But there is a sensitivity, a compassion in Mick Tuttle that Edward lacks entirely.

'He told me that reclamation of colliery spoil was old hat. Definitely out, he said. As if conservation is some kind of trend to go in or out of fashion. He asked me if I'd heard that just about all of the deep-pit mines in Britain had been closed.'

Helen draws up a chair and sits opposite Mick. 'What about open-cast mining?' she asks.

'That's what I said. He laughed. Suggested I look for a more promising area of reclamation.'

She feels a thud of hurt on his behalf. 'Mick, I don't know what to say.'

'Talk to him,' Mick urges. 'He'll listen to you.'

Helen looks, startled by the frankness of the request, into those dark eyes. His face, which is normally so controlled, as if denying the effort each step costs him, is flushed with agitation.

'I really don't—'

'It's not like I'm asking you to fiddle the departmental budget,' he says, with such sudden anger that she sits up, increasing the distance between them. 'I'm sorry, Helen. I know it's not your fault but — you know what he said to me? "You wear those callipers like a badge of distinction, Dr Tuttle. But in my book, there are only two criteria for selection: academic excellence and commercial viability."'

Helen feels a wave of hatred for her husband. She hears Edward's voice as clearly as if he had been in the room, calling Mick by the name he uses only in the privacy of their home: 'The cripple.' A simultaneous image floods her visual cortex — a knife slicing neatly through the intercostal muscles, meeting the smooth, slippery resistance of heart muscle, puncturing it with a faint pop.

'I do everything I can to make people look at me instead of at these!' Mick slaps his knees and Helen winces at the rattle of his metal callipers. 'So I'm asking you to try and convince him.'

'I'm not sure I can convince him on my own behalf, Mick. What makes you think I can argue your case for you?'

* * *

'I acted like a brat, storming out like that,' Tuttle said.

'Edward had that effect on people,' Helen said, shaking herself out of the daydream, the action replay. 'He made us all act out of character, one way or another.'

Mick stood, and Helen wondered if she had offended him again. Then he picked up the freshly printed text of her proposal and said, 'I'll phone you when I've had a read through.' He made his way to the door and stood looking at her for a few moments. 'If you need me—' he began.

'I know where you are.'

He stared thoughtfully at her as though he doubted that she would ask for help. 'Or I could pop by, see how you are.'

Helen felt a small contraction of her heart. Mick Tuttle didn't just 'pop by' anywhere. In the first five weeks of the academic year he set up in the lecture hall before most of his students had stumbled to the refectory for breakfast. He volunteered for the early lectures so that he could be there before they started drifting in, he remained seated throughout and waited until they had all left before packing up to leave. He once told her that his first tutorials were make or break for most of his tutees: either they had already accepted him as a person and it was no big deal, or they were offended that they had been tricked all this time by a *cripple*.

Helen blinked, realizing that she had let another silence develop, that he must have seen her drift off like some sad psychotic. 'Yeah,' she said, rallying. 'Fine. I'll make us some coffee.' She tried to adopt the same careless tone Mick Tuttle had tried. And failed, as he had failed.

* * *

'I've just been talking to your boss.'

Hackett slowed his pace, half turned, waited for Ruth Marks to catch him up. He had chance to appraise her in the fifteen metres or so distance between them. Rangy, lean, fit. A woman who chose clothes for comfort and warmth, rather than fashion; today she was wearing faded jeans with ankle length, low-heeled boots. The blue check of her brushed cotton shirt was mismatched by the brown wool of her sweater.

'You know,' she said as she drew level, 'if I had a German Shepherd with eyes that shade, I'd have it put down.'

Hackett bit the side of his cheek. 'I take it you didn't get on too well,' he said, electing understatement as a defence.

'He's mad as a rabid hound and twice as dangerous. Are you on your way to hassle some other poor bastard or do you have a moment?'

Hackett was not in the mood for idle chat. He had just finished interviewing David Ainsley, who had confirmed that his wife and Professor Wilkinson had been having an affair. Ainsley claimed to have known nothing about it until the news article, and said he wouldn't have the first idea how to break into a colleague's computer. But then he would say that, wouldn't he? DI Nelson had counselled diplomacy in the matter of the Apocalypse file. 'Listen carefully and wait for someone to slip up,' he'd said. Meanwhile, they would ask the computer services department to locate whose PC had been used to modify the file.

Hackett was weary; his home was not the normal haven of quiet and comfort because of his mother's frequent calls, and the new argumentativeness in Lisa. He was worried about Daniel, as well; he had become secretive, evasive, refusing to tell them where he had been the previous night. 'Just out,' he'd said. The fact that this case was keeping him away from home was not helping the situation.

'You've given your statement to DI Nelson, Dr Marks,' he said. 'I'm sure that will do.'

'Please yourself.'

Something in her manner made him ask, 'You *have* made your statement?'

'I made *a* statement.' She gave him a level stare. 'I *told* him bugger all.'

Hackett found her constant amusement obnoxious. He took a breath, ready to say what he thought of her light-hearted dismissal of their murder investigation, but she spoke again before he had a chance to begin:

'I'm sorry, Sergeant, but I don't *like* him. He has crazy amber eyes and a nasty mind.' She paused, as if regretting the passion with which she had spoken. He thought he discerned a slight shrug, then she resumed in a more bantering tone, '*Your* eyes, on the other hand, are a very nice shade of green. Cats' eyes. Sexy, if you want to know.'

'So my wife tells me.'

Ruth Marks laughed. She edged closer and whispered. 'It's all right, Sergeant. I'm not going to ravish you — you're not my type.'

Hackett huffed a little laugh. 'All right, I can give you ten minutes.'

He conducted the interview in the college refectory, partly because it was lunchtime and partly because it was the place Nelson was least likely to turn up.

'So,' Hackett said, trying not to show surprise at the four doughnuts Ruth Marks had picked up from the buffet. 'What can you tell me?'

'What do you want to know?' she asked, biting into a doughnut and unselfconsciously licking the sugar from her lips as he watched.

Apparently, she wasn't going to make it easy for him. 'Tell me about Professor Wilkinson,' he said.

'An unmitigated, selfish egocentric shit.'

'The newspapers are carrying a story about an affair—'

'Privatization has gone too far if you're relying on the tabloids to direct your enquiries,' Ruth said, sinking her teeth into the jam centre of the doughnut and groaning with pleasure.

Hackett smiled obligingly and began on his sandwich to give himself time to think and Ruth Marks an opportunity to say more. She chewed thoughtfully and then nodded, pouching the mouthful of doughnut into her cheek and mumbling 'Clara Ainsley.' Noting his surprise with a self-satisfied smirk, she added through a doughy mouthful: 'Clara and Ed had been at it for a year or more.'

'And his wife didn't suspect?'

'Suspicion of adultery is one thing, proving it is another. And Ed was so convincing he sometimes fooled even himself.'

'You knew him well?'

'Too well.' She took a swig of black coffee and swallowed. Hackett had to look away; there was an indecency in the way she abandoned herself to the enjoyment of her food, cramming the sweet, vanilla-scented cakes into her mouth. 'Is that why you're leaving?' Hackett asked.

For a moment Ruth seemed confused, as if working through the idea in her mind. She picked up the third doughnut and licked it, as a child might lick an ice cream. 'It that why I'm leaving . . . ?' she repeated, then bit thoughtfully into the doughnut, taking time to suck the jam from between her fingers. 'Oh, you mean . . .' She wiped her face and hands with a paper napkin, laughing into it. 'My reasons for leaving are purely academic. I'm afraid *Ed* wasn't my type, either.'

'And what were *his* eyes like?' Hackett asked, surprised and amused to find himself flirting with this wide-mouthed, blunt-talking, messy eater.

'Brown, like velvet. But if you caught him when he wasn't ready — when he hadn't time to strike a pose — when he was being himself—' She shrugged. 'They were flat and dead — the inward-looking eyes of an arrogant narcissist.'

'And Helen Wilkinson? Do you like her?'

'I *adore* Helen.' It was a simple statement of fact. 'Everyone does who knows her well. Ask her students.' She went on eating, apparently unaware of the effect her words had had on Hackett.

'If you care so much about her, don't think that you should have told Dr Wilkinson of her husband's infidelity?'

Ruth laughed, blowing sugar crystals from the last doughnut. 'As a *friend*, you mean?' She bit, chewed, swallowed hard. 'Helen didn't need telling, any more than David Ainsley needed telling about Clara. Helen knew.' She chewed the next bite more slowly, her expression thoughtful.

'I saw them once — Edward and Clara — by the river. They were having a picnic. He was pretending to be asleep. Just lay there, looking pretty, driving her wild making out he couldn't feel her kisses, her caresses, her plaintive, humiliating pawing of that splendid body of his.' She caught the sergeant's startled look and added. 'What I'm trying to tell you is the man was a sadist. A subtle one, perhaps, but no less damaging for that. If I sound bitter, it's because I've seen what Edward did to people.'

'Why didn't Dr Wilkinson confront him?'

'She did, more than once. Which is more than most women would have the courage to do, given Ed's temper.'

'He was violent?'

'Physically, no. But I've seen him lacerate a few tough hides with that tongue of his. Edward Wilkinson made it his business to find a person's weak spot and he would attack it without compunction.'

Hackett listened to this, thinking how Wilkinson's cutting remarks must have filleted the delicate tissue of this strangely insecure community.

'You didn't like him?'

Ruth laughed. 'You have a genius for understatement, Sergeant. The question is, did anyone? Except Clara, that is — and she's a fool. Ed Wilkinson was despicable.' She sucked her thumb thoughtfully for a moment.

'Clara,' she said again. 'Perhaps she's not so big of a fool as I'd thought.'

Hackett waited and Ruth ran her tongue between her gums and her upper lip. 'Valerie Roberts worked as Edward's secretary for ten years, putting up with his sarcasm and his unreasonable demands on her time, smoothing ruffled feathers for him, getting him to where he needed to be — lectures, meetings, or mistresses' beds — on time, properly prepared.' She waited for the distasteful reality of her meaning to hit home, then went on: 'And he was planning to get rid of her and install that silly, vain little bitch, Clara, in her place.'

Hackett felt a tingle run from the back of his neck and down both arms. How the hell did she know all this? What was *Ruth Marks's* relationship with Professor Wilkinson?

'Ed felt safe discussing sensitive issues with me,' Ruth said quickly, as though she'd sensed his suspicion. 'Ed was a sucker for glamour, you see. And before long, I'll be doing glamorous research on state-of-the-art technology in that *most* glamorous of locations, the USA.' She smiled at him over the rim of her coffee cup. 'He told me things he probably never even told Helen.'

Hackett stared at her. 'You realize you've removed Clara Ainsley's motive for killing Edward?'

'The fact that he told David he was not to have his contract renewed? God forbid that I should put that round-heeled slut in the clear.'

So, she knew about Ainsley's dismissal, too. Could Ruth Marks have access to the professor's password? And did she feel sorry enough for Valerie Roberts to have changed the Apocalypse file entries?

Ruth was playing with a little mound of sugar on her plate, all that remained of the doughnuts. 'Try this,' she said, drawing the crystals together into a small, slightly pink-tinged peak. 'Clara thought Ed was going to dump her.'

'Why would she think that if he's just offered her a job working closely with him?'

She tilted her head on one side, working on the sugar mound. 'Ed played the game by his own rules. He might not have told her — kept it as a surprise. David gets home from his interview with God on Monday, tells her he's out of a job, she assumes that goes for her, too.'

Hackett watched, fascinated and repulsed, as she took a pinch of the sugar mound and trickled the sticky crystals onto the tip of her tongue.

'Ed would have told her the good news eventually,' she said. 'But it was his way to withhold information; to make the people under him sweat a little—' She paused. 'Which when you think of it, was literally true for Clara. It would be typical of him to let Clara think he was about to dump her, so Clara would be more grateful when he did offer her the job — there's nothing like gratitude to put a woman in a giving mood. But what if he didn't get chance to tell her? What if she stormed round to his place and topped him before he had chance to explain?'

Hackett stared. 'You really don't like Mrs Ainsley, do you?'

Ruth laughed, slapping sugar grains from her hands onto her plate. 'Ask her where she was on Monday afternoon, Mr Hackett.'

CHAPTER 11

Isaac Smolder wrote in his diary: 'I saw Helen standing in the quad this morning. She was talking to that policeman. She nodded her head, smiling in that sad, sweet way. I don't think she was listening to him — not really. She hadn't put on an overcoat and was shivering. Her breath condensed around her face as she talked, turning back, caressing her skin. I felt a stupefying surge of emotion. I wanted to go to her, to put my arms around her. To make her warm. Foolish, really: one shouldn't go against one's nature, it only brings trouble, complications.'

Although he was close by, she hadn't seen him. He had found this difficult: the need to make contact was becoming stronger, more urgent. He thought that she might understand, but human emotion being something of a mystery to him, he was unwilling to make this bold step, for fear of spoiling what was, for the time being, a delightful indulgence.

He knew that his preoccupation with Helen was becoming an obsession, but he could not help himself. He wondered what it would be like to experience her senses, emotions, urges. He had a dizzying notion that he would like to be inside her head, to feel the shock of synaptic electricity. Would it be different, seeing the world as Helen saw it? Watching her, unobserved, from his vantage point above the quad, her delicate gestures, her aching vulnerability, he thought that for Helen the world must seem a terrifying place.

* * *

The door to Helen Wilkinson's office opened and Detective Inspector Nelson slowed his pace a little. He made a mental note — the guy with the callipers was on his way out. Tuttle closed the door behind him then turned away, and Nelson watched him start his slow journey down the corridor.

Dr Wilkinson's office was opposite the staircase and Nelson glanced at the fire doors as he drew level with them; a survival instinct he'd retained from earlier and more dangerous days when he had spent time in the drugs-ravaged housing estates. He saw a flicker of movement, a face pulled back from the wired glass of the door. Nelson shoved the door hard, grunting with satisfaction at the indignant cry of pain.

'You bloody idiot! Who do you think you are?'

'I think I'm Detective Inspector Nelson, Cheshire CID. Who do you think you are?' Nelson turned a nasty smile on the scrawny looking youth, his eyes flashing an amber warning.

'Oh, I — I'm sorry, I didn't . . .' Then, realizing he hadn't identified himself, the youth said. 'Ellis. John Ellis. I'm just a PhD student. I really don't know — that is I *didn't* know Prof Wilkinson very well.'

Nelson raised his eyebrows, amused. *Ellis*, he thought. *Referred to the Senate House Overview Panel. And who'd asked him for his life story, any road?* 'You know his wife better do you?'

'Sorry?'

'Or is she your supervisor — isn't that what you call it?'

Ellis's laughter sounded brittle in the shrill acoustics of the stairwell. For a fleeting moment, Nelson saw someone else, and flinched at the recognition. 'No, nothing like that.'

93

Ellis's Adam's apple bobbed. 'I — Dr Mallory is my supervisor. I . . . er . . . I was just passing and—'

'Dr Mallory? But his office is in the other building, across the quad. Surely you can't have been just passing.' Nelson could sense terror in the boy — and so far, he'd been quite polite. Ellis blinked.

'Shall we begin again?' Nelson asked softly. 'Why were you about to visit Dr Wilkinson?'

Ellis opened his mouth to speak, but another voice carried, echoing up the stairwell: 'He came to pay his respects.' Nelson knew the voice — even on such short acquaintance, Dr Marks was not an easy woman to forget.

'Seems to be a lot of it about,' Nelson observed, thinking of the labouring figure of the crippled bloke retreating down the corridor a few minutes earlier.

'What?' said Ruth. 'Respect?' She appeared on the second landing, her shoes making short rasping sounds on the stone tiles of the steps. 'Nice to hear a copper say that. You're not one of the hang 'em and flog 'em brigade then, Inspector?' She was smiling.

Nelson wondered if she used this strategy as a regular thing, wrong-footing the opposition — diversionary tactics. Well, he wasn't about to enter into a philosophical discussion with Ruth Marks. He turned to Ellis who stood sweating, trapped between the handrail and the door. He looked guilty as sin.

'You were about to tell me why you were here.'

'It's like Dr Marks said. I'm here to—'

'Pay your respects.' Nelson's gaze flicked from the woman to the youth. 'Like Dr Marks said.' He stared the boy down, which was not difficult, but Ruth Marks looked back at him amused, interested. Nelson pulled open the door. 'Don't let me keep you, Mr Ellis.'

Ellis blanched, glanced down the stairwell.

'I was about to visit Dr Wilkinson myself, but I'll wait till you've *paid your respects*.' He saw the whites of Ellis's eyes as he looked to Ruth Marks for help, but this time, inexplicably, she held back, apparently content to watch the play unfold.

'I don't think I'll bother—'

'No,' said Nelson. 'I insist. We can't have you making such a long journey for nothing now, can we?'

Ellis wiped his upper lip. Nelson could see he was seriously considering making a break for it, but abruptly he subsided, meekly edging past Nelson through the fire door which the inspector considerately held open for him. He knocked at Helen Wilkinson's office door — a fumbled, multiple rap because his hand was shaking too badly to control it. Nelson listened to Ellis's mumbled message while staring at Dr Marks. Ruth stared back, a look of open curiosity on her face. Ellis shuffled out of the room a few moments later, blushing to the roots of his hair.

Nelson could only imagine Dr Wilkinson's bewilderment at the visit. He stood square in front of the fire doors so that Ellis had to edge around him.

'I'm afraid *you'll* have to come back later if you're after paying your respects to Dr Wilkinson,' Nelson told Ruth. 'I've got a few questions I'd like to ask her in private.'

Ruth stared past him at the nameplate on the office door. White etched on black. 'No problem,' she said, the corners of her mouth curving up into a smile. 'I've just remembered something I need to do.'

She caught up with Ellis in the courtyard. He was almost in tears. 'Bastard!' he hissed.

'Take it easy,' Ruth said, putting a hand on his arm.

He jerked away. 'Bloody bastard!' he repeated, but he slowed up a little. 'She looked at me like I was mad.'

Ruth laughed explosively, throwing her head back and catching, from the corner of one eye, a blue patch of sky in the jumble of grey and white cloud over the quad.

Ellis stopped, jammed his hands into his trouser pockets and stood hunched over her like an overgrown schoolboy. 'What's so bloody funny?'

'I was just thinking,' Ruth said through her laughter, 'it'd be a nice change for Helen, looking at someone like *they're* mad instead of vice versa.'

Ellis walked on, muttering.

'Okay.' She shrugged. 'You don't think it's funny.'

They crossed the courtyard, avoiding the rainwater puddled on the Yorkshire stone flags, hunching their shoulders against a fresh spattering of sleety rain. The foyer of the zoology building smelled of wet umbrellas and formaldehyde and years of dissections. The fish lingered for the greatest time: skate and mackerel, occasionally squid, always slightly off because the students' inexperience led to dissections taking days instead of hours. Some were returned to the freezer; after several sessions they dissolved into a sodden mush.

Ruth breathed deeply and then asked, 'So why *were* you visiting Helen?'

In the gloom of the poorly lit foyer she thought she saw Ellis twitch. 'Nothing. No reason. I just — I wanted to ask her about my research proposal.'

Ruth moved in closer, trying to read his expression. The foyer was walled in on either side by thick sandstone. Before and behind were heavy oak doors, and the only light was from two dim lamps set high in the ceiling.

'Look, I know I told you Mallory wouldn't be any use to you, but what makes you think Helen'd be any more help?'

Ellis looked over her shoulder, his feet moved restlessly, and his lower body pointed at an angle away from her. 'I suppose I thought Dr Wilkinson might — might know something.'

'About what?' Was he blushing? His body language suggested extreme unease, but the inadequate lighting protected him from close scrutiny. Ruth quelled an urge to drag him into the entrance hall and hold him under the lights. Ellis stirred himself under the intensity of her stare.

'My research grant finishes in the summer. I was hoping to ask her about the availability of posts here. Interview tips, that sort of thing.'

'From Helen?'

If anything, his head sunk even lower.

Ruth shrugged. 'All right, why were you lurking at the top of the stairs? Why didn't you just go into her office and speak to her?'

He fiddled with his tie, then brought his hand down, trying to control the nervous restlessness of his movements. 'Dr Tuttle was in there. I didn't like to interrupt. Anyway, he makes me uncomfortable. I never know what to say to him.' He glanced at his watch. 'Look — I have to go. Thanks for — you know — with that bastard Nelson.' He hurried off through the heavy doors and ran up the central staircase as if Ruth might grab him by the scruff of the neck and drag him back. She watched him go and mused that the acronym SHOP might have another, quite different meaning.

* * *

Ellis ran on, past the postgraduate research laboratory, down the corridor, sweating. Tuttle had been with her. Mick Tuttle had been waiting in Mrs Roberts's office when he had left after his interview with Professor Wilkinson. He must have heard the row. Did he know? What had he told her? What had the prof told her? 'Christ, what am I going to *do*?' he whispered.

He ran up another flight of stairs, out of breath, close to tears, trying to recall exactly what had been said. Not enough, perhaps, on its own to implicate him, but if Tuttle had seen him in the labs when he should not have been there, he might make connections.

* * *

When the doorbell rang, Helen was standing at the bedroom door. She thought she had heard something. A noise. Something. The police had taken away the bloodstained bedclothes and duvet. Ruth had done her best to remove the stain from the mattress, had washed and turned it, had put fresh sheets and blankets on the bed, but Helen could see through the layers to the darkening rusty patch. X-ray vision. The stain would remain forever. On the mattress. In this room. On her conscience.

She shuddered as the bell rang again, more furiously. Half a dozen reporters had been waiting for her at the college gates. The security staff had kept them out, but they could not protect her beyond the walls of the college and the reporters had followed her home, continuing their constant barrage of questions as she walked to her front door. Questions about Edward. Their relationship. Had she known about his affairs? About Clara? Could she account for the knife that was missing from the kitchen?

Helen covered her ears against the insistent ringing of the doorbell. She screamed: 'Leave me alone!'

Abruptly, the bell fell silent. A voice, thin, frightened called up to her. 'Helen? Come to the door, love.'

Her heart began pounding. She turned, ran down the stairs, fumbled the chain from the door and flung it wide open. Someone stepped forward before the rest of the hacks and Helen blinked in the light of the flash. A picture of her with a vague look of irritation on her face would later appear in the *Chester Recorder* under Dermot Molyneux's by-line: Molyneux got.

Helen turned to the woman on the doorstep.

'You shouldn't have come,' she said. Then: 'You'd better come in.'

She took the overnight case without comment and set it down at the foot of the stairs. 'You'll be wanting a cup of tea,' she said, falling unthinkingly into the old patterns of speech. 'You must be perished.'

'Your dad sends his love—'

'What were you thinking of, coming on your own?' Helen burst out.

'I got the train straight through — and a taxi from the station to the door. I'm not incapable, Helen. I can fend for myself. *He'd* have come but—'

Helen did not want to think about why her father didn't feel able to make the short train ride from Manchester to Chester. 'I think Ruth got some food in,' she muttered, turning to the refrigerator.

'Helen — love.' Her mother waited while Helen continued, frowning, sorting the cheese from the cooked meats, extracting the salad from the bottom compartment.

'Ready-washed — just open and serve.' She read the instructions on the pack aloud as if they could ward off her mother's questions.

'We were worried — your dad and me, when you didn't phone back. We tried to get through—'

Helen started guiltily. 'I unplugged the phone. Reporters. Crank calls . . . I meant to call again — to let you know I was okay.' She shrugged helplessly. Her mother smiled at her over the jumble of packages on the kitchen table, her concern, as always, an accusation.

'Are you?' she asked. 'Okay, I mean.' This, said too brusquely, encouraging a simple affirmative in answer, as though any admission of illness or unhappiness — even in bereavement — would be judged an imposition, a play for attention.

'Hmm.' Helen shied away from her mother's caress, saw the hurt in her eyes and regretted it but, powerless to recall the action, instead fussed over the preparation of food. 'I can do you an omelette — or would you prefer a sandwich?'

'Omelette'll be fine. What do the police say?'

'They don't *say* anything. They just keep asking me questions I can't answer.'

'So they don't have any idea who—'

Helen faltered, feeling a cold wave of dread. She wanted to say *Not unless you count me,* but that would be too cruel, so she said simply, 'No. They don't seem to.' She could not keep the tiredness, the exasperation from her voice and her mother withdrew. Helen knew that her mum must be thinking she was the cause, and part of her wanted to reach out — to comfort and reassure her mother. But she saw the small changes in her mother's appearance that signalled her disapproval: a tightening of the lips, hands crossed protectively across her abdomen, and she knew that any attempt to engage her now would only drive wedge between them.

She reached for the short-bladed knife she preferred for slicing vegetables and recoiled when saw the empty space in the knife block where the boning knife should be. The police had returned the others, but they had not found the missing boning knife.

'Why don't you make us a brew?' Helen asked keeping her voice level, 'While I sort this.'

She chopped the vegetables while her mother performed her tea-making ritual. As she waited for the kettle to boil, she filled the teapot and two mugs with hot water from the tap. By the time Helen was ready to whisk the eggs her mother was standing at the sink poised ready to tip the hot water out of the pot and add the tea bags at the exact moment the kettle clicked off. Of course, she preferred proper tea, loose leaf, like they all used to have, but she could make do when necessary. Helen watched her mother, to distract herself from thinking about the glutinous mix of yolk and mucilaginous albumen in the bowl, to take her mind from the smells of hot butter and fried onions and tomatoes in the pan. She would not allow herself to check for tell-tale flecks of red on the yolks, but added ground pepper and salt, a dash of Worcester sauce and a spurt of cold water, and began to beat the eggs.

The thick, liquid sound, a comforting rhythm in childhood, now made her stomach lurch and roll with every flick of the wrist. She tried not to think of the slimy liquid falling from the fork in ropy strands, but focused on her mother, adding the water to the tea bags, stirring the pot, placing the lid on it, looking around for a cosy and finding none, making do with a tea towel.

She's grey, Helen thought. *Quite grey*. And she looks exhausted. Only a couple of years earlier her mother had been dark, as dark as Helen; people had mistaken them for sisters. Now Helen could see in her mother the grey ghost of her future self.

'Can't the police do anything about those vultures outside?'

Helen was nibbling at a cheese sandwich while her mother worked through the omelette. 'I don't know that they want to.'

Her mother's anxious look of enquiry forced an answer. 'A knife is missing from the block.'

Her mother's head began to turn, then snapped back to look at Helen. 'They can't think that you—'

'Why not? I had motive enough. I even wanted to.' This was dangerous territory, this honesty. Who was she spiting, her mother, or herself? She felt herself hurtling towards an admission she did not want to make.

'Helen! You mustn't talk like that.'

'Why mustn't I, Mother? It's the truth. And it was just as I'd visualized it.' *Except for the blood!* She closed her eyes, but the image of Edward dead, white sheets and dark blood, was too strong and she gasped, standing, picking up the plates, throwing her half-eaten sandwich into the bin and taking the plates to the sink.

'What do you mean, how you'd visualized it? How could you think such wicked thoughts?'

Wicked thoughts! Didn't her mother know how she had fought over the years to repress the fury inside her — the wickedness — the natural unthinking urge to lash out?

'Mum, you must have seen the papers—'

'Lies. They make up stories to get people to buy. Surely, they must be lies, Helen?'

Helen sighed. 'I wish they were; then at least I could get angry instead of feeling this burning humiliation. It's true, Mum. All of it.' She wanted to say more, to explain, but her mother had been charmed by Edward, his middle-class manners and Oxford education, his easy, confident way of making small talk, appearing interested when he wasn't listening to a word. Edward had made sure that they saw her family infrequently and fleetingly, so the illusion had remained intact.

'Helen, we thought — your dad and me — we thought you and Edward were happy. Edward was such a nice man, so clever—'

Helen smiled. Tears pricked at the back of her eyes and nose. 'Handsome is as handsome does, eh, Mum? Anyway, what could you have done? I'm all grown up now.'

'I know love, but you're all we've got . . .' She faltered, stopped, biting off her words.

Helen plunged her hands into the scalding dishwater to stop herself finishing the sentence in her head: *You're all we've got since . . .* The unspoken implication: *And you're a poor substitute,* the question unasked a million times, but always there, as a reproach: *Why him and not you?*

'I'm sorry, love,' her mother said, breaking the silence. 'I never meant—'

'I know.' The silence descended again, and Helen's mother picked up a tea towel, ready to help, anxious to make amends. 'Let them drain,' Helen said. 'Why don't you go and lie down? The spare room's made up.' She had made it up for Ruth, whom she was expecting later, but Ruth would understand.

Her mother folded the tea towel with elaborate care, giving herself time to say something, but was unable to find the words. She hung it up on the rail next to the cooker and left the room. Helen could feel the distance between them, the silence, tug at her. She wanted to go to her mother, to comfort her. But how can the guilty bring comfort? What could she say that would change anything? So, she waited until her mother was too far away to hear and then she whispered softy, 'I'm sorry, Mum. I'm so very, very sorry.'

* * *

A sharp rap at the kitchen window made Helen start violently. She closed her eyes and concentrated on her breathing.

A second rap, something metal, perhaps a coin, then David Ainsley's voice, muffled and tearful.

'Oh, God.' Helen leaned against the sink for a moment, still trying to regain her equilibrium.

'Helen, *please!* Let me in.' Not muffled, slurred: he was drunk.

She opened the scullery door, shielding herself behind it, in case of photographers. He stumbled in and she slammed the door.

David stood, swaying slightly, blinking in the light. 'It's quite all right,' he said, enunciating carefully. 'They didn't see me. I waited until they weren't watching. Came down the side passage, the gate was unlocked.'

Helen looked at him, unshaven, his suit badly rumpled, the collar and cuffs of his shirt grubby, and wondered where he had been sleeping. 'You must be bloody mad, coming here.'

He grinned foolishly. 'Create a splendid photo opportunity, wouldn't it?'

She led him through to the kitchen and cupped both hands around the teapot. It was cold. *Crystal-gazing*, she thought, *fortune-telling. And what does the future hold for me?* She frowned at the incongruousness of the idea. 'I'll make you some coffee, then you can go home.'

His eyes filled with tears. 'Can't go home.' He sounded like a pettish child. 'You knew, didn't you?' His voice was high pitched, accusing. 'It's in the papers — have you seen? You knew and you said nothing.'

'Are you saying you didn't know?' Helen spooned coffee into two mugs, her eyes fixed on Ainsley. He looked away, muttering something incoherent.

'Sit down, David,' she said.

He dragged a chair out and collapsed into it heavily. 'Bloody bitch!'

Helen set down a mug in front of him and sat opposite. He was, she decided, referring to Clara.

'Clara was another conquest for Edward,' she said. 'He notched them up and then moved on to the next challenge. She'll realize that soon enough, if she hasn't already.'

'Oh, she has,' he said viciously. 'I made sure of that.' This, muttered into his coffee mug as he lifted it to his lips, moving it too fast, miscalculating the distance so that the porcelain clicked against his teeth and a little coffee slopped out, scalding his chin. He wiped it away with the back of his hand, swearing. Then, in a deliberate motion, he placed his hand on hers. Helen jerked away. He looked, startled, into her face, ready to weep. His eyes were bloodshot and sore from drink and crying and sleeplessness. He let his head fall forward, his hair flopping in front of his right eye. 'I thought you'd understand,' he said.

'I think I probably do.'

'The police think *I* did it.'

'Did what?'

'Killed him. Stuck the knife in the bastard bloody home wrecker.'

Edward smiling up from his bed, warm with the afterglow of sex. A kiss, a quick, firm push, and the knife went home. His gasp of surprise and pain . . . His hands grasping the sheets, spoiling their pristine smoothness.

Ainsley flicked his hair from his forehead. 'Some of his files were altered—'

'I know,' Helen said quietly.

'He was going to get rid of me. Us. You'd've had him to yourself.'

'I was past wanting him, either shared or all to myself,' she said. 'I wanted him out of my life.'

'What are you saying?' He tried unsuccessfully to bring the blurred outline of her face into focus.

Helen paused, wondering how much she wanted to tell him, then decided he had a right to know. 'You're wrong about Edward planning to get rid of both of you. He was going to offer Clara Valerie Roberts's job.'

Ainsley's eyes widened. His brain, steeped in alcohol, could not take this in. Then he saw Clara's face as he had told her that Wilkinson was going to have his contract terminated. 'No.' He shook his head slowly, feeling the liquid swirl in the vestibular apparatus of his brain, seeing the room rotate alarmingly even with this slight movement, 'No. She would have said.' She had been shocked, angry, when he had told her Edward had been planning to sack him. Was there also regret? If she had known Edward's plans, she would have said anything to hurt.

'She didn't know,' Helen went on. 'But he did plan to retire Valerie early, and he had recommended Clara as replacement.'

'Bloody, sodding bitch!' Wasn't he allowed even the satisfaction that Edward would have abandoned her? 'It's his, isn't it? Why else would he want to look after her? Shag 'em and leave 'em's his motto.'

'I know she's hurt you, David, but you have to look to the future. What about Henry?'

David snorted into his coffee mug, took another slurp. 'Let her take care of the little bastard. Better if he'd never been born.'

Something changed in the room. The cold tap dripped steadily into the sink, as it did before, the pale lemon walls reflected the blue-white glow of the fluorescent lighting but momentarily the darkness seemed to close in and the air grew hot despite the bitter easterly wind which rattled the window sashes. David frowned, feeling the change, chanced a look at Helen. Her face had grown solemn and still.

'I think you should leave now,' she said, quietly.

'I didn't mean—' He reached out to touch her.

'Leave me alone. I can't help you.' She stood and moved to the side of the table. He lunged forward, made to grasp her hands, missed, his hands fumbling at her waist. 'Helen—' She pushed with both palms, flat on his chest but although he swayed, he did not yield, and Helen felt a clammy apprehension. He bent forward, his fingers straying lower now, gripping the tops of her thighs, cupping her buttocks. His face near hers, stale, smelling of cheap wine and vomit. She began to fight, knowing this to be the wrong thing to do, but the smell, the confining proximity of him was too much for her. She shoved hard and he staggered back, catching the base of his spine against the kitchen table.

'Fuck,' he muttered, releasing one hand from her buttock, flailing, knocking a chair over. Helen began to fall, but he caught her by the waist again and she swept her arm in a wide semicircle, connecting with a crack to the side of his face.

David responded slowly, looking first at her, shocked by the strength of the slap, then raising his hand to his face. 'Bitch,' he said, softly, astonished, as though realizing the truth of it for the first time. '*Fucking* bitch!'

'Go back to your wife, David.' Helen's voice was harsh, her breathing ragged. 'Go back to your son.'

He laughed, belching a sour cloud on his breath then he turned quickly, almost losing co-ordination, but steadying himself against the door frame before he drew himself up in an effort to regain some dignity and stepped carefully into the scullery. He paused at the back door. Helen stared at him. His face was contorted with hatred. 'You didn't realize how much you had in common with Clara, did you? She thinks you despise her for not having a job — relying on my income. And there *he* was, banging away at the both of you. It didn't seem to matter to him. Like a dog, he followed any bitch on heat.'

'*David!*'

'It's a pity you didn't carry full term,' he said, enjoying her outrage, the pain he was causing her. 'Clara's little bastard would've had a half-brother to play with.'

CHAPTER 12

Helen leaned against the back door, trying to think past the trembling that shook her body, above the pain in the middle of her ribcage, beyond the screaming in her head, to a small, white patch of nothing, where there was no pain, no guilt, no tomorrow. Edward had told Clara about their baby; had even told her it was — would have been — a boy. And Clara had told David. She felt a surge of fury at Edward's continuing malign influence. When she thought her legs would support her she took a step into the kitchen. She gasped as though struck.

'Mum—'

Her mother looked at her, her head slightly lowered, angry, unapologetic, unembarrassed for the first time since she had arrived. 'What were you waiting for, Helen? For us to read about *that* in the papers as well? Couldn't you have told us — me?'

'How could I have told you? I've hurt you enough. I couldn't—'

'You mean you *wouldn't*. I'll get my things,' she said. 'I'll not trouble you any longer.'

Her mother's cold look of dislike was too much for Helen and she burst out, 'Mum!' her voice rising in panic.

She took a step, tripped over the fallen chair, and her legs buckled, she felt herself falling, spinning and she snatched at the tabletop, missed, heard the sound of her fingernails scratch the wood.

Her mother was bent over her, crying. Helen saw a tear fall and felt an urge to catch it, but her limbs wouldn't work. Then she felt a sharp stab of pain in her cheek and everything returned to reality. Helen blinked, thinking, Real? Yes, I think this is real. But the impression lingered for a while longer that if she had caught that teardrop, she might have made everything right between them.

'Get Dr Patterson.' Her mother had not spoken. Ruth had arrived at last.

'Help me up,' Helen said. 'Then call Sanjay.'

Ruth gave her a long, speculative look. 'I didn't know you were on first-name terms.'

* * *

Patterson had wanted her admitted to hospital for observation, but Helen had refused and he had compromised with her mother and Ruth taking turns to watch her throughout the night.

'It's a nasty bruise,' he said. 'She's lucky she didn't catch herself half an inch higher or she might have lost an eye.'

Helen lay on the sofa of her den and let the discussion go on around her while she determined what she could say to her mother, how much she dared tell her.

'I'd like to speak to Mum, please,' she said quietly. Ruth and Dr Patterson stopped talking to look at her. They exchanged a glance; the agreement was unspoken, and they left in silence. For several minutes the only sound in the room was the impatient spattering of wind-driven rain on the windows.

'I'm sorry, Mum,' Helen said at last. 'I was trying to protect you both.'

'From what?'

Helen closed her eyes. *From more pain*, she thought. *From letting you down again. Another loss, with me at the centre.* What she said was: 'I was only four months on.'

Before answering, her mother took her hand. 'Only four months.' It was said as a judgement. Only Helen's lapsed Catholicism would allow her to say such a thing. Her mother had read the statement as a dismissal of the worth of the child Helen had been carrying.

Helen tried again: 'He was perfect, your grandson . . .' She couldn't go on.

'Grandson.' Her mother tried out the word. She sighed.

'I know all about foetal development,' Helen went on. 'I knew what to expect. But I was totally unprepared for how perfect he was, how complete. They let me hold him—'

'What did you expect?' She seemed to regret the sharpness of her tone and after a moment, she asked, 'How did he die?'

'He didn't die. Not in the real sense. Because he'd never really lived.' For a moment they were both thinking of someone else. 'And that's the tragedy of miscarriage.' Helen searched her mother's face. It was closed. Her mother had decided: Helen's failure of faith; her immoral views on abortion; her inadequacy as a wife — the sins of her past had returned to punish her. Just before she looked away, Helen thought she saw an exultant glint in her mother's eye.

'It can't be helped.' This was said firmly, and Helen wondered if her mother wasn't referring to that other time, that other tragedy.

Helen closed her eyes, fetched a sigh that became a sob and turned her face away. 'I didn't want him. Not at first. I was furious with Edward.' She knew it would do no good, but Helen needed at least to try and make her mother understand, to see just once, the pain she felt. 'I think he wanted me pregnant so that I was out of the way.'

'The affair?'

Helen nodded. 'And I'd just won backing for my project from one of the pharmaceutical companies. I think he was jealous.' She risked a glance at her mother. Although she looked puzzled, lost almost. The dislike was gone, and this gave Helen the courage to continue. 'I did it.'

Her voice was no more than a whisper, but her mother's head jerked up as though she had screamed.

'It was my fault. We'd argued about Clara. I took a swing at him. I wanted to *kill* him!' She paused for a moment, breathing heavily. 'He dodged and I fell. I began haemorrhaging.'

'You didn't mean it to happen.' It was meant as a reassurance, a comfort, but the inflexion was wrong. It came out as a question, despite her. Helen felt it as a physical blow.

'Old excuse. Wears a bit thin, doesn't it?' She could not keep the bitterness out of her voice any longer.

Her mother looked away.

'No, Mother, I didn't mean it to happen,' Helen went on. 'By then I wanted him. My baby. My son.' Her voice trailed off and the room was filled with the throbbing grief of loss. The two women looked at each other, each aware for the first time the depth of the other's pain and regret, but aware that the years of estrangement had rendered them powerless to breach the gap.

CHAPTER 13

Nelson seemed preoccupied, even shaken. Hackett tried to engage his attention and, failing, shrugged and drew up a chair for Dr Wilkinson. He leaned back against Mallory's desk, his legs stretched out in front of him, fingers curled around its edge. It had been cleared of its ornaments — living and dead. The tarantula would inhabit some other office until Mallory's temporary exile was over, and the skull, cigarette still drooping insouciantly from between its upper and lower mandibles, now squinted down at them from the shelf opposite.

Nelson had requested an interview with Helen Wilkinson. It was in all the papers; the Don Juan story had taken a new turn: the tragic loss of his wronged wife. They had somehow got hold of information that Helen Wilkinson had miscarried a child in January, and it seemed that her behaviour since had been strange, to put it mildly. The mood of the reports had changed: they were becoming more sympathetic to Helen, and Hackett wondered if she was capable of feeding them the story herself.

Hackett looked at Nelson. He was standing at the window, feet slightly apart, hands in his pockets, staring out at the rain.

'Sir,' Hackett said. There was no response. He shrugged and turned to Helen.

'Are you all right?' He gestured to the swelling and discolouration on her cheek.

'I fainted. Fell against a table. I'm fine.' She tilted her head forward, so that her hair hid the bruising under her left eye. 'Why did you want to speak to me?'

Hackett watched her for some time, before asking, 'You've seen the papers?'

'Yes.'

'You didn't tell us that you'd had a miscarriage . . .' Hackett began gently.

'Why the hell should I?'

'Well . . . because it could be relevant — if you were depressed for example.'

'Of course I was *depressed*. I'd recently lost a baby and my husband was having an affair with the wife of a colleague! Wouldn't you be depressed?'

Hackett looked into her pretty, elfin face. This was something new, this fieriness, this sparky aggression. Ruth Marks had told him that the fey, dreamy, damaged quality that he had seen up to this point was not the true Helen Wilkinson. Is this, he wondered, closer to her real self?

'I think if it was me,' he said, continuing in a warm, gentle tone, 'I'd want to get back at him.'

She tilted her head on one side as if seriously considering the notion. 'You don't seem the type for revenge,' she said.

Hackett looked over at Nelson, but he had moved to the door and was standing with his head bowed, apparently deep in thought. Hackett turned back to Dr Wilkinson, irritated that Nelson, who had insisted on the interview, had apparently lost all interest in it. He nodded, even forced a smile. 'You're probably right,' he said. 'But I might be tempted to do something just to make the awfulness stop.'

She frowned.

'It must have felt like there was no end to it,' Hackett went on, his voice quiet, its tone mesmeric. 'The loss of the baby. The taunts.'

Helen looked into his face. 'I longed for one kind gesture from Edward,' she said. 'One act of gentleness. If he'd uttered a single word of regret—' She broke off, and just as he was about to prompt her, she spoke again. 'Would you understand if I told you that the simple truth is that I would have been grateful even to have been left alone to grieve?'

Hackett was shaken. What kind of monster would deny a woman that?

She nodded, as if accepting that he was beginning to appreciate the pain her husband's coldness had caused her.

'Shall I tell you what Edward said to me after I lost my baby?' She didn't wait for a reply but went on, 'He said that a female's worth is measured by her fecundity and her child-rearing skills. Apparently, I failed on both counts.'

Hackett tightened his jaw against making an utterance of disgust at the professor's cruelty, or sympathy for Helen — it wasn't his job to sympathize, it was his job to get to the truth.

'How did you respond to that?' he asked.

Helen blinked, startled, as if she hadn't realized she had spoken aloud, then she looked away. 'We argued,' she said. 'Again.'

'Did you ever fight? Physically, I mean.'

She gave a sad smile. 'Edward was far too subtle for that. He didn't need to resort to anything so crude as physical violence.'

'But surely, when you lost the baby—'

Helen swallowed. 'That was the only time. And it was me, not him. I threw a punch. Missed—' She took a breath as though she could not get enough air. 'And killed my baby.'

Hackett sat in the chair opposite Helen's. 'That must have been . . . difficult for you.'

Helen laughed. A sudden, harsh sound, without humour, like a cry of pain. 'Difficult. Yes.'

He went on: 'It wouldn't be surprising if you'd wanted to hurt him the way he'd hurt you.'

'Edward was fireproof,' she said quietly. 'Nothing could hurt him.'

'Something did,' he said quietly. 'Someone.'

'*I* did,' Helen said.

Hackett saw Nelson's shoulders tense and willed him to stay quiet. *Don't you dare interrupt now*, he thought. *Let her speak.*

'I hurt him a thousand times after that day,' she said. 'In daydreams. In fantasies so *real* that I would have to seek Edward out, to convince myself that he was all right. And when I found him in his study, or watching TV, or reading in bed, notes scattered around him, a supercilious look on his face, it wasn't *relief* I felt.'

Hackett waited, and after a long pause, Helen said with quiet dignity, 'I don't know who killed Edward, Mr Hackett. But I'm not sorry he's dead.'

* * *

'Sir?'

Nelson twitched at the sound of his name, then shook himself. 'Oh,' he said, looking around the room. 'You've let her go.'

'Are you all right, sir?'

Nelson's eyes were watery, their colour less intense than usual. 'That bloke,' he said.

'What bloke?' Hackett said, thinking sourly that Dr Wilkinson's vagueness must be contagious.

'Ellis,' Nelson said. 'He was hanging around again. When we brought her in. What is it between them? Are they having an affair an' all?' He tried to make a joke of it, but he seemed uneasy.

'More likely he's looking for her to put in a good word for him.'

Nelson frowned.

'With the selection board,' Hackett said.

'God, these people are ruthless!' Nelson exclaimed. Then, 'What did you get out of the mistress?'

'Clara Ainsley's more carved up about Wilkinson's death than his wife,' Hackett said.

He had interviewed Clara Ainsley earlier, at headquarters — it seemed kinder than bringing her in to the university where speculation and gossip had already reached fever pitch. A neighbour had agreed to look after her baby for a couple of hours. Mrs Ainsley looked a hundred years old. Hackett was reminded of the winter when Lisa got one damn cold after another and would cry all night and most of the day. Even when she was quiet, they would need go to her and check that she hadn't suffocated on the terrible congestion in her lungs and nose. Sheila, haggard, wild, frenzied, had been driven to the point of screaming in the end, and he had felt the urge more than once himself, despite the fact that, for ten or twelve hours of the day he would be away from the noise and the upset.

He gave Hackett a precis of the interview.

'So, she's torn up,' Nelson said. 'With guilt, or grief?'

'She claims she saw Wilkinson at the university after he'd completed the staff interviews,' Hackett said. 'She *says* that she told him they were finished. That she thought he was messing about with someone else.'

'She said, "I wasn't about to let him treat me like the others, like some tart he'd picked up on a street corner."'

Nelson grunted. 'Colourful image.' He pondered a moment. 'A pity, though, her dumping him like that, when he was planning to set her up in her own little office, right within pawing range.'

'I got the impression she felt the same way.'

Nelson sniffed, turned, and stood staring into the empty eye socket of the skull for a few moments. 'Spilt milk,' he said. 'On the other hand, we only have her word for it that she dumped him. What if it was the other way around?'

'He was setting up the secretarial job for her,' Hackett said. 'Why would he get shut of her?'

Nelson nodded, an irritated crease appearing in the middle of his forehead. 'Okay, what if she *thought* he was going to dump her? One of his little games — like Marks said.'

Hackett thought about it. 'Then I'd say that Clara is just about untethered enough at the moment to've taken a knife to him.'

* * *

The rain and sleet had abated for the time being and although small, sodden melts of snow clustered around the bases of the daffodils, the sky was a flawless cobalt blue and the sun sparkled on raindrops trembling on the buds of the birch trees.

'Hey, slow down!' Ruth caught up with Helen and put a hand on her friend's arm.

Helen stared at the clumped of flowers in the grass. 'Forty-five degrees,' she said.

'What?'

'The flower buds of the daffodils — they're angled at forty-five degrees to the stems. There must be a reason, don't you think?'

Ruth glanced around and then edged Helen towards the doorway of the environmental biology building. Helen's office was housed in the comparative modernity of this Edwardian building, the patterned tiling of its floor had long since worn thin and many of the tiles were cracked, but it held a certain charm; its square, unfussy design was well suited to the department's needs: a combination of office accommodation and laboratories — indeed, it was one of the few purpose-built departments in the old university.

'Helen,' Ruth said, putting some edge in her voice. 'Don't start flaking out on me again.'

Helen frowned, still considering the puzzle of the daffodils, then with a sigh, she turned and made to go through the door.

Ruth stopped her. 'This is a smokescreen,' she said, losing patience. 'Going off on a tangent like that — it's a bullshit smokescreen to avoid unpleasant truths.'

Helen blinked, and it was as if a switched had been flicked. 'How's this for facing the truth?' she said, her eyes cobalt blue and sharper that Ruth had seen them in a long while. 'One time — I think it was a month or so after the baby died — I found a kitchen knife — *the* kitchen knife, the one that's now missing — in my bedside cabinet. I couldn't remember putting it there. Still can't.' Her eyes, staring into Ruth's own, were hard and unforgiving.

'Shall I tell you how many times I took that boning knife from its slot in the block and sharpened it? Shall I describe how I took comfort from the song of metal against metal? And when it was sharp enough to carve wood, I would rehearse every step, from start to finish, carrying out my intention in my mind and soul and heart because I *hated* him with an intensity that cannot be described in words.'

'Shh!' Ruth gripped Helen's arms at the elbows and glanced over her shoulder, praying that no one had overheard.

Helen drew herself to her full height and gently disengaged herself from Ruth's grasp. Then she entered the building and walked past the stairway leading to her office, towards the staff common room.

'Where are you going?' Ruth said, following her.

'I have to get my coat.'

'Helen, for God's sake—'

Helen turned suddenly and Ruth was confronted again by that hard stare.

'Who would tell the press all those things, Ruth? About the baby. Who would know?' She stared into Ruth's face as though she would find the answer to her question in the fine lines around her mouth, or in the blue-grey of her eyes.

'Ed didn't exactly keep it a secret,' Ruth said, shrinking slightly under her unflinching gaze.

'Maybe. But he wasn't interested in the specifics — Ed was a broad brush-strokes man. There were *details* in the papers—'

'Clara? David? Who knows?' Ruth caught her hand. 'Helen — it doesn't matter.'

'It does matter.' Helen shook herself free. '*It matters.*'

'All right. I'm sorry. It matters. Now will you tell me where you're going?'

Helen's eyes roved around the main entrance and Ruth did the same, hoping for some clue to her friend's change in mood. The wide foyer was empty except for a porter and two postgraduate students who were checking the wooden racks of pigeon-holes for mail.

'Will you just *tell* me what the hell is going on?' Ruth whispered.

'I don't confide in many people, Ruth. There aren't so very many people I feel I can trust. I confided in you.'

'You did. So . . . ?'

The two women stared at each other for a full half minute, then Ruth, suddenly assimilating the implications of what Helen had said, burst out, 'Is this an accusation? You think I'd spread those sordid stories about your husband's grubby little affairs? Jesus, Helen! Who helped you sort yourself out when you lost the baby? Who suggested the switch to tissue culture when you couldn't bear the sight and smell of blood any longer? Who smoothed your worried brow and took your calls at two in the morning and convinced you otherwise when you found the knife in your bedroom cabinet — it was a couple of weeks after you lost the baby, by the way — your timeline's off.'

Helen turned her wedding ring round and round on her finger.

'Who looked after you? Who helped you to sort out what was real from what was in your head?'

More than once, Ruth had tracked Edward down — in a meeting, or a seminar — and insisted that he talk to Helen, because she had convinced herself that this time, she really had done it, that he was dead.

'It was *me*, Helen, all those times. Your old faithful friend. Always there, like a big St Bernard, lolloping after you — whistle and I come running.'

'Don't patronize me, Ruth.' The words spat out, angry.

'Then stop talking like a bloody lunatic!' Ruth said with sudden ferocity. She closed her eyes for a moment. 'I'm sorry. I really am. But you are making me *crazy*. What are you trying to do? Drive away the only friend you have in this temple of misogyny? Is that what you want?'

'I just want to know what happened,' Helen said, her voice calm.

Ruth shook her roughly. 'I'll tell you what happened. Someone did you a fucking great favour. Edward is dead and you're free to do whatever the hell you like. Get used to it and stop whinging.'

* * *

Isaac Smolder, skulking in the shadows, almost broke cover. Almost shouted to Ruth Marks to take her mauling hands off Helen. But he knew that now would be the wrong time. Once, animal activists had got into his laboratory. Security had discovered the break-in and called the police before they'd had chance to do much damage. All of the cages had been unlocked and the doors were wide open. He had arrived two hours later and from a total of over a hundred experimental animals, only a couple of rats had escaped; the rest, habituated to captivity, had remained passively in their cages, doing no more than sniffing anxiously at the open space where the door should have been. All he had to do was secure the latches. Helen would not go far. He could wait.

* * *

Helen stared at Ruth, shocked by her outburst. The two students had turned to look at them and the porter took a tentative step towards them. He cleared his throat. 'All right, ladies?' he asked.

Ruth let go of Helen. 'Fine,' she said. 'Everything's under control — isn't it, Helen?'

Helen shrugged and smiled, embarrassed. They were arguing. Why was that? Ruth was right — it was crazy. But who else would know all the awful, humiliating details the press had printed? Could Ed really have told his mistress the sordid particulars of his previous flirtations and affairs — and worse — the sad, intimate circumstances of her miscarriage? Had he thought so little of her?

At that moment, Helen felt the need of her mother. She knew it was childish and pathetic, knew how unsatisfactory the encounter would be, but she wanted comfort, uncompromising love, even though she knew her mother was incapable of giving it. Anyway, she had returned to Bolton on the nine-thirty train; Ruth had dropped her at the station after Helen had persuaded her to go home with the promise that she would visit at the weekend.

You're on your own, now, she thought. *You have to do this alone.* But looking into Ruth's face, she saw concern and love, as well as frustration — perhaps even a little fear. *Poor Ruth,* she thought.

'That bloke Nelson has a funny effect on me,' she said. Then turning back toward the door out, she added, 'I think I'll take a walk.'

Ruth hesitated, then followed, a few steps behind, uncertain of her welcome, but Helen dawdled, despite the cold of the day and she was soon walking beside her friend, feeling shaken by the sudden change in Helen. After a few minutes of silence, Helen spoke.

'I've been thinking,' she said. 'About the people on the list.'

'The Apocalypse file?'

'Could *they* have done it, Ruth? Would anyone kill, just to keep their job?'

'It isn't just a job to some of these people,' Ruth said, relieved to be on safer ground. 'This university is home, career, status. Ed knew that and would most likely have worked on their inflated egos. He really had a way of flaying the flesh from the bone, and Marks's Paradox states that *in*flated egos are easily *de*flated — the rate of deflation being directly proportional to the original distension.'

Helen smiled, and Ruth drew her arm through her own. Her hand was frozen — she hadn't fetched her coat, after all — and Ruth turned into a more sheltered area with paved paths and raised flower beds, riotous with pansies and polyanthus.

'Look at Mallory,' Ruth went on. 'He must've seen it coming, but he was devastated when Ed told him his contract wouldn't be renewed.'

'How do you know?'

Ruth grinned. 'Valerie hates gossip, but she's soft-hearted. Take a sympathetic line and she'll tell you anything you want to know. "Poor Dr Mallory, after all those years of devoted service . . ." You get the idea. And speaking of Valerie, she had a motive her own.'

'Ruth! You can't be serious! Valerie Roberts?'

'Never underestimate the fury of quiet women,' Ruth cautioned. 'Especially quiet, middle-aged women. They feel the slings and arrows, the contumely of the young and arrogant far more acutely than the rest of us. And they don't suffer the insults lightly.'

'I understand the argument,' Helen said. But *Valerie Roberts*?'

Ruth returned Helen's outraged stare for a few moments, then they both burst out laughing. 'All right,' Ruth agreed. 'Maybe not Valerie.'

'It's a ridiculous notion,' Helen chuckled.

'But reasons for murder often are ridiculous — or at least they seem so to the outsider,' Ruth argued. 'The objective, rational observer can't take the imaginative leap, because they haven't had to put up with the years building up to the event. Ten years, in Valerie's case.'

'Even so,' Helen said, clearly unconvinced. 'What about Clara, or David? If Edward didn't tell Clara his plans, she might have lost her temper.' She shrugged. 'And David has not been exactly rational since the news broke.' Her hand went involuntarily to the bruise under her eye.

'Bloody madman.' A sudden cloud darkened the little garden where they had been pacing for the last few minutes and they heard the first hailstones fall like broken rosary beads onto the stone flags.

'Shit,' Ruth said eloquently.

They ran for cover and found themselves a couple of minutes later inside the Horace Shelby library, shaking melting ice from their hair and continuing their speculation.

'Either of them could've done it,' Ruth said, her voice echoing in the high, empty space of the foyer. 'And what about Mick Tuttle?'

'*Mick?*' Helen blinked.

'It's no secret he hated Edward. He's strong enough. If he surprised Ed in bed—'

'Come off it, Ruth. He may be strong, but he could hardly be described as fast. And how the hell would he surprise Edward in bed wearing those callipers?'

'If it was nearer Christmas Ed might've thought it was the ghost of Christmas future coming to haunt him,' Ruth said with a sardonic smile. 'But you're probably right — Mick isn't a strong candidate. It'd help if we knew who'd altered the files. Who had access to Ed's password?'

Helen flushed slightly. 'Valerie, Me, Clara? Anyone with a bit of know-how can get access to a password, Ruth. And to make it really easy, Ed used to keep it on a slip of paper in his wallet — I've found it lying around on his desk a few times. He never agreed with the computer services' policy of expiring the passwords periodically — said he'd only got used to one when they forced him to change it.'

'Ellis is a keen computer user, isn't he?' Ruth said, in answer.

'So what?'

'So, he might know how to hack in to Ed's files — to alter them.'

'But *why?*'

'I'm working on that,' Ruth said. 'We know that Mick had a blazing, ding-dong, toe-to-toe, eyeball-to-eyeball confrontation with Ed the morning of the murder. If we knew why, then perhaps the rest would all come clear.'

CHAPTER 14

The entire plan was perfectly executed. The practice run-through had been just like the real thing, except that his eyes wouldn't stay closed. I couldn't bear him staring up at me from under those unevenly closed lids, like a tipsy judge, so I held them down with two fifty-pence pieces until they stuck. I can hear those two coins jingling in my pocket as I walk, I took them with me, a memento, and a private joke. What are they? No more than loose change. But what have they done? Where have they been? Next time I speak to the police, maybe I'll buy us a cup of coffee with these fifty pences. 'Sugar, Inspector? No, Inspector, I can't imagine why anyone would want to kill poor Edward. Please — let me get these . . .' Or maybe I'll keep them as make-weights, ringing out like leper bells: Unclean! Unclean!

* * *

'I'd like to question her with her GP present,' Hackett said.
'Who?'
The discussion of strategies had been going on in this distracted fashion for a full fifteen minutes, with Hackett making suggestions and Nelson either missing the point or deliberately obstructing him, and Hackett was beginning to weary of it.
'I'm talking about Dr Wilkinson.'

An innocuous statement in itself, but there was a suggestion of impatience, a whisper of insubordination — he'd heard it himself — and distracted or not, Nelson was sensitive to such things. He flashed a warning, his eyes kindling to gold for a brief moment, but quickly fading to dun brown.

'I'd like a chat with Ellis,' Nelson said. 'A real chat, I mean. Formally.' There was no emphasis on the 'I', no indication that he had heard Hackett's suggestion at all.

'Why?' Hackett asked.

'*Why?*' The heat of Nelson's glare was searing, but still Hackett could not force an apologetic 'sir' and after a second or two, Nelson went on: 'He's shifty, hiding something.'

'So is half the academic staff of the college, from what I can make out.'

'Got guilt written all over him.'

'He's edgy, sure, but—'

'Edgy my arse,' Nelson interrupted. 'He reeks of guilt. It oozes from his pores like sweat.'

Hackett had noted the nervy, twitchy movements of Ellis's hands, the constant tightening of his jaw muscles, but he was a PhD student with everything to prove, and nobody fighting his corner, from what Hackett could make out.

'He can't even look me in the eye when I speak to him,' Nelson added.

Hackett shook his head. Nelson generally took sustained eye contact as a challenge to his authority.

'He lies,' Nelson went on. 'Obvious lies. He can't even be bothered to lie convincingly. Said he was looking for Mallory when I caught him hanging around her office yesterday, but Mallory says he's been trying to catch up with the lying toe-rag for a couple of days. And he was here, loitering outside, just before Dr Wilkinson's interview.'

Hackett took a breath. 'We've got Helen Wilkinson practically begging us to let her confess,' he said. 'Ainsley's so beside himself with rage at his wife's infidelity he can't bring himself to set foot inside his own house. So, what makes you think Ellis—?'

'Don't use that tone with me,' Nelson snarled. 'Your inquiries into those two haven't exactly come up with signed confessions. If Helen Wilkinson is falling over herself to confess, why is it that all you've got is "I'm not sorry he's dead."'

Hackett was mildly surprised — Nelson must have been listening, at least to that part of his debriefing on the interview.

The two men fell silent,

'You spoke to Wilkinson's secretary,' Nelson said, at length.

'Twice,' Hackett replied. 'Once about the staff interviews and once about the professor's files being messed about. The professor certainly didn't mince his words on their relative performances in the Research Assessment Exercise — and of course the merging of faculties means some departments simply won't be viable.'

'Let's get her in again, see what she knows about our Mr Ellis.'

Hackett suppressed an exasperated sigh. 'What about Dr Wilkinson?'

'What about her?' There was no mistaking the look: Nelson was not about to tolerate any further discussion in the matter. Hackett, however, was not a man to give up without a fight.

'I just think, sir, that you should consider—'

He got no further. Nelson was on his feet and shouting and Hackett, permitting himself a heavy sigh, decided he had better do as he was told.

* * *

Mrs Roberts had been brought in a second time immediately after Ruth Marks's revelation that she had been earmarked for early retirement. She was, after all, the person most likely to have access to Prof Wilkinson's password and hence the Apocalypse file. Initially, she had denied any knowledge that Edward was planning to pension her off, but she was a woman not used to deception, and the dishonesty had proved hard for her to sustain, especially when they had discovered that she'd made discreet enquiries to the heads of several departments about the availability of secretarial posts. She had confessed, then, but although she had admitted to lying about the security of her job with the professor, she was unrepentant. It was not, she had told them, because of any inadequacy of hers that Professor Wilkinson had planned to get rid of her, thus implying that the inadequacy was all his. She vehemently denied having tampered with the Apocalypse file and although she was almost certainly hiding something, they could get no further.

Today, Mrs Roberts was discretion itself. Hackett had unwittingly prepared her for the ordeal of a third confrontation by manifesting in the short walk from their temporary base in Mallory's office to hers, a terseness, ill-temper and rudeness that was untypical of him, but which approximated, if rather pallidly, to Nelson.

She had arrived at Mallory's commandeered office some ten minutes after the summons, girded mentally with the steeliness and unassailable pride of a middle-aged Boudica.

Yes, she told them, a number of academics had exchanged heated words with the professor. No, she did not know the details of their disagreements. 'I think,' she said, settling back in her chair in a physical intimation that she would sit there all day if necessary, without betraying a single secret, 'that you really ought to be addressing these questions to the staff concerned, and not me.'

Nelson let her go after half an hour, disgusted with her.

Ruth Marks was more forthcoming, although no more helpful, as it turned out. She stood at the threshold of Mallory's office, her arms quite relaxed at her sides. 'Well,' she said. 'Isn't this a transformation! Incredible, isn't it, what a flick with a duster and a new perspective can do to enhance a place?'

Hackett covered a smile, but Nelson was not in the mood for levity. 'Dr Marks—' he began, but Ruth swept past him and began a deeper assessment of the alterations they had made to the office.

'The tarantula, for instance. Now I knew that wouldn't appeal to you, Inspector Nelson. All those beady eyes on you.' She gave a sensuous little shudder. 'As for the skull . . . To be frank, if it were my office, I'd rather have it sitting on the desk scowling out at my visitors than on the shelf glaring at me.' She tilted her head. 'But you know best.' She perched on the edge of Mallory's desk, staring thoughtfully up into the empty eye sockets of the skull. 'Most people assume it's an attempt by the old curmudgeon at humour, but in fact it's a reminder of *what could happen*. The cigarette? It's the last one from the very last pack of Capstan Extra Strength that Mallory ever smoked. There's even a family resemblance, don't you think?'

Nelson, who was not incapable of patience when the occasion demanded it, had listened to all of this with his head tilted on one side. 'I'm intrigued that you seem to know so much of the personal histories of your colleagues,' he said. 'Perhaps you can be as informative on the subject of John Ellis.'

She laughed, shaking her head, still with her back to him. 'Amassing a body of knowledge about a staff takes time and energy.' Her eyes twinkled and Hackett again sensed that edge of sexual mischievousness he found both stimulating and disturbing. 'And in the departmental hierarchy, Ellis, as a doctoral student, ranks just above an amoeba.' She looked over her shoulder, adding in a confidential tone, 'I don't like to waste my energy.'

Nelson gazed at her with half-closed eyes. 'Nevertheless, you did lie for him.'

She faced him, now, raising her pale eyebrows and placing one long-fingered hand across her chest in a dramatic gesture. 'When could I *possibly* have—?'

'Yesterday,' Nelson said. 'Dr Wilkinson's office. He wasn't there to pay his respects.'

'Oh,' she said, pretending wide-eyed innocence. 'Wasn't he? Are you sure, Inspector?'

Nelson stared at her, and Hackett saw a dark creeping flush of red spill from his neck onto his face. What was it about Ruth Marks that constantly put Nelson off-balance?

'I can't say that I know why he wanted to see Helen. He didn't confide in me,' Ruth said soberly.

'What do you know about him?'

Ruth turned down the corners of her mouth, thoughtful now. The flippancy, the sly humour vanished, if only momentarily. 'As I said — he's a postgraduate student, doing doctoral research.'

'What kind of research?'

'Behavioural ecology,' she said promptly. 'Animal physiology. Invertebrates. Mallory's his supervisor — he'd be able to tell you more.' She gave a short laugh. 'On the other hand . . .'

Hackett wondered what she meant by that, but Nelson interrupted his question: 'He's worried about this research project or thesis, or whatever you call it?'

Ruth Marks jutted out her lower lip, considering. 'He's built a certain notoriety for himself on the basis of a bit of dodgy maths. If he can't back it up with actual data, he's going to upset a lot of people who have personal investments in his theory.'

'Investments — you mean cash?' Nelson said.

'Not up front, but he's working on the trendy — and possibly lucrative — idea that population dynamics is linked to a self-regulating mechanism within the biosphere. Mother Earth protecting us from ourselves — a comforting notion, and quite popular in these post-Darwinian, post-atheistic, quasi-religious times.'

'What, you mean Gaia, that sort of thing?' Hackett asked.

Ruth's eyebrows shot up. 'You astound me, Sergeant!'

'My son's into all that New Age stuff. Can't get him to church on Sundays, but he believes in Gaia, all right.'

'I shouldn't worry too much. For Gaia, read God. *Homo sapiens* is neurotic by default — ever since we became sentient, we've been trying to make sense of why we're here. It — sorry, *she* — for Gaia is a she — is simply a trendier variant on the theme of deity. God with science PR — Saatchi and Saatchi style.'

'I'm sure this is fascinating,' Nelson said, 'but can we get back to Ellis?'

Ruth narrowed her eyes at the inspector, and for a moment, Hackett thought she might clam up, but after a pause which made her point eloquently, she went on, 'John has upset the vast majority of behavioural ecologists, physiologists, zoologists, environmentalists — in fact just about every species and subspecies of biologist *except* the crackpots who would like Gaia to be true. He has quite a following on the Internet — you should see the email he gets. If he's right — which any real scientist must seriously doubt — he could revolutionize our view of population dynamics.'

'And if he doesn't find the proof for his theory, all these people will be disappointed?'

'That's far too bland a term for it, Inspector. They'd be crushed. Humiliated. Mortified. Devastated. And you know who they'll blame.'

'What would happen to him?' Hackett asked.

'He'd be finished before he really got started.'

'So,' said Nelson, 'He's a worried man.'

'They all are, about the one thing or another,' she said. 'The Senate is talking in terms of thirty per cent wastage. Redundancies — in a university — I ask you!'

'*You* don't seem particularly worried.'

'Me?' She slid a sideways glance at Hackett. 'Didn't your sergeant tell you?'

Hackett shifted his weight from one foot to the other, trying not to look like he'd been caught out, and reflecting ruefully that Nelson wasn't the only one Ruth Marks put off-balance.

'I'm off to the United States as of August,' Mark said. 'I've been invited onto an interdisciplinary team working with neural nets — specifically the development of a part-biological and part-silicon-based brain. I'm going to be helping to develop the wetware — that's the biological side.'

She laughed. 'Don't look so horrified, Inspector. It won't be a human brain, although they do use human brain cells — from donated cadavers. The brains are packaged and shipped to the research facility before the neurones start to degenerate. You can keep clusters of cells alive for a very long time, given the right tissue fluids and stimulation.'

Hackett had never seen her so animated, so enthused about anything. He had thought her incapable of rising above her cynicism, but apparently this was something she believed in. Nelson, however, had heard enough. It seemed he disapproved of the whole concept of digging out people's brains and then sticking them in jars and giving them electric shocks.

'Yes,' he said testily. 'Thank you — that will do.'

'Oh, well, that was easy,' she said, heading for the door.

'I didn't say you should go,' Nelson said, and the harsh grating of his voice seemed to give her pause. She turned, with a smile to face him once more.

'So you didn't fall out with Professor Wilkinson on the day he died?' Nelson said, returning to his original theme.

'I'm one of the few who can say that, hand on heart, and mean it,' Ruth replied, solemnly miming the action.

'Would Ellis have cause to argue with the professor?'

Ruth considered. 'Edward loved to pick fights with people, just to show how completely he could win.'

Hackett sensed that the academic might be willing to say more, given the right sort encouragement. 'You, um — couldn't speculate as to why Ellis might argue with the professor?' he said.

'I *could*,' Dr Marks said. 'But would it be ethical?'

'We really would appreciate some help here, if you think you can give it, Dr Marks,' Hackett pressed, seeing that Nelson's meagre reserves of patience were almost exhausted.

'I'm afraid I haven't got a confession to the murders for you, Sergeant.'

'But . . .' Hackett prompted, thinking that her sharp perception really must rankle, if she was as unguarded in what she said to her colleagues.

She smiled. 'But I *will* tell you this: John Ellis is a troubled soul.' She looked from Hackett to Nelson, revelling in having their undivided attention. 'He has bad dreams.'

Nelson invited her to take a seat, and Hackett moved to lean against the cabinet of beetles so that he had a better view of her.

'At first, they were simply rehashed versions of his interview with Edward, but apparently he's started having a recurring dream. Now, I know it's only a matter of days since Edward was murdered—'

Hackett thought, *How easily she says that word*. Most people couldn't bring themselves to use it at all, and those that did would hesitate, or look away, a reflection of their embarrassment or disbelief. Yet Ruth Marks used the word unflinchingly. For her, it was just a word, the most suitable one for the situation.

'—But poor John has been sleeping badly, and whenever he falls asleep, he has this dream. He describes it as a "terrible dream". He finds it deeply troubling. He can have it four or five times a night, and he wakes from it in terror. It's disturbed his sleep patterns so much he's taken to cat-napping during the day — and the instant he falls asleep he starts to dream.'

'A nightmare,' Nelson murmured, and Hackett and Ruth both glanced at him, but he seemed engrossed in some abstract thought.

'The content of this recurring dream?' Hackett asked, thinking she does seem to have a talent for gaining people's confidence.

'Why don't I tell it to you, verbatim?' she said. She closed her eyes for a few moments and sat upright, clasping her hands lightly in her lap. Opening her eyes, she began:

'*I'm sitting on jagged rocks; at my feet is a net full of oysters. I'm opening the oysters with a knife and scooping out the pearls. Helen*

Wilkinson is watching me and I suddenly realize that I'm using the knife that killed Prof Wilkinson to prise open the oysters. I can't stop, because I don't want to draw attention to the fact and I don't want to upset Helen, so I carry on, opening the shells and casting the pearls into the sea, which is lapping at my feet. I've counted one hundred and twenty-five so far.

Then Helen is gone, and Edward is standing over me. He says, 'How many?' and I answer, 'One hundred and forty-seven.' He dips his hand into the water and scoops out a pearl, then he drops it into a beaker of water. But it isn't water, because it fizzes and Edward says, 'Drink it down. It'll set you right.'

I want to run. I know, you see, that the drink must be acid to make the pearl dissolve, but I can't move. I take it and he makes me drink. It tastes bitter. Then I wake up.'

There was a silence of three or four seconds and then Nelson demanded, 'Well?'

Ruth raised her eyebrows. 'Well what?'

'What the hell is it supposed to mean? What am I supposed to make of it? Does it mean anything?' Nelson demanded. 'You must have some idea.'

Ruth shrugged. 'I'm a neurologist, not a psychologist. You're the detective. You work it out.'

CHAPTER 15

Fear had made Dr Patterson timid: 'I'm not your priest,' he had said, regretting it even as he spoke. 'Whatever you tell me cannot be held an inviolable secret.'

Dr Wilkinson had accepted his anxious warning with a small nod, as though it was only what she had expected, and had left without another word.

He had almost followed her into the hallway of the large old house which served as both surgery and home to the practice partners, but Sanjay had fought hard for what he had achieved, and he was not about to risk losing it over a scandal. He was ashamed to think this way, but he couldn't change the fact that he didn't want to hear what Helen Wilkinson had to say. It was, he knew, by an uneasy intuition, dangerous in a way that Inspector Nelson, for all his ill-suppressed violence could never be: what she wanted to tell him was the stuff of ruined reputations — perhaps not his, at least not directly — but such secrets, once out, had a way of tainting all they touched, even incidentally. He did not want that risk; the burden of sharing her secrets would, he was convinced, prove too hazardous.

This refusal to share her secrets, even as an observer, had come as a shock to him. Until the moment that she had begun to take him into her confidence he had convinced himself that he would do anything to help. He had seen Helen Wilkinson through the first few months of pregnancy; the morning sickness, her doubts about having the baby, and her eventual acceptance and joy. Her husband's affairs had been common knowledge throughout the university. He had admired Helen's courage and dignity and sympathized with the hurt her husband caused her. He had attended her when she had been discharged from hospital after the miscarriage and had been deeply affected by her quiet strength despite an intense and poignant sense of loss. But friendship could be taken only so far, and only so much could be expected of him professionally, he reasoned. Nevertheless, he could dispel the feeling that his refusal to listen was cowardly, that he had failed her.

* * *

Helen had returned to her office just after four without any specific task in mind, but unable to face battling through the disorderly ranks of reporters outside the college gates in order to go home. They would, she knew, be there no matter how long she put off leaving, but she needed time to recover from Sanjay's Patterson's rebuff. She didn't blame him; within the confines of the university, an Asian doctor was viewed in the same light as a woman academic: exotic, an amusing diversion from the norm, but to be treated with caution and regarded with suspicion, since either or both could bring the deadly spores of liberalism and change. So, although Sanjay had a good Celtic surname, inherited from his Scottish father, he was not, in the eyes of the college establishment, entirely to be trusted.

A phone call from Edward's father had demonstrated unequivocally how entirely she was alone. She was crying when Mick Tuttle came into the room; weeping silently, tears of loss and confusion and self-doubt and exhaustion. The cynic in her asked what precisely she had lost, and

Edward's image was supplanted by a fleeting vision of her baby, small enough to fit into the palm of her hand, so terribly, immutably still.

After a brief confusion over the bruise on her face, Mick had accepted her explanation that she'd had an upsetting phone call and had made coffee in silence, giving her time to recover. She mumbled a 'thank you', accepting the mug, and he lowered himself into the chair opposite her, waiting for her to begin.

'I'm sorry,' she said. 'I thought I was finally getting myself together.'

'Who was the call from?' he asked.

'Edward's father. He and his wife are staying at the Chester Grosvenor.' She looked wildly about the room. 'Oh, Mick — what can I tell them?'

He didn't reply at first, but regarded her thoughtfully, his dark eyes brimming with sympathy. 'You don't have to tell them anything,' he said. 'They just want to be near their son, and now you're the closest they can get.'

Helen shook her head. Tears glistened on her lashes. 'They want answers — they've read the papers, heard the speculation. The knife missing from the kitchen, the infidelity, my miscarriage — oh God!' She covered her face with one hand. Mick gently prised the coffee mug from her grasp and set it on the desk, then he knelt beside her, and she thought of the pain in his knees and begged him not to.

He put both arms around her and held her to him. She drank in scent of his cologne, feeling the heat of him through his shirt, grateful for the comfort of human contact.

After a time, she subsided. The coffee was cold, and he made some fresh. She winced with him as he got slowly to his feet, testing the strength of his joints before putting his weight on them.

Helen washed her face at the little vanity basin, and he passed her a towel from the hook next to it. They returned to their seats and at first she avoided his eye, but after a few minutes she looked up tentatively, nursing the coffee mug in both hands.

He returned her look, his calm eyes unflinching, unjudging. Sunlight came and went in breathless bursts, barging out in brilliant ebullience and then disappearing, swallowed up by clouds which threw occasional drops of rain onto the windows. In these brief rushes of dazzling light, his eyes danced with colour, tawny flecks and hints of hazel and chestnut sparked from the dark, almost black depths of his irises, colours of warmth and compassion.

Helen swallowed, took a breath and began. 'Edward's parents worshipped him. He's an only son. I mean, he was. They have a daughter, but—' She shrugged. 'It seems archaic — implausible — doesn't it, that boys should still be valued above girls?'

'It's sad, and it's wrong, but implausible?' he said. 'No.'

'Edward always had whatever he wanted, so he never learned that there are some things you can't — *shouldn't* have. He assumed that what he wanted was his by right, and his looks and his public-school charm ensured he always got it.'

Edward was young when they had first met, and she still in her teens, a student, insecure. Edward had made something of a pet of her, liked to coax a smile from her. Not such an easy task in those days. She had felt singled out, blessed; his attention was a mark of distinction, it gave her confidence and eroded her self-hate. So, when he had pretended not to know her on her arrival at St Werburgh's, she had been hurt — stricken even. Of course, it had been a pretence, she had realized that when the excitement of his subsequent gallantry and courtship of her had begun to fade, after the gloss of marriage had accumulated a few months' dust. After that, she began to see Edward for what he was, and she despised the trick as infantile and cruel — a measure of his superficiality. Perhaps not all at once, but in small, shocking revelations, she saw his vanity and his monstrous narcissism.

When she first knew him, as a student and acolyte, he had an angelic look in repose, which she had mistaken for innocence. She couldn't have known then that the statuesque composition of his features had been carefully rehearsed in a mirror. With age, he had managed with this conscious control of his facial muscles to maintain a smooth, almost flawless mask, but the few lines and wrinkles he had been unable to avoid betrayed his inner self, emphasizing the meaner aspects of his nature. The deep grooves over his left eye gave him an effortless expression of superciliousness and a line, fine and indistinct as yet, from his right nostril to the corner of his mouth would, had he lived, have become a more or less permanent sneer.

'His parents couldn't see the flaws in his character, the casual cruelty, the way he used and manipulated people,' Helen went on. 'For them Edward was — will always be — perfect.'

'And you can't make all the things he did and said unhappen. You can't tell them all those things in the press are lies, is that it?'

Helen sighed and nodded, relieved not to have to explain this, at least. She took a swallow of coffee to slake the terrible dryness in her throat. 'After the—' She took a breath. 'After I lost the baby.' She frowned, fighting for control. 'I couldn't think straight. Sometimes I couldn't remember what I'd done or said. There were blanks. Blackouts. Some days, I couldn't find the energy to get out of bed. And all the while he was carrying on his affair with David Ainsley's wife' — she couldn't bring herself to say the name — 'and tormenting me with my failure, as he saw it.'

Mick gave a low, choked exclamation.

'There was only one thing I wanted at that time.' Helen was completely calm as she reached this part of her story. 'I wanted Edward dead. I wanted to kill him myself. I even planned how I would do it.' She brought her gaze level with Mick's. 'A knife between the ribs.'

Mick's expression was serious, attentive, but it held no hint of repugnance and this gave Helen the courage to continue.

'It was a fantasy, Mick, no more. Then one day I found the knife — the one that's disappeared from the block, the one the police are looking for. I'd put it in my little cabinet by our bed. Except I couldn't — still can't — remember putting it there.'

Perhaps he read the pain and confusion in her face, because Mick reached out and took her hand. 'What did you do with it?' he asked.

'I returned it to the block. But, Mick, it's gone again, and the police think—'

'And *you*, Helen. What do you think?'

She passed one hand wearily over her eyes. 'I wish I knew. I wanted him dead — for the death of my child. I wanted to kill him.' She looked at Mick. 'A life for a life.'

It wouldn't be the first time she had felt that way. On that other occasion she had failed, but only just. And this had been better planned, carefully rehearsed. She shook her head, trying to clear her mind.

'I'm so confused. I can't separate the fantasy from—' She frowned; she had been about to say, 'from what really happened', but she didn't know what had really happened, she didn't even know if she had been there.

'I keep thinking, every time I open a cupboard or a drawer, that I'll find the knife hidden—' She stopped. The whole thing seemed too wild, too crazy.

He considered, then nodded as though coming to a decision. 'How about checking over the house together?'

Helen looked up, startled. His hand, warm against hers, strong, increased its pressure slightly. She smiled, thanking him silently.

* * *

Isaac Smolder watched from his office window. Mick Tuttle had returned to his office, and Helen was standing alone in the quad.

Those eyes! She glanced up at the windows, with their hundreds of glinting panes, reflecting fleeting cold light, and

139

she seemed almost to look through and beyond Smolder. Yet he was certain she could feel his presence.

He experienced again that compulsion to know her thoughts, to see inside her mind. What would she do without Edward? That man was foul, destructive, but perhaps she had needed the dubious security of his tyrannical control. He nodded to himself. He thought he was beginning to understand Helen Wilkinson: her confusion, her timidity and abhorrence of change had led her to accept less than she deserved.

Her hair fell forward, curtaining her face. It gleamed with a warmth that seemed almost to challenge the feeble sunlight. He willed her to see him. To acknowledge him. She stood with her head tilted on one side, as if listening; an unconscious pose, but beautiful, like a carefully composed photograph, and he had a sudden, wild urge to capture that unstudied, natural moment.

He glimpsed a movement in the doorway from the main building and looked down, simultaneously pulling a little away from the window, out of sight. Someone had joined her. From his vantage point above the quad he had seen a number of comings and goings: Helen and Ruth; Helen and Ellis; Ruth and Ellis, Helen and Detective Sergeant Hackett, but none was stranger, none more devastating than this. Helen with Mick Tuttle. Smolder felt a pain radiate like a starburst in his chest. He wanted to tear at it with his fingers, to excise it, but instead he turned back to his room and sat at his desk to begin writing his journal entry. To anyone passing his open door, the suffering in his face might seem no more than a dyspeptic spasm, but his heart was lacerated and it felt almost that he was bleeding internally.

* * *

In the refectory, Ruth Marks tore another cob of bread from her roll and smothered it with margarine. She opened the tiny jam pot, still holding the knife and watched the drama unfold. Ellis had flounced in moments before. His eyes were raw-looking and the dark circles beneath them attested to his lack of sleep.

He threw an acid-damaged and dirty lab coat onto a table nearby, shaking with rage. Teacups were overturned and two of the technicians at the table jumped up, knocking over their chairs and protesting loudly.

'Who took it?' Ellis was red in the face, barely in control.

A voice somewhere behind him grumbled, 'It's bloody disgusting, bringing that filthy rag in here.'

Ellis wheeled on the man, a fellow graduate student with whom Ruth knew Ellis had a long term, low grade feud. 'Mind your own bloody business.' Breathless with fury, he turned back to the table. 'Who took my money?'

A post-doctoral student, dark-haired, lightly tanned from a brief trip to his parents' time-share in Spain, relaxed, sure of his welcome, strolled over, carrying a tray. 'What's up?' he asked, casually pushing the lab coat to one side and sliding the tray onto the table.

'Ellis is bitching again.'

The graduate student had spoken up a second time, deliberately baiting Ellis. He was bigger, a rugby player, also fitter than Ellis, and he looked like he'd put up with about as much griping and foot-stamping as he was prepared to from the smaller man.

'I just want to know who stole my money!' Ellis shouted, addressing this statement to those seated at the table, as an appeal to their decency and a means of deflecting the anger of the rugby player.

'No one stole it.' The woman who had spoken, a small, mousy-haired Masters student, riffled through the pockets of the filthy lab coat and finally fished out a one-pound coin. 'We swapped it for a couple of fifty p's.'

Ellis's eyes grew rounder, emphasizing the dark circles around them. 'You took *my money*. My personal *property*.'

This was an old grouse: in the research lab, a good deal of 'swapping' went on, but most people, both students and staff, were philosophical; the odd filched biro or stick of chewing gum had to be balanced against a pleasant working relationship with the rest of the crew. Ellis could not — could never — accepted this. What was his was private; no one had the right to touch his property, borrow his lab coat, rummage through his pockets, or swap one coin for another. To a man of his closed mentality, it was intrusive at best and criminal at worst.

One of the technicians spoke up, smiling foolishly. 'I needed fifty p for the coffee machine. You know it won't take one-pound coins—'

'You bloody bastard!'

The post-doctoral student seemed unruffled by Ellis's exhibition. 'Listen, man,' he said, smiling the crooked smile that the girls found so irresistible. 'You've got to get used to give 'n' take in a research lab. Graham didn't mean anything by it. Chill out, will you?'

Ellis's eyes bulged. Ruth could see a blood vessel standing out on his temple.

'He'll burst something,' Ruth muttered, scooping more jam onto the last little ball of bread without taking her eyes from the scene.

'You give it back. I need those fifty p's. You had no right! They're my personal property!' he was screaming now.

Graham, the technician who had taken the coins rolled his eyes. 'Oh, for fuck's sake, John, get a *life.*'

* * *

Helen telephoned Ruth from home, some hours later. Mick had helped her search every inch of the house — supervised her might be a more accurate description, since she insisted on Mick checking with her every cupboard and drawer, every bookshelf and box file, no longer trusting the evidence of her own eyes.

'Do you want me to come over?' Ruth asked.

'No . . . I think I'll make an early start in the morning, see Edward's parents and then go and visit mine — try and shake off the tabloid hacks for the weekend and get my research submission completed. Thanks for your comments, by the way. I'll incorporate them into the discussion.' Her face grew hot, hearing her words as Ruth would hear them: forced, stilted.

'About to schkip town, huh, schweetheart?'

Helen smiled. She could imagine Ruth drawing her lips back from her teeth to get the Bogart lisp just right. 'I've told Sergeant Hackett where he can reach me. He suggested leaving a few lights on at home and slipping out the back way.'

'He's such a *nice* man!' Ruth exclaimed. 'You know, if he wasn't already spoken for, I'd set my cap at him myself.'

Helen shook her head, smiling. Ruth was irrepressible. 'I've told him you have a key, in case of emergencies — I hope you don't mind.'

'A key? To my place, or yours? Hey! And what about Mick Tuttle?'

Helen was stunned for a moment. She *had* given Mick a key to the back gate so that he could let himself in and out without being noticed by the reporters camped outside. 'Mick?' she faltered.

'Well, did he pop in for coffee as he'd threatened?'

'Oh!' Helen laughed, realizing her mistake. 'Yes. He was very sweet.'

Ruth made balking sounds at the other end of the line. '*Sweet!* Helen, really. Why don't you call him *nice* and be done with it?'

'What do you mean?'

'Sweet, nice, bland, nondescript, boring, tedious, vapid—'

'Yes—' Helen interrupted. 'All right. I get the general idea.'

'Well, talk about damning with faint praise!'

'Ruth—'

'All right . . .' Ruth sighed. 'But at least admit that you like him as a man.'

Helen said nothing, and she heard Ruth catch her breath. 'Oh my God . . . is that where you've been all afternoon? He wasn't in his office, either. Helen, you *minx*—'

'He helped me search the house,' Helen blurted out, just to make her stop.

'Search the—? Oh, Helen, you're not still obsessing about that bloody knife?' Helen heard a choked laugh. 'Sorry — bad choice of words.'

Helen took the phone away from her ear and glared at the receiver. Ruth had been impatient that Helen persisted in her self-doubt, or rather in the possibility that she might really have killed Edward and had refused to help her search the house, 'checking for non-existent evidence' as she termed it. She was about to hang up, when Ruth said:

'You didn't find it.' It was a statement of fact.

Helen now discovered a lingering and, she knew, unwarranted resentment against her friend, tempered by embarrassment and tinged with relief, that she and Mick hadn't found anything. Mick had left exhausted and she suspected in pain, but at least he had taken her seriously, had understood her need to convince herself once and for all, that the knife. The murder weapon — was not hidden somewhere in the house.

'If you *did* find it, I'd fall on it myself as an act of penitence for not having believed you,' Ruth said.

'I wish you wouldn't make jokes like that,' Helen said, wincing, but at the same time recognizing it as one of Ruth's veiled apologies.

'Who's joking?' Ruth replied. 'Look at it this way, they say some women fantasize about rape — not my scene, I have to admit — I see myself more as a dominatrix, but that's not my point. Just because they *fantasize* about it, does it mean they actually *want* to be raped? Of course not. Because in their fantasy, they're in control. They know exactly who the guy is — and more than likely they fancy him. They determine the moves, the duration, what he does or does not do, because the fantasy is theirs. But the *real* thing is someone else's fantasy; it's brutal and ugly. Like murder.'

Helen's eyes snapped to Ruth's.

'What?' Ruth said. 'I'm only telling it how it is.'

'I'm tired, Ruth,' Helen said, suddenly exhausted, and wanting to avoid an argument about Ruth's lack of tact.

'Okay, I'll pick up some wine and Chinese food, bring it round. We'll get hammered.'

Helen knew she would feel differently after a good night's sleep, but for now, she could not take another moment of her outspoken friend.

'I need some sleep,' she said.

'So,' Ruth said. 'You don't want your old buddy, your mucker, your pal—'

'Look,' Helen said, interrupting what she feared would become another of Ruth's thesaurus-mode monologues. 'If you'd really like to—' She regretted the words even as they tumbled out of her mouth. She really did need sleep, she hadn't been lying about that, but before that, she needed to think about Mick and her unexpected reaction to his presence in the house. His proximity as they searched through the seemingly endless boxes and bookcases had acted as a balm. A male presence that did not threaten or challenge, but which soothed and reassured, it was all the more shocking when they had touched as he climbed the ladder behind her to check the top shelf of the bookcase in her study and the contact had felt like an electric charge.

After a brief silence, Ruth said, 'I don't know about you, but I'm bushed. I've been holding John Ellis's hand for the last few hours.'

'John? Is he all right?'

'Don't ask. Suffice to say that counselling neurotics takes its toll, you know?'

Helen felt the muscles at the back of her neck tighten. 'Yes, I suppose it does,' she said.

A pause, then 'Oh, Jeez, Helen, I'm sorry. I didn't mean—'

Helen relaxed. 'It's all right, Ruth,' she interrupted. 'We're both tired.' It was a typical Ruth comment, unintentionally hurtful, retracted in an instant and probably worried over for hours afterwards. 'Forget it.'

'No,' Ruth insisted. 'I've put my size sevens right in it again, haven't I?'

Helen laughed. 'Who's being neurotic now?'

'Last offer. Do you want me to come over and keep you company?'

'Ruth, I'm fine. I've got a bit of sorting to do, then I'm going to bed.'

'Before you do, check out the fridge. You'll find something mouth-watering.'

'Ruth!'

'So, tell me you've eaten.'

Helen laughed. 'I promise I'll check out the fridge before I go to bed, Mum. But I can cope for one night on my own.'

There was a hesitation before Ruth said, 'To tell you the God's honest truth, I was hoping you'd say that. What I lust after most just now — picture this, if you will — is to curl up with a large gin and tonic (heavy on the gin) and tipple myself into oblivion.'

CHAPTER 16

Nelson's close scrutiny burned his skin. He felt it in tiny splashes, not enough to leave a mark, but sufficient to make his arms and upper body jerk in a hundred minor spasms. Like hot fat, it seemed to continue burning, layer on layer, until he could feel it freckling the pale flesh of his face, marking it. His cheek muscles twitched with each explosion of heat; he would be scarred by the encounter.

He covered his own eyes to protect them from the light coruscating from Nelson's in short, searing radioactive bursts. He knew there were gamma rays emanating in deadly particle-waves, penetrating the dermis, mutating irretrievably the Malpighian layer, burrowing deeper into his body, poisoning his liver and destroying it. He knew with a feverish helplessness that toxins were building up to dangerous levels.

Orange light pierced his fingers, he could see the glow even though his eyes were shut tight. He breathed hard, sobbing with each breath, and Nelson kept up his incantation of muttered words, arcane magic.

He fled to the window and stared out through the mesh, willing Nelson away. The entire room was now bathed in the unnatural sodium glare, it intensified and pulsated, gaining power from his neural circuits, piercing the protective carapace of his skull, probing the delicate pathways of thought, shorting the synaptic connections, destroying millions of cells in the ferocity of its heat.

A sudden scream roused Nelson and he became aware that he must have been staring. The stand-off between father and son had resulted again in a wordless battle of wills, the unspoken hostility that had characterized their every meeting. Hackett moved quickly across the room, anxious to stave off another outburst, soothing, calming, softly calling the boy's name.

'You're killing me!' the boy screamed. 'You're burning through my *brain*!' He turned to the metal grill on the window and plucked at it despairingly.

* * *

Smolder wondered how she could be so taken with that phoney, that invalid, that cripple. Helen always was easily moved to pity. Stray dogs, mangy cats, ragged people, the flotsam and jetsam of life. And now this — it's too obvious, too *hackneyed*, this elevated compassion, and for him!

He was consumed with disgust. She used her vulnerability like a pheromone. What is it? Some kind of exhibitionism? Wasn't she satisfied that she was free? What was she trying to do — drive him crazy? Smiling at that policeman — after all, he's oh so polite. And now that damned mutant, Tuttle! Letting him talk to her. Listening to him, taking his advice, throwing her door open to strangers. She'd be giving the press an exclusive before long. He flung down his pen, unable to concentrate. He knew what was right for her, why couldn't she see that?

* * *

Helen lay awake for a long time, listening to the muffled sighs and occasional creaks of the old house. She tested her feelings as one might test a bruise — gently, approaching the tender area obliquely. She had felt safe tonight with Mick Tuttle, protected in a way that she had longed for, but never felt, with Edward. It was something approaching trust; a warmth, an emotional security that Mick had summoned like a charm by his unquestioning, unjudging presence. With Mick, there was no need to keep up the defences she had built high to keep Edward at bay.

Soon, she would tell him the rest: about Robbie, but also about the night she had gone out, looking for the man she held responsible for his death, and finding him, had—

The moon flashed suddenly from behind a cloud, and she saw again the sharp glint of light on metal, the slow, arrogant walk, the easy smile, and she experienced the same searing rage that had made her want to kill.

Helen groaned and turned over. Pale, cold moonlight shimmered dimly through the curtains, casting shadows from the pear tree onto the window. She had arranged to meet Edward's parents the next morning and she had no words of comfort for them, no tears, no regret to share with them, no sense of loss. And now she was being drawn to the one man in the college whom Edward had despised more than any other! For hours she watched the pear tree's shadow see-sawing in the wind.

* * *

The exchange was quick, money for a twist of something wrapped in silver foil. 'Bold as you like,' the locals said, but this was not bold, it was discreet, a business transaction. No one wanted to get caught and, the trade completed, he left. Daniel Hackett couldn't see the harm in that. He wasn't shooting up in anyone's doorway. He didn't rob grannies on their way home from collecting their pension, and he resented being made to feel like a criminal just for the sake of the occasional tab of E, and maybe enough weed to roll a couple of spliffs.

Nevertheless, he walked quickly away from the housing estate. He'd been relieved of his purchases more than once on the dusty route back to the outside world, and if there was nowhere to run, it was best to give in with good grace: less chance of getting hurt.

The wind whipped up bits of grit, and he turned his face away to protect his eyes. In the darkness, chip papers and polystyrene boxes lifted and skittered along the road towards him, sinking as the wind dropped, as if in exhaustion, only to rise and dance a few fluttering yards more with the next gust. He tasted grit in his mouth and thought, this is excitement. This is real life. The comfortable, lazy existence his parents called living was like a long sleep, a living death.

A noise to his left made him whirl round, but it was only a tin can, skittering along in the wind, bouncing hollowly from gutter to roadway and back, overtaking him in its bustling urgency to be elsewhere. It was darker that the streets of home: lads with air rifles put out the streetlamps, sometimes for sport, and sometimes for money, or a little twist of paradise — the pushers didn't like to be too closely observed. Daniel laughed suddenly and started to run, chasing the tin can in the wind.

* * *

Nelson drove around the city aimlessly, first heading for home, but the thought of the empty house was unbearable, and he turned the car towards the city centre and the County Headquarters. The sight of the shabby, glass-fronted building depressed him further and he drove past, unable to stop the automatic glance upwards, the check on which offices were lit.

He flicked on the radio, punching the off button immediately to silence the nasal whine of a jilted cowboy. Finally, unable to stand his own indecision, he pulled over and jumped out of the car in a fury and landed a satisfying kick to its offside front wheel, screaming 'Fuck!' a few times for good measure.

A car full of youths cruised by, windows open, stereo thumping an insistent, meaningless beat: noise to attract notice. They hung out of the windows, laughing, asking if he had a flat tyre. 'Use the spare!' one wag yelled. 'The one keeping your trousers up!'

Their laughter, the noise, the erratic swerving of the car was enough. Instantly, Nelson was back in control, he didn't need to remind himself that he was a professional, these boys had welded him seamlessly back to himself. He watched their car edge past at a strolling pace and memorized the index number, even smiling a little as he put the call through to Traffic to have them pulled over and checked for drugs and booze.

Feeling much better, he drove on a little further, then swung off the road by Grosvenor Park and eased the car into the kerb in front of St John's church.

The night was cold, and the wind blew in petulant bursts, subsiding from time to time, before whipping up again to bring in a few spots of icy rain. Between the clouds, the Plough was just discernible, shimmering in the orange-tinged sky. He locked the car and walked down the narrow path between the ruins of the old collegiate church and the park. Its closely mown lawns were damp and sparkled in the ghostly light of a low-energy streetlamp.

Nights like this, he used to ache to be home. But that was when Beth was still alive. He always called her if he was going to be late and the miracle of it was that she never seemed to mind. She had made an adventure of those nights, listening to the radio while she ironed or sewed. Sometimes she would bake bread.

He still couldn't walk past a bakery without having to suppress a bubble of emotion, remembering the warmth of the house as he opened the front door, the air fragrant with yeast and malt and the faintly beery promise of the loaves proving by the hearth. And Beth, waiting for him, so cross with herself if she'd dozed off that he'd quickly learned to slam the door as he came in, to avoid disappointing her.

She was truly lovely, his Beth, with her thick brown hair and her creamy skin. Full-lipped and generous-spirited. She

151

had seemed to glow with an inner happiness during the pregnancy. Her skin was furred with the faintest hint of down, an ethereal phenomenon, which he could feel with his fingertips and his lips, but which suggested itself to the eyes only as a reflection of light from her face, like a golden aura.

And with the baby, she had died.

Not immediately, it wasn't a sudden demise: she wasted away, body and soul. Soul first, before the rest, in stages, one merging with the other until he couldn't be sure exactly when she reached the point from which she could not be recalled. It was as if the child had drained all the life out of her. She ignored it and of course it had keened like a lost kitten, endlessly, hopelessly. Even when he had succeeded in coaxing her into holding it, she had only looked at it with a kind of dull disgust.

Nelson thrust his hands deep into the pockets of his raincoat and trotted down the steps, slowing at the bottom to negotiate the stone sets that glistened, treacherously wet in the lamplight.

Baby Blues, the doctors had called it. In those days they had simply waited until the woman snapped out of it, hormone imbalances and biochemically induced depression as yet unheard of. So it went on for two years and eventually their GP had prescribed antidepressants, and the boy learned in infancy to mistrust, when he should have known only certainty. Even the provision of comfort and food, which he should have been able to take for granted, were provided sporadically, unreliably, for in Nelson's absence, when he went to work, or to buy groceries, there was no one to remind Beth, and Beth needed reminders. More importantly, the boy learned that he had no right to love. He was neither loved for himself, nor for what he did. His mother was unpredictable, except in her coldness towards him, and so he learned also to fear. He could not know that as he looked up at them with those huge fearful eyes, his fear and unhappiness was both an accusation and a reproach, but Beth felt it, and finally she could take it no more.

Nelson turned instead of crossing the footbridge and followed the path beside the river. At this late hour the riverside was deserted. His footsteps echoed in the quiet moments when the wind was still. He continued, deep in thought, only dimly aware of the sound of his footsteps ringing out on the flags and the biting cold nipping at his ears and his fingers.

He had found her, lying on the sofa, a bottle of whisky empty on the floor beside her — his whisky — a bottle of paracetamol beside it. Ever practical, she had placed a bowl beside her on the floor, but she hadn't the strength to lift her head, so she had lain in vomit half the night. The boy had been playing quietly on the floor beside his dead mother, and Nelson's overriding urge had been to yell at him: *Why didn't you stop her?*

They had pumped the child's stomach in case he had swallowed any of the pills and Nelson had felt a perverse, shameful, sadistic satisfaction in the boy's pathetic cries as he balked on the tube.

She had left a note: '*I thought it would be so perfect—*' The sentence was unfinished, the note unsigned.

Nelson paused at the bandstand to catch his breath and looked down at the black water. He hadn't allowed himself to think of this since the day it happened, since Beth's suicide. He had blanked out the details of that night, but it was there, always, like a haunting, if not the images of Beth, grey, repugnant in death, as she had never been in life, then the feelings he couldn't suppress: pulsating, fearful waves of emotion. He thought of all the times he had sat, staring at the boy in silence, hating him for taking Beth from him. The boy had curled up, shielding his eyes, hiding from him, from the hatred that must have flowed from him in tidal surges. Nelson uttered a cry of anguish and jerked away from the rail, walking quickly in the direction of the weir, wanting its roar to silence these newly awakened thoughts.

'He's burning into my brain!' the boy had babbled. 'His eyes. The fire. Make him stop! I can't think. *Help me!*' The screams had pursued Nelson into the corridor, down the staircase, out into the car park of the hospital. They echoed now in his head. He felt they would follow him — accusing him, cursing him for ever.

* * *

Helen surfaced briefly from a light sleep of confusing dreams, sighed and sank again. Moonlight and shadows played over the bedding, the dark jagged lines of the twiggy branches, and the pale blue reflections from raindrops on the window, dripping like melting wax down on the covers.

Her eyes opened and she was instantly awake, totally conscious. The hairs on the back of her neck stood up. A faint noise, no more than a creak and a dull thump, had roused her. She held her breath, waiting, listening, and imagined the intruder on the other side of the door, also listening, tense. The phone was in the hall, and that would be cut off by the intruder, but perhaps she could get out of the house by the patio doors. She eased herself into a sitting position and then stood. A floorboard creaked under her foot and she drew in a breath, her heart pounding. The presence grew stronger, an almost palpable menace filled the room. Helen saw the door handle begin to turn. She hadn't locked the door! She looked over her shoulder at the patio doors. If she got out she would be trapped in the back garden — the key to the side gate was in a drawer in the kitchen — would anyone hear her if she screamed for help? But if she surprised the intruder . . .

She went to the side table by the front window and picked up a statuette in bronze, a slender woman in diaphanous, clinging silk, but surprisingly, comfortingly, heavy. Helen moved to the door and raised the figure. As the door opened, she prepared to strike, then gasped in dismay and relief as the tall, muffled stranger yelped:

'What the f—?'

Ruth.

'Jesus, Ruth — I might've brained you!'

Ruth took the bronze statue from Helen's trembling hand and placed it on one of the bookshelves.

'I should bloody well brain *you*,' she growled. 'So much for alcoholic oblivion. Know where I've been?'

Helen stared at her friend. 'Ruth, what the hell are you doing here? Why didn't you call first — or at least ring the bloody doorbell?'

'You sound pissed off, Helen.'

'I am! You scared the shit out of me.'

'Good,' said Ruth. 'Why didn't you say something, Helen? Why didn't you warn me?'

'Warn you about what? For God's sake, Ruth, I thought you were—'

'What? The murderer? Or the dear departed Edward?' Ruth laughed, and Helen shuddered at the harshness of the sound. 'He wasn't particularly dear to you, though, was he, Helen, though his departure was dearly, devoutly hoped for.'

'Ruth, what *is* it?' Helen had never seen Ruth so angry.

'I've spent a couple of hours in the company of the lovely Sergeant Hackett, accounting for the fact that my computer was used to alter the Apocalypse file.'

'Oh.'

'Oh? Is that it? I lie through my teeth to protect you and all you can say is "Oh"?'

Helen went straight to the phone in the hall. There was no point in apologizing to Ruth in her present frame of mind. Neither Inspector Nelson, nor Sergeant Hackett were available — hardly surprising since it was the middle of the night, but the officer she spoke to suggested Helen come in and make a statement at a more acceptable hour. Helen hung up and turned to face Ruth.

She was still angry, but Helen could see that some of the heat had gone out of it and she was left with an overwhelming sense of Ruth's disappointment.

'Don't you trust me, Helen? After all we've been through together?'

'Ruth,' Helen reached out to touch her friend's arm, but Ruth flinched from her.

'You let me speculate about the people on the list — Valerie Roberts, Ellis, Mallory. Did you think it was some kind of game? Were you *laughing* at me, trying to make a fool of me?'

'Ruth, no!' Helen knew that Ruth's flippant humour and twisted irony were defensive measures, an armour against the snipes of colleagues who regarded women scientists as little more than window dressing, light, mindless froth, and yet, with typical inconsistency, condemned her research as unfeminine, immoral, projecting from it a terrifying future of cyborgs and cybernetic control. 'I just didn't want to involve you. I thought I could help a few people by altering Edward's records.'

'David as well — such Christian good will, Helen.'

'He has a child to support. And there's nothing wrong with his work. Edward simply wanted him out of the way—'

'Whose child?'

Helen was stung, but hadn't she thought the same herself? That Henry was Edward's son?

Ruth glared back, and Helen saw in her friend's furious gaze how much she had wounded her.

Helen sighed. 'Come on,' she said. 'We'll try for oblivion together.'

Ruth hesitated, then, shrugging, followed Helen through to her study. Helen poured two large measures of whisky and handed Ruth one glass. She took it begrudgingly.

'You're thinking what right have I to judge other people's work,' Helen said. 'Who am I to say David should stay on and Mallory go, right?'

'It might've crossed my mind.' Ruth flopped into a chair and scowled at Helen.

'The Senate were going to get rid of Mallory with or without Edward's say-so. He wanted to break the news himself, that's all, wanted Mallory to think it was all down to him.'

'I saw him leaving Ed's office on Monday,' Ruth said. 'It was not a dignified exit. Ed really was a bastard.'

Helen had no argument with that. 'If I'd changed Mallory's entry,' she went on, 'the Senate would've been onto it immediately. While I was waiting for you in your office, Valerie Roberts came in. She was looking for you.' Helen stretched out, pointing her toes, tapping her friend's foot with her own. 'Poor Ruth, folk are always seeking you out to unburden themselves. Valerie told me she'd lied to the police about Edward wanting to keep her on. She was afraid they'd find the file and suspect her — well, I know it's ridiculous, but I wasn't thinking straight.'

Ruth sucked her teeth and refused to respond.

'I was trying to put things *right*, Ruth. Trying to redress the balance a little. I thought maybe if the selection committee accessed the file they might be influenced — that they might respect Edward's last wishes.'

A glimmer of amusement lit Ruth's features and Helen lifted her shoulders and gave a rueful smile.

'I know,' Helen said. 'Pretty naive, huh?'

Ruth's faint spark of humour became a grin and they laughed. Ruth took a swallow of whisky and swilled it around her mouth before swallowing with a slight wince. 'Thing is, Helen, they're likely to suspect *you*, now. After all, you get a promotion out of it.'

Helen almost choked on her whisky. 'I didn't change *my* entry, for God's sake!'

'*The thing is,*' Ruth repeated, 'will the police *know* that?'

Helen chuckled. 'For someone who's at the cutting edge of intelligent computer systems you know very little about the basics of the software.'

'I'm strictly wetware, the *bio* of bionics. And anyway, neural nets aren't programmed in the same way as your standard UNIX system.'

Helen bowed her head, conceding the point. 'They can tell which entries have been edited and which haven't.'

'Well,' said Ruth. 'That's all right, then. So long as you're in the clear.'

Helen's smile faded. She wished she were in the clear, and that it was all as simple as checking databases — if her own memory were only as accessible! What was it in her that so mistrusted people that she hadn't even told Ruth that she had altered the files? Was it because she feared that the hidden part of herself might become visible to Ruth, and that, through Ruth she would be forced to see the awful reality of what she was, and of what she had done?

CHAPTER 17

Nelson seemed subdued, perhaps even reflective. The brooding anger was there still, unmistakably, seething beneath the skin but it had an altered complexion. He looked ill, and when Hackett had commented, he said that he'd spent most of the night thinking. Hackett believed this, although he would have given Nelson's ponderings another name: the inspector's present fixation on Ellis as a suspect was becoming an obsession and Hackett believed it was more than tenuously linked with his boss's visit to the hospital the previous evening.

The inspector had shaved, but badly, and his skin, always uneven in texture, and suffused with an angry glow, was nicked in several places and had a shiny, scalded appearance. His breath smelled of peppermints, but there were undertones of heavy alcoholic consumption and his movements were a little too controlled, a little too precise.

Hackett understood Nelson's frustration. It wasn't as if they didn't have anything to go on — there were, perhaps, too many people who would have liked to see Professor Wilkinson dead. And it wasn't as if the exhaustive list of suspects had watertight alibis — Helen Wilkinson had given conflicting stories as to where she had been at the time of the murder: first she had said that she had been with Ruth Marks all afternoon, then she had remembered that she had left work a little early and stopped briefly at the supermarket before walking home. David Ainsley and his wife were, separately — neither wishing to corroborate the other's story — at liberty and unobserved at the approximate time of death, Dr Ainsley working in his study at home and Mrs Ainsley walking the baby in a fruitless effort to lull the child to sleep. Ellis, whose behaviour was growing increasingly bizarre, had been working in the computer suite at the Horace Shelby library, again unobserved. Hackett wondered at the insular and rather lonely life these academics seemed to lead, that they could spend hours of each day sequestered in some silent spot with not a single soul knowing or caring where they were or what they were doing. Perhaps it was a symptom of the escalating paranoia surrounding the reorganization of the departments, together with the consequent 'staff wastage'.

Whatever the cause of the overwhelming atmosphere of secrecy and suspicion at St Werburgh's, it didn't help their investigation when all they had were a few smudged and useless fingerprints. The murder weapon was still missing and the high hedge at the front of the Wilkinsons' house and an even higher brick wall which enclosed the back had prevented even the most assiduous neighbourhood watchers from observing the murderer entering or leaving the premises.

'So,' Nelson said, breaking the silence at last. 'Is she covering for Ruth Marks?'

'Ruth has the least to hide,' Hackett said. 'She's leaving for a much better paid and resourced job in the States in a few months. She wasn't even listed on the Apocalypse file. What motive would she have?' They were seated at opposite sides of the desk in Nelson's cramped office. Helen had just left the headquarters after being interviewed. It was still early; Nelson had called Hackett in as soon as he'd got the message she had left during the night.

What motive? Nelson repeated to himself. He shook his head, and Hackett noted that his gaze seemed unfocused.

'What about one of the others?' Nelson smoothed a hand over his face. It trembled slightly over the short distance between desk and forehead. He looked terrible.

'Like who, for instance?' Hackett asked, distracted momentarily by the tremor.

'Clara Ainsley, for instance,' Nelson said with choleric impatience.

'Helen's unlikely to cover for *her*, of course,' Hackett said. 'She wasn't on the files, either, but Helen could be telling the truth when she says she was trying to help out the professor's secretary and do a few people a good turn in the process. Which means the alteration of the Apocalypse file might have nothing at all to do with the murder. Now if *Clara* thought Edward was going to get rid of her, what would she do? She said in her original interview that she saw Professor Wilkinson at the university, but Mrs Roberts says she wasn't listed in the appointments diary — and her story checks out. Of course, we know Mrs Roberts has no great affection for Clara, and that she has lied to us before. Neighbours saw no one enter or leave the Wilkinson house that afternoon. But the prof didn't commit suicide, did he? So, someone must've been there, and it's entirely feasible that Clara saw him at home, and not at the university.'

'In which case she's got some explaining to do.'

Nelson screwed up his eyes as if the light hurt his head. *He's got the mother of all hangovers*, Hackett thought.

'Fetch Mrs Ainsley in and talk to her again,' Nelson said. 'Give us a call when you're done. I'm going home for an hour or two.'

Hackett was glad of that, Nelson would not be much good in an interview the state he was in, and with any luck he'd think to shower and change before he came back. He wondered whether his boss had a single moment of contentment or peace, and thought that his own situation, despite its complications, must seem idyllic to a lost soul like Jack Nelson.

Hackett called in DC Tact to assist in the interview.

Clara responded to the young constable's vagueness, mistaking it for vulnerability. She combed her hair and insisted on getting changed before going with them. A university colleague agreed to look after the baby until she returned and as she slammed the front door shut, Hackett noticed that she had dabbed on a little make-up, but it couldn't entirely cover the dark shadows under her eyes and the grey tone of her skin. She declined her right to a solicitor, and the interview began at nine a.m.

'You say you saw Professor Wilkinson at his office on Monday,' Hackett said. His hand rested on a red leatherette-bound book.

Clara looked from Hackett to Tact, who was staring with intense curiosity looking at something a fraction to her left. Hackett saw her eyes twitch to the left, he wondered for a second if she would turn and follow his line of sight. But she blinked and sat up straighter and said:

'I've already been through all of this.'

'You told him you were finishing the affair,' Tact said, as though trying to fix the facts in his own mind. 'Is that right?'

Clara lifted one shoulder. 'It's already on record.'

'In his office?' Tact again.

Clara blushed.

'You told him you were finishing your affair, in his office,' Hackett repeated, approving of the line Tact had taken. 'Within earshot of the professor's secretary.'

Clara looked down at the tabletop. 'That's right.' She braced her shoulders and folded her hands demurely in her lap. 'I thought—' She stopped, seemed to consider the line she was about to take unwise.

'What did you think, Clara?' Hackett asked, leaning forward.

'I wasn't about to let him treat me that way—'

'What way is that?' Tact asked.

Two bright spots of colour grew and deepened on Clara's finely chiselled cheekbones. 'I thought he—' Hackett saw a tiny shake of her head. 'I'm *sure* he was seeing someone else.

I didn't want him to take me for granted. I couldn't bear to have people feel *sorry* for me as they did Helen.'

'I don't think there was any danger of that, do you?' Hackett said, slouching back in his chair, pausing so that the insult had more impact. 'Helen was his wife; she had a right to pity when her husband was unfaithful.'

Tact drew down the corners of his mouth. 'Mistresses don't have the same rights to sympathy,' he added, shaking his head regretfully. Hammering the point home.

Clara's eyes darted about the room, avoiding the two men. Her eyebrows were drawn together in a worried frown, and there was something in the set of her mouth that suggested tears were imminent.

'Professor Wilkinson's secretary has no record of you going to see him on Monday,' Hackett said, opening the red book and identifying it for the tape as Professor Wilkinson's appointments diary.

'I didn't need an appointment to see Edward,' she said with stiff dignity.

Hackett saw her swallow deeply and remembered from somewhere, the telly, or a course in interviewing techniques, that this was a sure sign that the interviewee was lying. Not that he needed to deploy such clever and close observation skills, since he had questioned Valerie Roberts on this very matter by telephone that very morning.

'Mrs Roberts says *everyone* needed an appointment to see the prof that morning — even his wife.'

'She *would* say that, wouldn't she?' Clara said with a sneer. But the colour in her face deepened.

'She did say you visited the prof that morning, or at least that you were on your way to see him. But someone was already with him.' Tact was staring in that focused, yet unfocused way over her left shoulder again. 'And you left.'

'I . . .'

'Come on, Mrs Ainsley,' Hackett said, gently. 'We're just trying to get at the truth here. You were fond of the professor, weren't you? You must want us to find out who killed him.'

Clara mumbled something, and Hackett asked her to repeat it for the tape. 'I said, I wasn't just fond of him, I loved Edward.'

'Well then,' said Hackett.

She looked into the Hackett's face and he could almost see her making the calculations, deciding of which snippets of information would throw suspicion off her.

'I had intended seeing Ed,' she said after a long pause. 'But when I arrived, he was having a terrible row with John Ellis.' She frowned and seemed to be trying to remember. 'No, that's not quite accurate. Edward's voice was only raised sufficiently to make himself heard over that lunatic's ranting. Ellis stormed out, screaming at Ed, threatening him, calling him names. "I won't let you do this to me. I'll sort you." Surely busybody Mrs Roberts told you? I didn't want her listening in on what *I* wanted to say to him. It was private.'

'So, you decided to see him later at home . . .'

Clara stared at Tact and he stared back. 'No, of course not. I was too busy with the baby.' But she had delayed too long, and everyone in the room knew that her hesitation was tantamount to an admission.

'When did you see him, Clara?' Hackett asked. 'At what time? We know he went home after lunch — sometime between one and two-thirty.'

She bowed her head.

'Someone murdered Edward Wilkinson, Clara.' Hackett leaned forward. 'Was it you?'

'No!' the flush drained from her face, leaving her sickly pale. 'Look I don't expect you to sympathize, but *I've* been bereaved, too—'

'I know this is difficult for you, Clara,' Hackett said. Then left a silence that lengthened, almost half a minute. They all felt the pressure of it; half a minute is a long time for silence between strangers. Clara felt it most, which was what he'd intended. Slowly, she began to speak.

'I — I'm not sure of the time.' Her voice was almost inaudible at first. 'Half one, two, perhaps? But I left Ed safe and well.'

She looked up at Hackett and her lashes were wet. 'I said some terrible things to him. I confronted him, said I knew he was being unfaithful to me. How could he *do* that to me?' Hackett searched her face, but the irony of what she had said seemed beyond her understanding.

'Now I don't know — maybe I was wrong. I don't understand why he didn't just tell me he was going to look after me — why he let me think those awful things about him?'

'More games?' Hackett asked.

'Maybe he *was* seeing someone else and wanted you as well,' Tact suggested.

She looked at him sharply, but he had that bland, vague look on his face. She shrugged. 'He didn't deny it. But then Edward never denied anything. "Never apologize, never explain." It was kind of a motto for him.' She fell silent.

'Clara?' Hackett prompted.

'He was so calm. It didn't seem to matter to him that I was going to leave him. I was so upset—' He gave a little sob. 'But he smiled and smiled and—'

'Did you have intercourse with Professor Wilkinson that afternoon?' Hackett asked.

'Of course not!' Clara gaped at Hackett, shocked. 'What do you take me for?'

Hackett left that question unanswered.

'Oh, my God,' she gasped. 'David said he'd been found in bed. You mean—?'

'Do you know who he was . . . seeing — apart from yourself, that is?' Hackett said.

She shook her head.

'What time did you leave?'

'I don't know.' Clara's hand went to her hair and she tugged at a strand, worrying and twisting it. 'I was only there about a quarter of an hour. I couldn't speak to him when he was like that.'

'Like what?' Tact asked.

She turned from Hackett to the young constable. 'Cold, distant, cruel.'

* * *

'He was found naked in bed,' Hackett said. 'Semen on the sheets. Clean sheets, fresh on that morning. He wasn't alone, either — forensic have got two types of pubic hair, and some fair or mousy hairs on the pillows, along with a few from his head. And from what Dr Wilkinson says, since her miscarriage there'd been no sexual contact between her and her husband.'

'D'you believe her, Sarge?' Tact asked.

'No reason not to. She hated his guts.'

Clara had been taken down to the cells after a tearful phone call to her babysitter. The babysitter would not hear of social services being called in and had agreed to keep the baby until Clara was released. Hackett and Tact had retired to the canteen to take a late, but well-earned breakfast.

Tact shrugged.

'Come on, Jem, let's have it.'

Tact carefully assembled a piece of fried egg, a sliver of bacon and a square of fried bread onto his fork, then dipped the lot in the yolk before sliding the lot into his mouth. 'I don't know what women see in that type.'

'Takes all sorts,' Hackett replied. 'Wilkinson was a clever — some say a brilliant man — women find that attractive.'

'No, I can understand that. But all the rest. The cheating, the lies, the power play.' He shook his head. 'Maybe that's where I'm going wrong.'

'Love life not up to snuff, Jem?'

Tact narrowed his eyes but chose not to grace the comment with a reply. 'Clara has no alibi, and plenty of motive,' he said. 'Aren't you eating those mushrooms?' Hackett was already regretting the fried breakfast he'd just eaten. He shoved his plate over and Tact scooped the mushrooms onto his own plate and continued. 'She now admits she saw Ed at home on the afternoon of his death and argued with him.'

'Closest we've had to an admission since the investigation began,' Hackett said. 'But Ellis *did* threaten the prof, so maybe we should have him in again.' Nelson would be well pleased. It was time to call him anyway.

Hackett accompanied Nelson to the university-approved accommodation at eleven o'clock on Saturday morning. It was a rambling Edwardian building, divided into flats and bedsits. The owners had made an effort to keep the paintwork in reasonable condition, but the occupants had put their own distinctive mark on the windows: coloured glass ornaments; stickers exhorting passers-by to legalize cannabis, to ban hare coursing, or organophosphates, or the second runway — this last was faded, the Sellotape yellowed and peeling from the window pane. Hackett reminded himself that this concern for the environment, mingled with rebellion against the constraints of conformity, were a natural progression, a modern equivalent of the rituals of rites of passage. It was just that Daniel, as the son of a policeman, had more to kick against than most teenage boys. He felt briefly consoled.

The front door was open. The two policemen wove past a motor bike and a rusting VW Beetle parked on the concreted front garden, and went in. For the moment, all was quiet. Several bicycles leaned against a large grey cupboard in the hall, in varying states of disrepair. The house smelled of lubricating oil, accumulated dirt and fried food. They climbed the stairs and knocked at number seven and were admitted by a dishevelled and disorientated John Ellis.

A quick glance around the grimy surfaces of the room confirmed Hackett's suspicions: that Ellis was undisciplined, disorganized — clever, perhaps — but without the dedication and single-mindedness required to bring his projects to a satisfactory conclusion. The room, in short, was a mess. Several days' dishes lay encrusted in the sink, several weeks' washing unsorted, smelling rankly at the foot of the unmade bed. Books and papers were strewn without apparent organization on around the spindly kitchen table that served as a desk. A few old-fashioned third-of-a-pint bottles lay on their sides on various surfaces around the room, their blue, slightly crusted contents had shrunk from the sides, desiccated, as were the remains of the tiny insects which had fed off it. A few of them were tangled in the cotton wool bungs and several more clung to the filter paper which must have served some purpose to the once-thriving colonies.

Nelson, Hackett knew, had made the same observations and come to the same conclusions he had. Hackett had stared for some moments at the logo on Ellis's T-shirt, proclaiming *E-quality for all!* waiting until Ellis was visibly squirming before asking with guileless charm, 'Something to do with *women's lib*, sir?'

They had taken Ellis to headquarters for questioning. Nelson had, with uncharacteristic candour, briefed Hackett regarding the shift to the station: its twin aims were to silence Mallory's bleating about needing access to his office, and to encourage Ellis to be more forthcoming, a possibility Nelson felt was more likely in the unsettling atmosphere of an official interview room.

* * *

Ellis sat, transfixed by the glare of Nelson's eyes. Sergeant Hackett stood near the door, his expression unreadable. Ellis tried to listen to what the inspector was saying, but the clamour of buzzing and sing-song twitterings in his head were distracting. The words formed like bubbles on Nelson's lips, they floated upwards, like lysosomes: tiny organelles filled with self-destruct enzymes, poisonous packets of annihilation.

'Something's been bothering me,' Nelson confided. Ellis turned his head, listening to the whispering somewhere to his left, trying to make sense of it. 'You keep turning up all over the place.'

Doesn't he know the word 'ubiquitous'? Ellis thought dreamily. His hands brushed at some invisible speck of dust, or fleck of ash on the worn surface of the interview room table. He giggled.

Nelson squinted at him, and Ellis saw that he was fighting a hangover the size of Cheshire. The signs were all there, pallor, a faint sheen of perspiration on the forehead, photophobia. The inspector's hands were folded in front of him on the desk, so he couldn't make out the incipient signs of DTs. And Nelson had sneered at his E-quality T-shirt — bloody hypocrite!

Nelson massaged his right temple and went on: 'You argued with Professor Wilkinson the morning of the murder. Well, that's not unusual. Most folk, from what I gather, had a fair old ding-dong with the prof that day.' He shook his head sadly. 'That's one of the things that's making our job so bloody difficult.'

Ellis nodded, sympathizing with Nelson's predicament; he knew their task had been hampered by the complexity of the situation, by Prof Wilkinson's despicable treatment of so many people. He had it in his power to help the police, but he did not like the way Nelson looked at him.

'Of course, the professor wasn't what you'd call a popular character — and that's another problem. But not yours, eh?'

Ellis blinked, unsure. Didn't they know that part yet? He relaxed a little. Perhaps he was safe after all.

'I mean, your funding is guaranteed to the end of your doctoral research. When is that? End of summer?' At Ellis's confirmative nod, Nelson went on: 'So by October you should have your thesis all boxed off.' Perhaps he saw the hesitation before his second nod, because he added, 'It is going to plan, is it, John?'

Whose plan? Ellis thought, but he hissed a 'yes', and Nelson took up where he'd left off:

'Still, it'd be nice to have something set up for the autumn, eh? Is that why you wanted to speak to Dr Wilkinson? To ask her to put in a good word?' Ellis swallowed, unable to speak, and Nelson seemed to feel the need to clarify: 'Twice, when I've been to interview Dr Wilkinson, you've been lurking about.' He flashed Ellis a shark-like grin. 'You see the kind of conclusions a man like me might feel compelled to—'

Nelson stopped, and Ellis thought he saw shock — perhaps even fear — in the inspector's amber eyes. He glanced anxiously towards Sergeant Hackett.

'Sir?' Hackett stepped forward from his position by the doorway and placed a hand on Nelson's shoulder.

Nelson shook him off, impatiently and Hackett let his hand drop. 'You must see how it could look, John?' he finished belatedly.

'How it could look,' Ellis echoed, tilting his head, listening more intently. If they didn't know, he might be in the clear. But ideas had been coming to him, recently. Dangerous ideas, and they made him afraid. He hadn't felt this way since his A' levels, since that other, terrible time . . .

'You've been . . . edgy — let's call it that — since we arrived. It does make me wonder—' Nelson pulled the corners of his mouth down in an apologetic moue. 'Bound to.'

Ellis sighed.

Nelson changed tack. 'There was a disagreement, a fracas — call it what you like — yesterday in the um, refectory.' He sounded embarrassed to use the word, like he wasn't sure if he was using it correctly.

Ellis sat completely still. The whisperers, by some miracle, were beginning to be comprehensible to him.

'Over money, was it, sir?'

'Who told you?'

'There were lots of witnesses.'

Ellis nodded. '*Technicians!*' He felt a little glow of pleasure at the disdain in his voice and found that he could now hold Nelson's gaze.

Then Nelson produced two fifty-pence coins from his pocket. 'Someone wanted them to buy coffee from the machine. There were ten fifty-pence pieces in the machine when it was opened. Unexceptional, ordinary fifty-pence coins.' He held up a plastic bag.

Ellis could see the coins clearly through the plastic but couldn't read the label. He leaned forward, reaching for them, stopping himself in time. 'An *evidence* bag?'

Nelson scrutinized the bag, resting his elbow on the tabletop, and speculating as if to himself. 'Professor Wilkinson's eyes were closed.'

Ellis stared, dry-mouthed at the inspector. What was he saying? What did he know?

'There's some people can't even keep their eyes closed when they're *asleep*, let alone . . .' He focused on Ellis, staring intently. 'Did you know that, John? The eyes tend to flit open — or at least half open. Now like I say, Professor Wilkinson's eyes were closed. He looked asleep almost, but for the blood.' Nelson tilted the bag and the coins jingled softly, sliding together into one corner of the bag. 'In the old days they used to keep 'em closed with pennies — the big old ones, not the piddly post-decimalization toytown tiddlers. The big, solid old-fashioned type — you probably wouldn't remember — with Britannia ruling the waves on the one side and often as not king George on the other. About the size of fifty p's they were, only round of course.'

Ellis looked into those dangerous eyes and knew it was hopeless trying to explain. His life was falling apart; his research was treated as a departmental joke by everyone except his supervisor — and that was only because Dr Mallory was so out of touch he couldn't see that it was a heap of shit. Everyone was waiting for him to fall: he had been *so close* to scientific eminence — and now nobody respected him, even the technicians tormented him.

Suddenly Ellis could stand it no more. He leapt to his feet and his chair shot back, bouncing off the far wall. He flung himself towards the door and Nelson was too slow to prevent him.

But Hackett grabbed Ellis as he scrabbled at the door handle and swung him round by the collar and the hem of his jacket. Nelson set the chair right and Hackett lowered Ellis into it. He was crying, muttering about *needing* the coins, that they didn't have the *right*, on and on. Nelson let him, waiting for the waves of nausea and the pounding in his head, brought on by the surge of adrenaline, to subside.

When, at last, Ellis was quiet, he said, 'Now then, Mr Ellis, perhaps you'd like to tell me exactly why these two coins were so important to you.'

* * *

Helen sat at the kitchen table of her parents' home, trying to make sense of the dream that had woken her from her afternoon snooze. Her father had taken his tea and his copy of the *Manchester Evening News* through to the sitting room as she came into the kitchen, mumbling something about catching up on the final scores on the telly. Helen tried not to feel the painful thud of rejection, but her face betrayed her, and her mother said, 'Now don't look like that, Helen. Your Dad's had a hard week, that's all.'

A hard week had been the standard excuse for years for her father's avoidance of Helen on her weekend visits. When she had been able to persuade Edward to come with her, he had made more of an effort to be sociable, to hide his feelings for her. She realized that her parents had seen Edward as a substitute, and now she had taken even that away from them. Her mother set about making tea and Helen, calmed and reassured by the familiarity, the predictability of the ritual, prepared herself to answer her mother's questions. She would not tell her about Mick, not yet — there was nothing to tell. Despite which, Helen found herself thinking of him constantly.

'You've had time to do some thinking, then,' her mother began.

'I suppose.'

'What have you decided?' The question was posed over the shoulder, face-to-face questions being difficult for

Helen's mother, as if she thought them impertinent, and eye contact rude.

'I haven't decided anything, Mum. I still don't know . . .'

'You're still not sleeping. Not eating?' Since she could not show Helen the affection that she really needed, her mother had fallen into the habit of nagging her about her health: at least it gave the appearance of concern.

'A little, of both. Oh, Mum, I am trying, really, but—'

There was a silent build-up of tension; the air seemed almost to crackle with it, as before an electrical discharge, then:

'When your brother died—'

Helen gasped. Her mother had broken an unspoken rule which, until now, had been inviolate.

'Mum, please.' Her voice was barely audible. She felt a prickling in her scalp, a tingling sensation ran from her chest to her fingertips. She tried to get up, but her legs would not support her.

'What happened to him was a tragedy.'

Helen was finding it hard to breathe.

'We've tried, Helen, but we can't put it behind us, not entirely.'

Helen shook her head, to dislodge the image of her brother screaming in pain and clutching his head.

'We can't blame you.'

As if blame, the apportioning of responsibility, would make it better, easier to bear.

'If we'd stayed and to hell with what his friends might think, maybe we'd've been able to stop him — or do something to help.'

This was a well-worn circular track, spiralling inwards to a claustrophobic centre. They blamed themselves, for Robbie's death. They might have stopped him taking the pill that killed him, where Helen had failed. They couldn't blame Helen, and yet they did blame her, needing someone to share the burden, despite all their rationalization, and this increased their guilt.

'It's such a bloody *waste*!' Helen burst out, suddenly angry.

A waste and a shame, and what happened after was a shame and a waste of two years of her young life. It had happened, and life would never be the same, but they still had to live it. Helen looked into her mother's face and saw the sadness of the years etched deep, and the unrelenting anger that she, whom they had trusted with their most precious gift, had proved unfit, had taken from them their only son.

Helen had suffered two years of black despair following his death. She would rather have died than let Robbie go through that terrifying pain, but she did not regret what she had done after his funeral.

It was unplanned. She had wanted to see the man who had taken so much from her family, to understand how he operated, and she had driven her car from the quiet suburban street where they lived through to the terraced houses of the estates on the rough side of town. She sat in her car, watching him in the dark winter night, and he had turned and smiled at her. That smile! His casual arrogance that made her want to kill, because he was alive, vibrant, and Robbie was dead. She had buried her kid brother the day before, and this thug was able to walk the streets, selling his poison, turning a profit.

Accelerating through the rain, the drops of water seemed to elongate as they streaked past her window — warp speed — but not fast enough.

Her mother broke the contact, disconcerted. She avoided Helen's eye, as one avoids the eye of someone disliked, and Helen disentangled herself carefully, feeling a solid pain in her chest, as real as the fading bruise on her face.

She returned home late on Sunday night, and to keep her mind from the thought that this would be the final separation from her parents, she mulled over the dream she'd had the previous day.

In her dream, Helen saw herself wearing a coarsely woven dress, sitting at a table while other women took food from her plate, each making the ritualized statement, 'At prisoner's request.' On waking, she had thought immediately of Margaret Atwood's book, *The Handmaid's Tale*.

Am I blaming myself for Ed's infidelities? she wondered. Then she remembered that Edward's mother had said something about her "allowing" Edward to have affairs. Perhaps that had been the trigger.

They had looked older, both of them. They had dressed carefully, as they always did, and were as well groomed. But the sleekness was marred; they were irretrievably diminished by the loss of their son.

'Edward wasn't a child,' Helen had told them. 'He didn't ask for permission.'

In the dream, the women asked her how she felt. She had replied 'Hard. Full,' and they had given her sideways looks, as if they knew she was pregnant.

Helen had been told in the dream that once a month the members of the community were allowed to vent their true feelings on an effigy of the 'lord' who ruled them. The lord was Edward. He rode on a white horse up and down the pavilion. The women charged on foot at a straw-stuffed doll which was dressed like Edward. They stabbed it again and again and Edward smiled down on them, unharmed, shielded in some magic way. Then the weapon was placed in Helen's hands and the pavilion fell silent. She looked at the long, thin steel pin, at its globular head, she knew she had the power to destroy him.

She had walked slowly, quietly through the hushed crowd while the lord on his horse had looked on in amusement. She went to the straw effigy and stabbed it again and again, the long shaft of the pin piercing through the breast and stopping only at the post to which the doll had been tied.

From each tiny puncture hole, a bead of bright red blood appeared.

Helen shuddered, and roused herself from her morbid thoughts, but the dream would not be shaken; she found herself returning to it again and again, wondering if she could have killed Edward during one of her blackouts — she had them even now. From time to time it happened that she would become aware of her surroundings, *coming to*, it seemed, and the discovery would be unexpected. She could not remember having gone into a particular room or, more disturbingly, having travelled from home to work. At these times she always had a dizzying sense of danger, and the danger was within herself.

CHAPTER 18

Jeff Townley had been looking forward to taking a short walk to the smoking room, but he now pushed the cigarettes to one side. In the last week Dermot Molyneux had come up with some first-rate pictures of Helen Wilkinson. Aside from the haunting *House of Death* picture, he had managed somehow to catch Ainsley, the cuckolded husband, and his wife, Clara. Touching one, that: her carrying the baby, looking startled and vulnerable. The Wilkinson shot and the last one of Clara Ainsley had been syndicated to most of the tabloids, one of the quality papers and the BBC. Dermot had earned more than enough in one week to pay for a computer with hi-tech imaging software, a bed scanner, a modem to connect him to the office from home, a zoom lens, and a lightweight camera holdall. As Dermot enthused about his latest piece of information, Townley had serious doubts that he would be able to entice the photographer to stay past the end of his one-year contract.

He eyed the packet of cigarettes longingly. Gone were the days when he could light up without fear of provoking a storm of protest. Smoking was now strictly limited to the smoking room, but what the hell good was that, when he needed a smoke to help him think here, now, in his office, talking to a photographer who was probably about to waste company time and money, but whom Jeff couldn't afford to upset?

'Wait a minute, hold on! Go back a few paces.' He had lost concentration for a second. 'You reckon this "contact" of yours says an arrest is imminent? Is that what he actually said, *imminent?*'

'She,' Molyneux corrected, his vanity unable to resist setting the facts straight. 'And she said she thinks they'll charge him.'

'She?' Townley repeated.

'Well . . .'

'Molyneux,' Townley said. 'Dermot. Don't, please, don't try to work that one on me.' He meant the coy smile; the roguish grin; the look from under his impossibly unruly hair which invariably won over the lasses.

'Sorry, Boss,' Molyneux said. 'Look, I know the story's straight. The police took this guy Ellis in and questioned him. They've tied some new evidence to him, so my contact says.' He held up both hands to placate Townley. 'I know what you're thinking, and I can tell you she's sure.'

'Not just trying to impress the *man?*' Townley asked, extending the vowel in an approximation to Molyneux's Dublin burr.

'Sure, she was trying to impress me,' Dermot said quietly, 'but don't you think I'd check me sources?'

Townley was affected by the pained restraint in Dermot Molyneux's voice. He buckled under the strain and reached for the packet of cigarettes, opened it and slipped one from the pack. Only two left. He rolled the pristine cylinder between his index finger and thumb, resisting — just — the urge to lift the cigarette to his nose and sniff the *Nicotiana tabacum* like a connoisseur sampling the aroma of a good Havana cigar. Molyneux was watching him hungrily, and Jeff surmised it wasn't the cigarette he was interested in.

'What the hell,' he sighed. If he refused, one of the nationals would encourage Molyneux to go for the story.

'If you don't turn anything up by tomorrow, the story is dead, is that clear?' Townley pointed with the filter end of the cigarette.

'And, Molyneux,' he called, as the Irishman headed for the door. 'Take a tip. You're far more convincing when you drop the BS.'

Molyneux grinned. 'I couldn't take a tip from you, boss.' He nodded at the cigarette. 'Those things are lethal without them.'

That surprised a laugh from Townley himself. 'That's just what my wife keeps telling me.'

* * *

Helen was interviewed at two p.m. on Monday. A pro-vice chancellor, the Dean of Faculty and Alice Chambers were present. They asked their questions kindly and with due deference, and twenty minutes later confirmed that she would be offered a post as senior lecturer in the new School of Life Sciences. She received a call in her office at three p.m. It was Ruth.

'You'll be staying, then.'

'Where else would I go?'

'Where indeed? I have to say you don't sound exactly thrilled. It *is* a promotion, Helen.'

'I know. But I don't feel much like celebrating, given the circumstances.'

'Ouch.'

'Sorry.'

'No, I'm sorry. Shall I come round this evening?'

They agreed to meet at seven thirty. When, ten minutes later, Mick Tuttle phoned, Helen felt an unexpected flutter of nervousness. She was smiling to herself as she hung up but snatched the receiver back at the last moment. The line was dead. What to tell Ruth?

* * *

They met in a restaurant in Watergate Row. Helen had walked the mile and a half to the city centre, doubling back on herself a couple of times to be sure she was not followed. She passed the squat, sandstone cathedral building of the university's namesake, St Werburgh, and approached the stone cross at the meeting of the old Roman roads.

She mounted the steps onto the raised wooden walkway that led to the restaurant. Ahead, a series of archways seemed to overlap, layering the covered path with increasing darkness. She could have continued along the road way and come up the steps at the end of the Row instead, but she was shivering, despite wearing a thick woollen coat, and the Rows, enclosed on one side by shops and offices and on the other by the black and white wooden railings so characteristic of Chester, provided shelter from the bitter wind. There Helen felt safe, unobserved within the twilight of wood planking, overarched by a low, plaster ceiling. The black paintwork of the studded timber doors, icing-thick with centuries of repainting, were reassuring in an indefinable way; perhaps giving a sense of perspective, of proportion to her present difficulties.

As she drew near to the restaurant, she glanced across Watergate Street to the copiously inscribed upper floors of God's Providence House. '*God's providence is mine inheritance*,' she read, and it felt like a prayer for strength. Taking a breath, she stepped into the warmth of the bar.

Helen had never seen Mick Tuttle so relaxed. He was warm, funny, and a remarkably good mimic, a skill he used to good effect in his description of his own interview with the panel.

The restaurant was quiet and the tables well spaced. Its wooden floors, oak panelling and low beamed ceiling sufficiently worn and battered to lend an air of permanence and solidity which added to Helen's feelings of security and safety; perhaps they had a similar effect on Mick.

He paused, studying her for a moment, then said, smiling, 'Go on then, ask.'

Helen blinked. 'Ask what?'

'Whatever it is that's making you look so bewildered.'

'Is that how I look?'

His smile broadened, then he concentrated on his meal for a few moments to allow her time to think. He had chosen vegetarian, deferring to her sensitivity with unshowy consideration, and Helen had been surprised that her appetite had been sustained throughout the first and well into the main course.

'I suppose,' Helen began cautiously, 'I was thinking how different you are outside the university walls.'

'Different?'

She blushed. 'It's hard to explain.'

He gave her a lop-sided grin. 'Or just hard to say?'

She raised her eyes to meet his and felt a thrill of something she scarcely recognized. Happiness?

'Less inhibited?' she said. 'Maybe more yourself?' She finished with a shrug; it was the best she could do.

He considered for a few moments and seemed to like her interpretation.

'At St Werburgh's I've always got something to prove. You know what it's like. In a way we're both regarded as physically handicapped — you, because of your sex, me because of my callipers, whereas here,' — he glanced around the restaurant — 'nobody would really care if I was held together by elastic bands and lengths of string, as long as I can pay the bill.'

Helen stared at him, appalled. 'That's horrible — I'm sorry we make you feel that way.'

'*You* don't, but enough do.' He reached across the table and squeezed her hand. 'Don't let it worry you. I can outlast them. I've got incredible stamina when it comes to that sort of challenge. The good thing is, we'll both be working for the newly Recreated School of Life Sciences — or R-SOLS, for short.'

Helen laughed, nearly choking. 'Arseholes?'

'Present company excepted,' he said, deadpan.

* * *

Dermot Molyneux moved swiftly and silently, shadowing Ellis as he made his way from his lodgings to the other side of the city. Dermot knew, before they had reached the halfway mark, exactly where they were heading. The evening was cold and blustery and ridges of velvety grey herringbone cloud formations had built up on the underbelly of the storm gathering from the east. It was a long walk and he was thankful for the lightweight material and broad shoulder straps of his new camera bag. He always felt a barely reconcilable sense of hilarity and excitement when following a mark: on the one hand it seemed ludicrous, boys playing at spies; on the other, it was risky and on occasions had even proved dangerous.

The house was now bereft of reporters; interest in the story had waned when, after a whole week, the police had made little progress. The last of the nationals had left on Sunday afternoon, disgusted to find that they had wasted the weekend freezing delicate parts of their anatomy waiting for something to happen, when in fact the Wilkinson house was empty. If it hadn't been for two of the more reckless (or more desperate) journalists bunking over the gate at the back of the house and peering in at Helen's study, they might have stayed a little longer and witnessed the arrival of John Ellis. Dermot held back at the corner of the street and got a good shot with his new, lightweight 100-300 zoom, of Ellis in profile as he hesitated, looking both ways before slipping down the side entry leading to the back of the house. He switched lenses as he walked on, working by touch, while keeping a keen eye out for Ellis.

There was little cover in the street, even though there were plenty of gardens, for in this area of the city, the houses were all occupied — by the families of the professional classes or housing the upper range of bed-and-breakfast accommodation — and as such were most kept in good order. Dermot reflected that he would be likely to attract unwanted attention creeping through gardens with a camera, and so he strode down the street purposefully. Drawing level with the house, he needed decide: walk on by or go in. There was really no contest: Townley had given him a day to find something worth putting on the front page and the closer he could get to the Wilkinsons' house, the more likely it would be that a good composition would present itself.

The house was semi-detached and each pair in the street was flanked by a side entry. He darted into the passage, glad that he had worn his air trainers, since the high walls on either side echoed and magnified every sound. At the back gate he listened for half a minute before trying the latch. It was locked.

He adjusted his bag strap to wear the camera crosswise and swivelled it until the bulk of the weight rested somewhere between his shoulder blades, then he reached up — not too much of a stretch — to the top of the gate, bracing one foot against the brickwork, a couple of feet up. He swung his right leg over the top of the gate and then eased himself into a sitting position, checking for signs of activity before dropping down quietly into the back garden.

It was well kept, unlike the front of the house. Tiny daffodils and pale-yellow primroses were massed with stubby-looking purple crocuses which struggled to keep their heads above the mat of grass at the base of the trees. The wooden framed greenhouse stood at the end of the lawn; painted dark green, it was filled with both mature plants in pots of various sizes and seedlings in trays. Beyond the greenhouse, through an archway of climbing roses in delicate new leaf, were carefully laid out oblongs of freshly tilled soil. There was a shed, too, at the far end of the garden, covered in ivy and some variety of climbing rose. The archway would provide good cover, but it was some twenty-five feet from the house—

Ellis's face appeared at the kitchen window and Dermot ducked behind the bins, hidden behind a screen of close-growing evergreen. Dermot braced himself, sweating, listening for the sound of the back door opening. Silence. Ellis had not seen him. He peered through the foliage; the door was intact, so Ellis must have let himself in with a key. Interesting.

Dermot altered the f-stop on his camera and estimated the focus he would need: there wouldn't be time for adjustment. The house and most of the garden were in shadow at this time of evening, which should cut the reflections.

A scurry of footsteps in the passageway almost made his heart stop, then he realized they were going away from the house. 'Stay calm, Dermot,' he told himself. 'Only the neighbour going out the back way.' He counted to three, then rushed at the window and fired off three shots, ducking down below the window frame panting, almost laughing to himself. Three near perfect shots, and of what? Ellis delivering some sort of confectionery for Helen Wilkinson? 'Jesus, Dermot,' he told himself, 'you'll have to do better than that!'

Dermot returned to his hiding place in the little enclosure of evergreens, taking a few shots of the upper windows, but didn't get anything he could use. At last the key turned in the lock and Ellis let himself out, apparently preoccupied and completely unaware of his presence. He dropped the key, and cursed, fumbling to retrieve it, and Dermot noted there were in fact *three* keys on the ring, together with a plain yellow fob. Front door, back gate and back door, keys, Dermot speculated. Ellis must be a trusted visitor, to have full access to the house.

As Ellis selected the correct key and slotted it into the door lock, a motor bike blatted down the road, and Dermot used the sudden burst of noise to risk a shot of Ellis locking up after himself, already working on a suitable caption, wondering if he could persuade Townley to run with, 'WIDOW'S SECRET TRYST WITH STUDENT?'

* * *

David Ainsley had been watching the house for an hour. He had sat, motionless, on cracked and mossy steps of an empty property, peering through a dense mesh of twiggy fuchsia and leafy hawthorn which had long since overgrown its function as a hedge. The hawthorn, though small and scrubby, was beginning to take on the form and height of a small tree. Still, the shrubs gave cover enough and he could observe, unobserved himself, using the patience and the observation skills he had learned from fifteen years of field and laboratory study. During his watch no lights had been turned on or off, no windows opened, and nobody had entered nor left the house opposite. When he was quite sure it was safe, he stood, giving the blood a moment to circulate through his cramped limbs, then, absently wiping the dust and detritus from the seat of his trousers, he crossed the street and let himself in. Half an hour should do it.

* * *

Dermot waited three or four minutes before venturing out. He tried the back door, but Ellis had been sure to secure it. A good interior shot of the *House of Death* would be quite a scoop, he decided. He scanned the windows of the upper storeys. One on the first floor was open a crack; if he could find a step ladder . . .

The shed was locked and there was nothing hidden inside the greenhouse. He was about to abandon his half-hearted attempt at unlawful entry when he heard footsteps approaching the back gate, and for a moment he froze. If he used the pathway to gain his hiding place by the bins, he might be heard. He retreated quickly across the lawn, leaving clear footprints on the wet grass, but perhaps Ellis would not notice. He hid behind the rose arbour just as the gate opened.

Dermot risked one quick shot: the wind was blowing in his direction and should carry the click and wheeze of the shutter and auto-wind away from the house, but his heart thudded so loudly in his chest that he was seriously worried it would give him away.

It wasn't Ellis, but the new visitor carried the same three keys on a simple fob with a yellow tab. What was going on? He waited a couple of minutes and was contemplating sneaking up to the house, when a movement at the study window caught his attention and he fired off another shot. The light was fading and there was probably too much shadow to make it worthwhile, but he already had one clear picture and he could try and improve the definition in the dark room, or on the computer.

He waited a further five minutes, wondering whether to leave or to try for another shot, failing to notice the face at the attic room window which overlooked the garden, didn't see that *he* was being observed.

* * *

'David.'

Clara had lost weight. Lost the sheen of good health and even better grooming which had cost him so much financially, and later — after she met Edward — everything he had ever wanted in life.

'I need some things,' he said. 'Five minutes, I'm on my way.'

Clara held the baby to her. He was asleep, exhausted no doubt, as she must be exhausted. She placed the baby carefully, almost fearfully, into his cot beside the bed then turned to look at her husband.

Ainsley eyed her cautiously, wondering how she might react. For a second she seemed ready to fly at him, then she smiled briefly and, sweeping an overlong lock of hair from her forehead with the back of her hand, she said, 'I'll fix you something to eat — you must be starving.'

'No. I won't stay.'

She laughed, a tentative, nervous sound that ended almost in a sob. 'Yes, you did rather leave in a hurry.' She half turned. 'Your cheque book's in—'

'I have it safe now,' he said, patting his jacket pocket.

'David, I would never—'

He had sounded harsher than he had intended, and she seemed wounded by the implication. 'I know,' he said, relenting. 'I know, Clara.'

She stood by as he placed folded clothing into binbags.

'You really don't have to move your things—' A desperate edge had crept into her voice.

'Yes,' he said, firmly. 'Yes, I do. I have to.'

Her mouth worked and she almost lost control. She looked about her, as if trying to find a distraction from her extreme distress. 'Where've you been staying?'

'Rutherford put me up for a few days, then I found a B&B.'

Rutherford, who so abhorred Ainsley's smugness, had been unable to resist his deep unhappiness. Ainsley had heard Mrs Rutherford had murmured a warning about appearing to take sides but had agreed that they could not allow David to continue sleeping in his office. Ainsley had quickly recovered from the heavy drinking — too ashamed to let Rutherford's children see him stumbling about the house, shambling and tearful — and from there, he had started piecing together a new life, of sorts.

'This is such a big house,' Clara said. 'We needn't be in each other's way.' It was said timidly, and Ainsley felt a sharp pain below his sternum. He pulled the drawstring on the third bin liner full of his clothing.

Clara laughed shakily. 'Funny,' she said, 'I always thought you didn't care about clothes. And look at all this.'

He half smiled, reaching to lift the first bag. Her hand closed over his, tightened, pulling against him. Their eyes locked, hers pleading, tearful. But he was beyond tears.

'I need you,' she said, looking away, and a tear fell onto the black plastic of the bin bag.

'I know,' Ainsley said quietly. 'But you don't love me. It's not enough, Clara.'

She nodded silently, moving out of his way. 'The police took me in for questioning on Saturday.'

He held his breath, waiting for the confession.

'I was with Edward, at his house, the afternoon he was murdered.'

'You don't have to tell me this.'

'I went there to tell him it was over between us.' She laughed, softly, tentatively, glancing over at the baby's cot to check for signs of restlessness. 'The police think I was the last to see him alive, and you know what that means.'

'Clara—'

'They can't prove anything. They haven't even got enough to charge me. They let me go after eight hours. They searched the house — our house — but of course they found nothing.'

'I don't know why you're telling me this.'

'I had to leave Henry with Cloe Sallis. She wasn't pleased. But the alternative was to bring social services in. She says he slept for six hours. That's more sleep than I've had in the last three days. It was humiliating, David, having to ask for her help, for that reason. She knew, of course. Everyone does.'

'It's not my problem,' he said, avoiding her huge, hungry, tearful eyes.

'No,' she said, with an effort of control. 'It's *our* problem. We can deal with it.'

'I'll see that you and the boy of provided for.'

'Your *son*!' she screamed with sudden ferocity. 'Henry is your son!'

He looked at her with real pity this time. Then, shaking his head, started to take his belongings down to the hired van below.

CHAPTER 19

They walked part of the way back along the Roman walls. Helen had been prepared to slow her pace to a shuffle and was surprised that Mick was able to stride along with her; she even had difficulty keeping up at times. The wind by now was fierce. It buffeted them, changing direction with capricious inconstancy, slamming into the walls and creating vortices which snatched the breath from their mouths. They conceded defeat, retreating, laughing, to the relative calm of the street below.

'Maybe we should phone for a taxi,' Helen suggested.

'Are you tired?'

Helen saw the concern in his face and felt a slight shock in the realization that he should think her frail. Did she really look so ill? 'Not unless you are,' she said, somewhat defensively, but was unable to suppress a smile when he laughed. 'Smugness doesn't suit you,' she added.

She was relieved that there were no reporters in evidence outside the house. 'Best thing I ever did, going to my parents for the weekend,' she commented.

'Best thing ever?'

She paused, with her hand on the gate, feeling that the genuine curiosity he had shown in asking the question deserved serious consideration. It seemed that her absence had deterred the reporters, resulting in a huge improvement in her quality of life. Also, a candid exchange between herself and her mother had been long overdue. She knew now that she could never be to her parents what they wanted her to be, simply because she was not Robbie. This had been a painful revelation, but it had also been a kind of deliverance from the years in which she had hated herself and had tortured herself with futile yearnings: if she had supervised him more closely; if she hadn't been so keen to appear the cool older sister; if she had called the ambulance sooner, or her parents . . . And yet there was unfinished business — the waste of two years of her life. It would shock her mother to know that Helen only considered it a waste because she hadn't achieved what she had set out to do, as far as Robbie's dealer was concerned. Helen was ashamed of her feelings, but she could not make them go away, and so she had told no one and tried not to think about it. Sometimes it worked, but not always.

Someone had finished the job for her while she was in prison — a drugs-related shooting, the police had called it. Helen had felt thwarted; she had had her chance and blown it. Perhaps there was something within her that was dangerous, bad.

Still, in all, the letting go of years of self-recrimination had given Helen strength. She had mended no bridges, dressed no wounds, but at least now she was reconciled to the fact that she would have to learn to go on alone, since her parents were stuck in the past, experiencing the same grief, the same pangs of suffering and remorse as they had more than ten years before.

She smiled at Mick; he was still waiting for an answer. 'If not the best, then certainly the most beneficial thing I've done in years.'

She made coffee while Mick fiddled with the radio, trying to tune in to Jazz FM. Mission accomplished, he sat back and watched Helen through half-closed eyes.

'Unbelievable!'

Mick roused himself from a pleasurable, if imagined, caressing of the curve of Helen's neck. 'What is?'

'Not what, who. Ruth.' Helen straightened up from the fridge. In one hand she held a bottle of milk and in the other a white cardboard box. 'She keeps bringing me little delicacies, trying to "tempt my palate", as she calls it. This looks like the latest. Fancy sharing a pudding with me?'

They had skipped the banoffee pie on offer at the restaurant and Mick had worked up a renewed appetite fighting against the wind on the walk back to Helen's house. 'Mind you don't drip!' he warned.

Helen set the box down on the scrubbed kitchen table. It seemed one of the cakes had leaked jam, for the base of the box was oozing sticky red juice.

'Doughnuts,' Helen said, smiling. 'Ruth has a thing for them.' She cut the string and opened the box lid.

'My God.' Mick looked up into Helen's face. It was frozen, ominously still.

Inside the box, on a square of balsa wood, was a white laboratory mouse. It was splayed in a way that always made him think of crucifixion. Each tiny paw was pinned through its centre and stretched out, to place the body wall under tension and facilitate the dissection.

Helen began to shake so violently that he feared she might convulse. Mick stood and put both arms around her, pulling her away. Once outside the door, Helen came to as if waking from a hypnotic trance.

She struggled free of him. 'I'm going to be sick.'

He let her go, knowing that his slow ascent of the stairs would only impede her. By the time reached the bathroom after her, she was already rinsing her mouth out. Then she had splashed her face with water.

'Helen, who would do this to you?' he asked.

'Did you see?' She ignored his question, focusing on something in the middle distance. Something so real and tangible, that he almost fancied that he could see it too.

He frowned, nodded. Yes, he had seen. So much blood! Whoever had done this, had killed the animal by severing a vein and allowing it to bleed to death slowly. Then it had been expertly dissected. The oesophagus and rectum ligatured with cotton before being cut, then the stomach and small and large intestines had been carefully lifted out of the body cavity, displaced to the left of the body and arranged in a lyre shape to display the mesenteric blood vessels fanning across the transparent connective tissues in a delicate filigree arrangement of red blood vessels and off-white adipose tissue. All this, he had seen, but what she had meant by the question was the last part of the dissection, the part calculated to hurt her most: the pouched uterus exposed — showing, beneath the thin, pink muscle of its walls the clear outlines of seven fully formed foetuses.

* * *

Sergeant Hackett's eyes roved about the room, searching for something unusual, something that might serve as a clue to who or why. The kitchen was neat and orderly, a prosaic picture of banal domesticity — except for the package at the edge of the table.

'The blinds?' he asked.

'I drew them when I arrived,' Ruth Marks answered. Helen's first instinct, as before, had been to call her friend before she called the police. 'I'm sorry if I've done wrong, sergeant, but the last thing Helen needs right now is her picture in the paper again.'

He nodded, a neutral acknowledgement of the facts, taking in, subliminally, the lack of one knife from the wooden block next to the window, a gap tooth, unsightly, obtrusive in its absence. It had not been found, despite an extensive search of the Wilkinsons' garden and all the gardens adjacent to it — they had even sifted through the mulch in the drains along the street, but the murder weapon had disappeared, dropped no doubt, in the canal or the Dee, where it would rust quietly until nothing remained but a reddish sludge.

There were no signs of a break-in, and the SOCO had found no fingerprints on the cardboard box.

'Who's got a key to the house — apart from Dr Wilkinson, that is?' Hackett asked.

'Me,' Ruth answered. 'Her mother, I think. That's all.'

Mick Tuttle cleared his throat. 'I have a key to the back gate.'

Ruth stared. 'I had *no* idea!' she exclaimed, and Hackett thought he caught an expression somewhere between amusement and exasperation.

'Helen was concerned about the press interest. The side passage generally wasn't watched too closely.' He shrugged.

'Do you have a key to the house?' Hackett asked.

Mick shook his head.

Ruth opened her mouth to ask a question, then seemed to change her mind, smiling a little to herself.

Hackett asked the question for her. 'When did she give you the key?'

'A couple of days ago.'

Hackett wondered if the professor was not the only Wilkinson who had been having an affair. Mick returned his stare calmly.

'Any ideas about who might've—' Hackett waved in the direction of the white box.

Ruth shrugged. 'Virtually everyone knows about Helen's miscarriage after the newspaper articles, Sergeant.'

'What I meant was who would bear such a grudge against her that they would break into her house and leave a butchered animal in her fridge. But you think the real message is the murdered pups?'

'Yes,' Ruth said firmly. 'I do.'

'And you think anyone who *knew* her would do this? I had no idea she had so many enemies.'

Ruth sighed, spreading her hands in a gesture of helplessness. 'I misspoke. Helen's students adore her. She's reasonably well liked among her peers — bearing in mind that

St Werburgh's is a bastion of chauvinistic, misogynistic fundamentalism.'

'It could be someone jealous that she got a senior lectureship.' Mick Tuttle said.

Ruth fixed her gaze on Tuttle, her eyes ice blue, now, analytical. She seemed to measure him against some paradigm and find him wanting.

'Could be,' she replied.

Hackett couldn't decide if it was mistrust or dislike that filtered through the cool blandness of Dr Marks's expression as she scrutinized her colleague.

A thump overhead broke the silence and with it the wordless exchange between the two academics. Hackett was out into the hall first. Helen was supposed to be resting in her study downstairs. He mounted the stairs two at a time, not pausing to think of the danger he might be running to.

Helen stood at the door to the bedroom where her husband's body had been found. She was pale to the point of deathliness. On the dimly lit landing her face seemed to glow with pearly light. She smiled tentatively.

'I'm afraid I stumbled,' she said. 'I'm feeling rather weak.'

Ruth pushed past Hackett and helped Helen to the staircase.

'What are you doing up here?' Hackett asked.

'It's her bloody house, Sergeant,' Ruth answered angrily.

Hackett had to concede. It was, as Ruth Marks said, Helen Wilkinson's house, after all, and he supposed this restless prowling was only to be expected given that her property had been invaded in this way. *Violated* was the word that came to mind. Nevertheless, Hackett walked to the end of the landing to check the two doors which stood slightly ajar. One, a box room: spartan, empty, soulless; Edward Wilkinson had used it as a study, but apparently had preferred mostly to stay in his university office when pressure of work — or Clara — demanded. The other door led to the front bedroom. Hackett felt an unaccustomed premonitory dread as he put his hand on the door handle of the bedroom and eased the door open.

The room was empty, undisturbed, expect by some turbulent spectre of fear which he felt had emanated from Helen.

When he returned to the kitchen the SOCO was clearing away the last of his gear and Mick Tuttle was pouring black coffee into mugs. He raised the pot and Hackett nodded his thanks. Helen was sitting at the table, staring at the spot where the box had lain; a damp patch remained, cleaned of blood, but darker than the rest of the old pine. A faint smell of bleach hung in the air.

The atmosphere Hackett had sensed in the room upstairs was here, too. Stronger, a solid, almost tangible presence. The SOCO glanced uneasily at him as he secured the clasps of his equipment case and Hackett set about trying to find something to say. Then the shrill chirrup of his mobile phone shattered the silence, and everyone jerked convulsively before relaxing, grateful for an end to the oppressive stillness.

Hackett spoke briefly, sharply, questioning, and then he was gone, taking the SOCO with him and leaving the three remaining occupants of the room bewildered.

CHAPTER 20

Hackett arrived outside the Victorian frontage as the ambulance was leaving. 'Smoke inhalation,' Nelson said. 'Plus a bloody great skull fracture. He's lucky they got to him in time.' He nodded in the direction of a small knot of firemen, greasy and black-faced, who had just come out of the house and now seemed to be conferring about what action to take next. Two of the men turned and went back into the house, stepping over the fire hose which trailed inside the building.

'Any other casualties?'

Nelson shook his head. The flare of the sodium street lamps and the sharp glitter of blue-red, blue-red in rotating splinters from two police cars and a fire engine cast unflattering shadows on his ravaged face. It was raining heavily now, battering down. The unpredictable gusts of the storm had made the job of fighting the fire more difficult, but it seemed to be contained more or less to one room and the fire service appeared to be bringing it under control. The one window billowed orange-tinged smoke into the night, but there were no flames.

'Molyneux's darkroom,' Nelson explained, hunching his shoulders against a cold trickle of rain that had found its way down the back of his neck, and thrusting his hands deep into his pockets.

Two hours later they were inside Dermot Molyneux's flat, crunching over debris and tasting the bitter, oily remains of the fire on their tongues. It was not yet light and both men carried powerful torches.

Tim Dignan, the Fire Investigation Officer, his face sweating and smeared in soot, had led them in. 'The fire started in the darkroom,' he said. 'Arson, no question of that. And there's been some damage done before the fire was set. From what we can tell, he came to long enough to get out of the dark room, but he passed out in here.'

'Where was he found?' Hackett asked.

'Near the phone. But the wire had been cut. The fire built to quite a pitch in the darkroom, but he'd got the door shut and that contained the worst of it — till the window shattered with the heat, but luckily people started to notice by then.'

Nelson was prodded the mess underfoot with the toe of his shoe. A family grouping — they'd have to be informed. A collection of CDs greasy with smuts. Bands he'd never heard of but guessed must be Irish from the Gaelic titles.

'Were there people around to notice after midnight on a Monday night?' Hackett asked.

'Studentland this, Terry,' Dignan said. 'They keep late hours.'

Hackett nodded, glancing over at the door to the darkroom, which stood open, its paintwork blistered and blackened in places. Most of the damage in the main living room of the flat was from smoke and water. He didn't envy the poor sods who'd have this lot to clear up.

'Aren't you supposed to get as much of the valuable stuff out before it's wrecked?' Nelson demanded. Equipment, some of it expensive by the look of it, lay broken on the floor.

Dignan took a moment before answering. 'We try to put people before property,' he said, looking hard into the rheumy Nelson's eyes. 'The photographic equipment was wrecked by whoever started the fire. What did you think? That we came in here wielding fire axes and smashed the place up?'

'Life's bloody work,' Nelson went on defensively. 'Wanton bloody destruction.'

Hackett wondered what had brought on this rare exhibition of empathy in the inspector. 'Surely not wanton, sir — I mean, if it served a purpose?'

Nelson fixed him with a look that would have pinned a lesser man to the wall. Hackett returned a bland, if vaguely expectant stare.

Nelson did not actually concede the contest, but his next words were spoken with an unexpected mildness. 'Perhaps "wanton" wasn't quite the word I was looking for,' he said, returning to a desultory prodding of Dermot's personal effects. 'Can that door be made secure?' He nodded towards the entrance to the flat. The door, though still on its hinges, swung open, while the lock side of the frame lay twisted on the sodden carpet.

'We'll see to it before we leave,' Dignan promised.

Nelson frowned, flashing the beam of his torch to one side of the door. 'Can anything be done about this?' Nelson asked.

Hackett and Dignan exchanged a surprised look.

'Done about it? Salvage, you mean?'

Nelson threw Hackett a withering glance. 'Evidence, I mean.' He directed his torch at the charred remains that had once been Molyneux's PC. 'Might be worth getting young Tact to have look at it.'

Hackett thought there would be precious little to look at, but he had to agree, it was worth taking a squint.

* * *

It isn't much of a room, John thought. All the same, it had hurt when that crazy policeman had looked around it with that expression of disapproval, of disgust even.

He picked up one of the culture bottles and shook it. The flies lay in clusters on the oatmeal growth medium, stuck fast, not one living specimen remained. He shook his head. It had all made perfect sense. He gathered the other bottles to his chest, sweeping them to him, anxious that this evidence of his failure should not be found, smudging the pristine whiteness of his T-shirt with dust. Never mind, there would be time to change. He was in control now. Back in control.

He threw the bottles into the waste basket and carried them downstairs, jingling as cheerily as a milkman's crate. Nobody saw or heard him — the tenants, most of whom were students, had already gone out for the night, and he had the house to himself.

Gusts of spiteful wind spat large chilly drops of rain. He hurried to the back, where the bins were kept, slipping once or twice on patches of slimy moss at the side of the house. By the time he was indoors again, a heavy shower was drenching the street and rainwater gurgled from a crack in the downspout next to the front door.

He ran back upstairs, shivering, and slammed the door of his flat behind him. It was cold. It was always cold in this room. He stripped off his T-shirt, now smeared with rust from the bin lid, overlaying the greyish dust from the bottles. He threw the shirt onto the pile of dirty clothing at the foot of his bed, then, visualizing the contemptuous expression on Inspector Nelson's face again, he bunched the lot into a ball and stuffed it into the bottom of his wardrobe.

Dispossessed of its clutter, the room looked sparse, grey, ordinary. He had once been proud of his *Drosophila* cultures, and of his skill in handling them — they weren't easy insects, not if you wanted the best from them, but he could etherize, sex, and type fifty in less than five minutes. Where other students routinely lost flies into the lab when they came round unexpectedly, or else slaughtered them by over-anaesthetizing them, he knew almost by instinct how much would be just enough to do the job. Where others made their culture medium too wet, so the insects fell prey to fungal infection, or too dry, so they died of starvation, or their eggs, desiccated, failed to hatch, John's *Drosophila* were robust, healthy, reliable experimental subjects — even the wild ones he'd brought in from his field studies.

He didn't know why he'd kept them for so long after everything had turned so disastrously against him, and he had allowed his carefully labelled batches to die. He had intended to throw them away, but, somehow he couldn't bear to, and after a while, they had provided a perverse form of comfort to him, like the smell of his own sweat, and the pile of unwashed clothing at the end of his bed.

He turned on the gas fire — no sense in being uncomfortable — and dragged a clean T-shirt over his head. Nearly ready now. He wondered if Helen had returned home and tried to imagine her reaction. Shock, anger, perhaps. He hoped she had understood the message, otherwise it had been nothing more than a petty act of spite.

* * *

Helen, alone at last, bolted the doors front and back of the house before returning to the bedroom. Soon first light would glimmer over the rooftops of the houses; already there were a few restless stirrings in the eaves of the front gable, where sparrows were nesting. This was something to be done under cover of darkness.

She overcame her reluctance to cross the threshold, taking a breath before stepping into the room. Her heart thudded painfully in her chest and she turned her head away from the bed, avoiding the image that she would see: Edward, half sitting, chest bare. No, she *would not* think of it.

She crouched beside the little wooden cabinet and braced one hand against the door, taking another breath, holding it, easing the catch with her thumb, opening the door a little at a time, cautiously as though afraid of some terror waiting to escape. A picture of the mouse, splayed, butchered, flashed into her mind and she felt her gorge rise. She pulled the door wide in her distress, dislodging the contents of the cupboard. Magazines, books, an audio cassette fell to the floor. And with them a knife. The blade was dulled, clotted with blood, and the handle smeared with the same rust-coloured stuff, dried and flaking.

Earlier, she had picked it up with her bare hands and thrust it back into the cupboard, now the thought of touching it filled her with dread, a childish horror of the supernatural. How had this happened? They had looked in every room, every possible hiding place, she and Mick together. She stared at the appalling spectre of the knife until she thought if she waited a moment longer she would go mad, then, carefully, she opened the food bag she had brought from the kitchen and tilted the magazine on which the knife had been resting. It slithered into the open mouth of the plastic bag with an unholy sound which drew from her an utterance of disgust and distress. She carried it at arm's length through the house, unable to countenance the thought of having it upstairs with her, close to where she would be sleeping, but equally unable to rid herself of it. What if the police came back, searching bins, digging up the flower beds as they had done before? She would put it somewhere out of the way until she had thought about what to do. Could she trust Mick, tell him? Or Ruth — would she think she had finally lost touch with reality?

She fetched up in the kitchen. The police had already searched here, dusting for fingerprints. Yes, here would be best. She opened the third drawer from the top of the sink unit, the drawer in which she kept oddments, keys, wrapping paper, measuring tape, bits of string. The knife nestled like a dangerous animal on top of a coil of coarse string. Helen wanted to bury it beneath the clutter, but she could not bring herself to look at its stained steel and the brackish brown remains of blood on the handle any longer, so she slammed the drawer shut and fled the room, afraid to look over her shoulder, unable to go to her bedroom until she had showered and scrubbed her hands and arms until they were raw.

CHAPTER 21

Ruth slept badly, dreaming of boxed doughnuts that turned into squirming, screaming mice as she bit into them. So, when the doorbell rang, waking her from a new permutation in which Helen was performing an operation on Tuttle's legs without anaesthetic, explaining with cold rationality that all that was required was a little self-control on his part, she tumbled out of bed gratefully.

Nelson and Hackett were taken aback at her wild appearance.

'You,' she grunted, ungraciously, and retreated, scratching her head and yawning.

She left the front door open which the two policemen took as an invitation and stepped inside. The hallway was cold, a grey, nondescript replica of rented accommodation in any town and city just about anywhere. The two men exchanged a look and then followed her upstairs.

Her flat was a maelstrom of ideas, themes and colours. Where Ellis's room had been chaotic, an undisciplined mess of unfinished work and insanitary slovenliness, without purpose, Ruth Marks's flat seemed to reflect a mind that held so many enthusiasms that it rebelled against the constraints of order and ordinariness, so that dour and disturbing prints of

Munch's work were displayed on the same wall as a poster of patchwork intensity by Klimt and watercolours of the Cheshire countryside were hung next to Picasso prints. On her crowded bookshelves popular fiction vied with texts on neural networks and the silicon brain. Hackett scanned the mantelpiece; it was cluttered with postcards, curling with age and filmy with dust. He concluded that Ruth Marks was something of a hoarder. Wooden carvings of the three wise monkeys were arranged in a semicircle, in a conspiratorial huddle, partly obscuring a photograph of Helen Wilkinson, bundled up in a dark overcoat, and looking upwards in a dreamy pose. The remains of a Chinese take-away lay discarded on the low table next to the sofa, bringing a faint savoury whiff of stir-fry and the jaded smell of cold bean sprouts. Over all hung the too-familiar sweetish smell of marijuana.

'Dr Marks,' Nelson began.

Ruth had her back to them. She scratched at her side with one hand and waved Nelson down with the other. 'Give me a minute, will you? I've had a bloody awful night.' She stumbled to the far end of the room to a bank of steel shelving, which was covered by blue trelliswork at one end, dividing off the kitchen from the living area.

Hackett raised his eyebrows, but Nelson seemed content to give her time while they took in details of her living arrangements. Her PC rested at one end of a folding dining table, in a rather elaborate turret-style bay. Journals and papers lay on the table and were arranged with seeming purpose around the typist's chair by the computer. At the other end of the table was a microscope with a binocular viewer. In a cabinet designed for displaying glassware and ornaments, there were more of the little bottles they had seen in Ellis's flat, but these contained vibrant communities of tiny insects which seemed to stream constantly in solid black rivulets along thin strips of filter paper, from the cobalt blue food matter to the cotton wool plugs. There was room for flight, too, in this microcosm of existence which Nelson found strangely claustrophobic.

Ruth had set a pot of coffee to filter. She stopped suddenly, setting down the mug she held with a clatter, and turned, her eyes wide. 'Helen?'

'She's all right, as far as we know.'

Ruth looked from the inspector to the sergeant, then drew the lapels of her slightly shabby dressing gown together and, tying the cord more tightly, reached for a loaf of bread from a large earthenware pot. She continued her breakfast preparations in a thoughtful mood. Within minutes the flat was filled with the dually tantalizing smells of coffee and toast. Hackett wondered fleetingly if this was an attempt to mask the smell of marijuana, but recalling the doctor's insatiable appetite for carbohydrates, he decided that the food preparations were intended to satisfy another, quite different need.

Ruth carried her meal and three mugs of coffee through to the living area, nodding vaguely in the direction of a large, grubby linen-covered sofa. Nelson took up position at one end, sipping at his coffee and eyeing Ruth with a speculative stare.

Ruth cleared some textbooks from an armchair covered in the same material as the sofa and dropped them at her feet; apparently, she remained immune to Nelson's intimidatory tactics. 'So,' she said, 'If it's not Helen, why are you here? What's happened?'

Hackett was almost relieved she hadn't made some flip remark which Nelson could use to cruel effect later.

'I'd like you to tell us about John Ellis's relationship with Professor Wilkinson,' Nelson said.

'Relationship?' Ruth seemed ready to laugh but perhaps their grim expressions guided her to caution. She eased herself onto the chair and rested her coffee mug on the arm. A little coffee had slopped over the edge and she wiped it on the linen before saying, 'Ed's narcissism may have bordered on the psychotic, but he was strictly hetero.'

Hackett saw a muscle twitch in Nelson's jaw at the use of the word 'psychotic', but he remained admirably calm, giving Hackett the nod to take the lead.

'Professor Wilkinson saw Mr Ellis on the day he died. We know there was an argument. Ellis made threats,' he explained carefully. 'We also know that Mr Ellis's research grant was guaranteed until autumn this year, so the row couldn't have been about funding. But they did have an almighty ding-dong and Ellis left the place screaming abuse at the professor. We'd like to know why.'

'Why don't you ask him yourself?' Ruth's tone was uncharacteristically wary, even apprehensive.

'He's beyond questioning,' Nelson replied.

'Beyond. Are you saying—?' Ruth asked sharply.

'John Ellis took an overdose of barbiturates and alcohol yesterday evening,' Hackett explained. He felt Nelson tense beside him. 'He died sometime between three and four this morning.'

'Poor, stupid bastard,' Ruth murmured.

'We have photographs,' Nelson said.

Ruth sipped her coffee. 'Photographs?' she said.

Nelson took two black-and-white pictures from his pocket and handed them to Ruth. Ellis entering the Wilkinson's house. Ellis placing a white cardboard box in the fridge.

Ruth studied them for a long time. 'Compelling,' she said, at last.

'So, you see why we would like to know exactly what went on in the meeting between Ellis and Wilkinson on the day of the professor's murder.'

'Oh, I see,' Ruth said, passing the photographs back to Nelson. 'You think John killed Ed in a fit of rage and then did himself in out of remorse, is that it?'

'We're not jumping to any conclusions, Dr Marks.'

'Why not ask Valerie, Ed's secretary?'

'Yes,' Nelson said. 'We know who she is. Professor Wilkinson gave Mrs Roberts strict instructions to work on a recording of a report he wanted typing up, so she was wearing headphones at the time. She heard voices raised, but not the details.'

Ruth smiled. 'Discreet as ever. Good old Valerie.'

'Dr Marks?' Hackett prompted, when it became apparent that she did not intend to say more.

'I don't honestly see what I can tell you, gentlemen.'

'Oh,' said Nelson, softly, 'I think you do.'

Ruth looked uneasily from one to the other.

Nelson's smile was like cheese wire: thin, sharp and potentially dangerous. 'We've spoken to Alice Chambers, the Senate representative who is managing the departmental reorganization. She says the Dean of Faculty got an anonymous email yesterday.'

'The message?' Ruth asked impatiently.

'Said Ellis had been cooking the results. It suggested a comparison of his lab book with the data he's due to publish in his thesis. Miss Chambers said she had called Ellis to a meeting with the Dean of Faculty and one of the pro-vice chancellors. It was scheduled for ten o'clock this morning. They wanted a satisfactory answer to the allegations.'

'Which of course the stupid little prick wouldn't be able to give them,' Ruth said bitterly. She shook her head. 'And you think I sent the message, is that it?'

'Anonymous mailings are traceable, given the right expertise and a little co-operation from the electronic mailer,' Hackett said, repeating what Jem Tact had told him just over an hour earlier.

For a moment, Ruth seemed furious, then she sighed and raised her hands in surrender. 'Helen's right, I'm not much good with the minutiae of cybertechnology. Academic life isn't nearly so cosseted and woolly as you might think, Inspector. These days it's about fulfilling quotas of one sort or another, a side effect of the Research Assessment Exercise we've just undergone. Staff have to justify their existence by pointing to recent research of national, or preferably international importance, but they also have to find ways of bringing money into the department. Then there's the increased teaching load to cope with. Lecturers don't always have time to do their own research, so they put their doctoral students under incredible pressure to come up with something they wouldn't be ashamed to put their name to. Of course, the same pressures mean that they don't have time to supervise the students properly, so sometimes mistakes are made which aren't noticed, and occasionally — more times than I'd care to think too deeply about — results are fudged.'

'You discovered that John Ellis was "fudging" his results?' Nelson asked.

'The dream put me onto it — counting so many pearls and then giving Ed a different number. Lies, you see. They trip you up, unless you're damn good at it. Ellis was disorganized, a bloody disaster when it came to collecting reliable data. Computers are remarkable machines — give them something reasonable to work with, say a quarter of your results, and they can manufacture a whole new set on a random basis, fill in the blanks. You can even write in a variation about the mean that fits in with the statistical evidence. Saves all the hassle of doing the reps.'

'Reps?' Nelson cut in.

'Replications — repeats of the experiment to check your first set of results wasn't just a fluke. But most fiddlers — Ellis included — just leave out the odd result that doesn't quite fit with the trend, or which might make their statistical significance less than impressive. That way their graphs turn out as nice straight lines or curves instead of dog-legs or something resembling a temperature chart. Ellis had dropped a few inconvenient points from his graphs, and to be frank, I don't think he had the skill to do even that the job properly.'

Nelson stared fixedly at a point somewhere over Ruth's left shoulder, then he nodded to himself. 'Miss Chambers says the panel was a formality. He would have been dismissed from the department immediately.'

'Well,' Ruth said, running her fingers through her hair, 'On this occasion it gives me no gratification to be proved right. None at all.'

'If that's how you feel, why report him?' Nelson demanded.

Ruth's eyes widened in shock. 'I'm a scientist. I search for truth — I'm sorry if that sounds callow, unworldly, but it's how I feel. What Ellis did discredits the whole scientific community. His research was bullshit, and I have to put up with enough of that from my peers without sanctioning the lies of a second-rate doctoral student. Anyway, if he'd published, the statisticians would've punched a hole the size of Antarctica through his data. And, there were other considerations: the reputation of the university would have suffered; thirty per cent job losses might've become fifty per cent. I didn't want that on my conscience.'

'Very public-spirited of you, Dr Marks,' Nelson said.

'Didn't think altruism was a part of my biological make-up, did you, Inspector?' Ruth said with a twisted smile. 'Well, you'd be surprised.'

'You seem to be saying that the argument between Ellis and Prof Wilkinson was about Ellis fiddling his results,' Hackett said, 'And yet there is no record of a complaint against him in Wilkinson's computer files.'

'I thought you'd seen the *shop* entry in Ed's Apocalypse file.'

Hackett remembered the list of academics in the file, each with a recommendation next to their name — the file that Helen Wilkinson had admitted to altering so that her colleagues got the happy endings they wanted from the departmental restructuring. The word 'SHOP' had been written next to Ellis's name, and given the professor's vindictive nature, they had assumed the obvious. But a member of the Senate had explained that it was a harmless acronym for a regular check on doctoral students. 'Senate House Overview of Progress,' he said aloud.

Ruth stared, her eyebrows raised. 'Sergeant, I'm astonished — I thought you police were a bunch of cynics!'

Hackett saw laughter brimming in her eyes. He took a breath, shook his head and exhaled. If it wasn't so bloody tragic, it'd be funny.

'Our original assessment was correct,' he said.

'I'm afraid so,' Ruth said. 'No acronym. Just plain, old-fashioned slang. Edward was going to shop the silly little sod. His mistake was letting Ellis know that.'

Nelson snorted. 'Didn't you say postgraduate students rated somewhere below an amoeba, Dr Marks? Why would Professor Wilkinson be interested in the petty cheating of a student who wasn't even under his supervision?'

'I think what I actually said was that he ranked just *above*, but you're right, most professors would have neither the time, nor the interest in the students not directly under their aegis. But Edward, you must remember, liked to control people.' A small puff exploded from her lips. 'People, Events, Policy. Edward's version of a PEP — and he got a good return on his equity — look how far he'd risen in a relatively short period of time. Edward was also something of a sadist. He was probably just toying with the poor sod, but he didn't bank on Ellis's instability.' She laughed. '*The value of investments can go down as well as up.* I can understand why Ellis would want to kill Edward, but I really can't say why he'd kill himself, unless he thought he couldn't live with the shame of fucking up his research so publicly. After all, as far as your murder investigation goes, he was virtually in the clear. It isn't as if you'd made a great deal of progress with the case prior to his suicide, had you?'

A thoughtful silence settled on the three, and Nelson, exchanging a glance with Hackett, rose to leave. He placed his coffee mug on the floor beside the sofa and straightened up. Perhaps it was the harshness of the light, or perhaps it was simply that he hadn't slept for a day and a night. Whatever the reason, Hackett saw beyond Nelson, the hardened practitioner of the law, not above bullying, cajoling, or deceit to achieve a result, to the lonely, unhappy and ageing man bewildered by the changes imposed on him by the emphasis on work quotas and lack of funding, equal opportunities and political correctness.

'The photographs,' Ruth said.

Hackett turned to her. He got the impression that Dr Marks had blurted this out, that she was, for once, uncertain of her ground, but he had been so absorbed in analysing Nelson that he had missed her facial expression. 'Where on *earth* did you get hold of them?' she finished.

'A journalist.'

'Press? I thought those bloody vultures had all flown. Picking over the bones of some other tragedy.'

'He's local — from the *Chester Recorder*,' Nelson said flashing her a look of — of what? Hackett wondered. Aggression, certainly. But was there also resentment? 'Ellis tried to kill the "vulture" who took these pictures.' Nelson went on.

She stared hard at him. '*Tried* to?'

'Torched his flat.' Nelson's eyes blazed suddenly as if with some reflection of the inferno.

'But we recovered the pictures,' Hackett said.

'How? I mean, if John set fire to the flat—'

'Molyneux had sent the pictures by computer fax. Scanned them into his computer and then zipped them along the information superhighway to the *Recorder*.' Molyneux's boss, Jeff Townley, had brought the photographs personally, as soon as he found them on his return to the office in the morning. 'That's how we found Ellis so soon. If it hadn't been for the photographs, the body might've been undiscovered for days.'

'As I said,' Ruth observed dryly, 'Computers are remarkable machines.' She frowned suddenly, chewing at the inside of her cheek. 'The photographer?'

'In a coma,' Hackett answered. 'He may not make it.'

As they left, clumping down the grey stairs unaccompanied, Hackett said, 'I can see why Ellis'd want to kill the prof, and it makes sense he'd have a go at Helen if he thought she'd dropped him in it with the Senate. But I don't understand why he'd bash the photographer over the head and try to destroy the photographs when he intended going home for booze and barbs.' He sensed a watchfulness in Nelson and murmured, 'Sorry, sir.'

'For what?' Nelson turned viciously on him and they stood at the foot of the stairs, locked in another duel of egos.

Hackett shrugged. 'Nowt.'

Hackett glared at him for a few seconds before continuing down the stairs.

'It certainly looks like Ellis planned to go home and top himself,' Nelson said, picking up where Hackett had left off.

Transgression forgiven, Hackett thought, relieved.

'So why would he give a monkey's backside if he'd been snapped in the act?' Nelson finished.

'Doesn't make an awful lot of sense,' Hackett agreed.

They lingered a few moments longer outside Ruth's house in a pool of rare warm sunshine. 'My feeling is, Ellis's trick with the mouse and the attack on Molyneux are unconnected.'

Hackett was less certain. He thought they were connected, though indirectly.

* * *

Hackett stopped off at the Countess of Chester hospital on his way home; Nelson had sent him to get a couple of hours' kip, but he couldn't rest until he had seen the young photographer. He checked his watch as he went in: Nelson would want him back at headquarters by mid-afternoon, but he hoped the house would be empty so that he could shower and get a couple of hours' rest. He needed to talk to Sheila about Daniel's continuing rebellion, but he also needed sleep, and right now that would have to take priority.

Molyneux was in the intensive care unit. A WPC had been posted outside the glass-fronted ward, with strict instructions to check and verify the identity of anyone entering. She duly scrutinized Hackett's warrant card but waived the formality of a phone call to headquarters.

'No need, sir. Saw you on telly with DI Nelson.'

Hackett stepped into the antiseptic air of the high-dependency unit. The nursing staff moved about quietly, checking adjusting the bewildering complexity of digital instruments, occasionally exchanging a word or two with the exhausted, silent figures seated next to most of the beds, afraid to leave, determined that if their mother or husband or child was to die, they would not die alone. There was no rush, no panic, even the lighting was subdued; the atmosphere was one of quiet efficiency. There were five patients in all, and Hackett quickly found Molyneux. He had a visitor. Hackett recognized him immediately as Jeff Townley, the editor of the *Chester Recorder*. He had turned up at Molyneux's flat when one of his reporters, sent to cover the story of the fire, telephoned him and told him who the victim was.

Townley looked pale and tired. He had a heavy growth of stubble on his chin and looked uncomfortable with it. He held a packet of cigarettes in his hand as though he had been distracted in the act of taking one out of the pack. A blood vessel throbbed in his temple and he gave the impression that he was both angry and upset.

'Any news?' Hackett asked.

Townley gave him a bleak smile. 'They say it looks worse than it actually is.' His eyes roved over the respirator tube, the drips and monitor wires, attached to the lean frame of the Irishman. 'Let's hope they're right.' He sighed. 'He's going to be so pissed off when he sees they've shaved off his hair.' Then, wincing at his own clumsy attempt at humour, he hurried on: 'They've sedated him because they're worried about him moving — the skull fracture could—' He stopped. 'I should never have allowed him to take on that bloody assignment!' His voice caught and he coughed. 'They say the next few days will be crucial.'

'His parents?'

'They'll be here by early evening.'

They listened to the click and hiss of the respirator for some minutes without speaking and Hackett offered up a silent prayer.

'Did you come just to see the lad, or was there something you wanted to ask me?'

'You mentioned an assignment. Did you have reason to believe it could be dangerous?'

'Bloody Ellis!'

'We went to his flat,' Hackett started to explain.

'I know,' Townley said. 'It's my job to know. Overdose.' He shrugged. 'Doesn't help Dermot though, does it?' He glanced apologetically at Molyneux before saying, 'He'll hate me for betraying a trust, but . . .' He shrugged. 'To be honest I was more worried it'd be a waste of time. He'd had a tip from one of your lot.'

'Police?'

Townley nodded.

'Did he mention a name?'

'No, but I could check with the news team — see if he mentioned her to anyone.'

'Her?'

'He was quite specific about that. D'you want me to . . . ?'

'I'd be grateful.' Hackett waited a few moments, then, registering Townley's hesitation and guessing its cause, he said, 'You go ahead. I'll watch him till you get back.' Townley had a cigarette in his mouth even before he had left the unit.

During his brief vigil Hackett had an opportunity to reflect on the events of the previous night. Something had been bothering him, some detail, teasing at the edges of consciousness and now, as he watched the steady rise and fall of the respirator and the fluctuating count of Dermot's pulse on the digital readout, the feeling became more tangible and it framed itself as Nelson's question:

Why *would* Ellis take the trouble to try and cover up his sick prank on Dr Wilkinson? Presumably he had killed himself, as Ruth had suggested, because of his imminent exposure as a cheat and an incompetent, but hiding the fact that he had put the butchered mouse in Helen's fridge would not have saved him from the humiliation of being dismissed from the university. In fact, it made more sense that he would *want* her to know who had left the box. Was this mendacity in the doctoral student force of habit, something that had become so much a part of his life that he didn't know when to stop?

Or was it possible that someone had set Ellis up? After all, leaving the dissected mouse in Helen's fridge didn't make him a murderer. It did, however, suggest a deeply unpleasant mind, and that might lead a plodding copper to think Ellis capable of more than this single, spiteful act.

He continued watching the rise and fall of Molyneux's chest, mechanically induced, an imitation of life and, in his depressed frame of mind, an intimation of impending death. Townley returned, breaking in on these morbid thoughts. His telephone conversation had proved unproductive. 'A woman, as I thought. A detective constable — that's all he'd said.'

Hackett groaned inwardly. Nelson would make of this an opportunity for griping about the unreliability of women detectives. 'We'll investigate from our end.' There weren't that many to choose from, so the task wouldn't be all that difficult.

He scuffed down the hospital corridors deep in thought. Where were Helen Wilkinson and Mick Tuttle between eleven p.m. and twelve thirty the previous night? They said they had taken the scenic route back to Helen's house, but could just as easily have taken a taxi to Dermot's flat, hit him over the head, and torched the place. Had they been wrong to rule Helen out?

A blast of cold air and icy rain roused Hackett from his reverie. He found himself outside the hospital, with his car on the far side of the car park, and in it, his overcoat. He turned up his jacket collar and made a run for it. If Ellis really *had* left cakes, either Helen or Tuttle were perfectly capable of performing the dissection on the mouse and switching it for Ellis's offering — although he had to admit, Dr Wilkinson did look pretty sick afterwards . . . But why would she draw attention back to herself just when pressure was beginning to ease off? Of course, she might've looked sick because she'd just got back from beating a man senseless and then setting his flat alight. In which case, the mouse was a suitable diversion to make her seem the victim instead of the aggressor. There again, was it really feasible that Ellis had popped into Dr Wilkinson's with a box of cakes and then went off to top himself? And where had he got the keys from? None had been found in his flat, and yet he'd let himself into Helen's house. So, either he'd stolen and then dumped them, or he'd been loaned a set, which meant Helen, or someone close to her, was in on it.

He sat in the car for several minutes, gripping the steering wheel in concentration, and dripping rainwater. Why would Helen attack Dermot Molyneux in the first place? Why not let him use the photographs of Ellis in the next issue of the *Recorder*, alongside the bizarre story of the dissected mouse? Perhaps Dermot had got more than he bargained for — but who else had he photographed? Helen? Tuttle? Or both of them? What the hell had they been up to?

And what about Clara Ainsley? They had an admission that she had seen Professor Wilkinson at home at around the time of the murder. Might she have gone back to the house to recover some evidence? What if Molyneux had photographed her? But this was pure speculation — Molyneux had computer-faxed two photographs, not three, and they had both been of Ellis. He fervently hoped Jem Tact would be able to work one of his miracles on Molyneux's computer.

* * *

Ruth picked at the chips on her plate. The refectory was noisy with lunchtime traffic; the same disparate mixture of foreign visitors, lecturers, technicians and doctoral students as before, although the students this week were Japanese, and they were quieter and more polite than the previous week's visitors. Ruth looked on with amusement at the dismayed expression on some of the faces as they picked at the greasy mound of fish and chips on their plates. 'I tell you, the chef is a sadist,' she remarked.

'What?'

Helen was finishing her far healthier choice of soup and a roll and looking down at her own plate, Ruth shoved it from her, disgusted.

'I just can't get that bloody animal out of my head. I mean is that how it is for you? Is that what it's like, constantly thinking of the blood and that poor mangled . . .'

'Don't do this, Ruth.' Helen seemed disturbed and her eyes showed too much white.

'Well I can't look at food without seeing that damned mouse crucified on a board.'

'Ruth, shut *up*.'

Ruth stared, arched an eyebrow.

'I'm sorry, but you do go on at the worst of times and in the grossest detail.'

Ruth beat her breast in penitence, levelling a sardonic smile at her friend. 'I hope you know who you should thank for the sudden emergence of the new, forthright you,' she said.

Helen flushed, and Ruth wondered what it meant. 'The angel of mercy who topped Edward,' she said, attacking her chips with renewed appetite.

* * *

Sweet sounds; sweet, mellow scents. Daniel lay back on his bed and closed his eyes, imagining himself on the Andean mountains. He visualized vast tracts of green and thin wisps of steamy condensation above the tree canopy. He took another drag from the inexpertly rolled spliff, which he had made using a diagram a friend had drawn for him; three pieces, two end-to-end, and one to bind them together. He sucked deep, taking the smoke to the bottom of his lungs, like he'd been shown, and held his breath, waiting for the chemicals to find their way into his bloodstream. Simple diffusion, he thought, inadvertently allowing his biology revision to intrude on his thoughts. He giggled, expelling puffs of smoke. THCs in, stress *out*!

Terry Hackett pulled into the drive and sat for a minute or two, his eyes closed, trying to find the energy to get out of the car. He had time to catch an hour's sleep, shower, and then back out to discover the truth of who had leaked information to the press, he told himself.

Daniel's bedroom window was open. 'How many times do I have to tell him that most burglaries are opportunistic?' he grumbled to himself as he found his key and let himself in. The bloody Yale wasn't double locked, either.

Daniel was beginning to float. Some of his mates at school didn't rate Rocky, because they said it just made them feel dizzy, they preferred Skunk, but they didn't have dads with noses like bloody Pinocchio. Anyway, this — He sighed, smiling to himself — this was more than dizziness. This was special. He took another pull on his joint and relaxed to the South American music he had picked up on his last protest weekend. An Ecowarrier called Treecreeper had sold it to him. She was *gorgeous*. He listened to the breathy tones of the pan pipes, and pictured himself with Treecreeper on one of the platforms of the tree she was protecting, smoking dope, listening to music, kissing . . .

She had two rings in her lower lip, and he tried to imagine how it would feel, tonguing the thin rim of gold, probing deeper into her mouth, his hand around her waist, straying under the rough edge of her woven waistcoat, beneath the coarse linen of her shirt, to flesh and bone. He groaned.

Hackett stamped upstairs, feeling increasingly irritated with Daniel. The boy had no regard for their feelings: he sneered at their perfectly reasonable requests to switch off lights, or to close doors and windows, and yet he constantly lectured them about their exploitation of the environment with their use of two cars, and the washing machine and God knew what all else.

He opened Daniel's bedroom door.

Daniel leapt from his bed, yanking the radio, still attached to the headphones, from his bedside table. It fell with a clatter and the tape ejected. Daniel fastened his trousers, mortally embarrassed to have been caught in an erotic fantasy by his father.

Hackett strode over to his son and dragged the remains of the spliff from his hand, then pulled the headphones off. 'What the hell do you think you're doing?'

Daniel was too shaken to sneer.

'You should be in school. Why aren't you in school? Where did you get this?'

Daniel didn't know which question to answer first. He stood, blushing to his ears, wondering with agonizing distress if his father had seen him with his hand down his trousers.

'This is illegal, Daniel. Who's your supplier?'

Daniel regarded him in mute rebellion.

'Do you know what this stuff does to you? Do you know the lasting damage marijuana can cause?'

Daniel recovered enough to say, 'No one calls it *that* anymore, Dad.'

'I don't give a *monkeys* what you call it,' Hackett yelled. 'Where's the rest?'

He started rummaging through Daniel's things.

'Dad!'

He turned on the boy. 'Empty your pockets,' he demanded. '*What?*'

'You'll bloody well do it here and now, or you'll do it down the nick.'

For a moment, neither moved. Daniel stared at him with absolute hatred, then he began emptying his pockets.

* * *

Hackett tried to contact Nelson at headquarters and at home. His mobile was out of action and he wasn't answering on his home number. No one had seen him or heard from him since they had split up after reporting in briefly that morning.

Hackett had taken a frightened and sullen Daniel to school, and had spoken to the headmaster, requesting that any and all absences be reported to him or his wife immediately. Sheila had gone to visit her sister in Leeds for the day, which was why Daniel had thought he wouldn't be disturbed.

218

Hackett arranged for his mother to be at home when school finished and had left his mobile number so that she could let him know if Daniel was late. She had been delighted to be of use, and, mercifully, had not asked any awkward questions. He would talk to her and to Sheila that evening, and they would decide what sanctions to impose.

In the meantime, he could not rest, and decided to drive around to Nelson's house. He rang the bell and, turning his back to the door, cast a critical eye over the garden. Hackett helped Sheila with their garden when he could spare the time, actually enjoying it; he even knew the names of a few of the plants. Nelson's garden consisted of a square patch of lawn, well-trimmed, the border ruthlessly weeded, but without a single flower or shrub. A barren suburban square.

He returned to headquarters and sought out Sergeant Brinckley. Jane had known Nelson a long time and Hackett had noticed that he tolerated her more easily than most.

'He got a call,' she said. 'Sounded urgent.' Hackett understood from her quick, frowning glance around the room that there was more to say, but not here under the eyes and within the hearing of people who, by profession and habit, were unashamed eavesdroppers.

He waited a couple of minutes, sifting through his memos to make it look like he had something to do other than track down his boss, and found the long-awaited search on Helen Wilkinson's background. A rapid skim through the report increased his unease that they had been so quick to dismiss her as a suspect, and also prompted him to telephone his mother and tell her that Daniel was not to go to his room when he got in, but get started on his homework with her in the kitchen.

He followed the sergeant out of the open-plan office and into the corridor. She pushed through the door leading to the back stairs and waited for him.

'His son?' Hackett asked, saving her from the ignominy of betraying the inspector's trust so directly.

Jane nodded — a slight flicker of movement, no more.

Hackett considered asking — actually opened his mouth to speak, then decided against it. 'Thanks,' he said. 'If he gets in touch, tell him I've gone to question Wilkinson and Tuttle. Ask him to contact me urgently.'

'Sure, Terry.' She seemed relieved that he had not asked for more.

'Jane—' Brinckley's expression quickly changed to one of pained wariness. 'It's not about Nelson,' he reassured. 'But I do have a favour to ask.'

'You can ask . . .' she said.

'Someone's been leaking info to the press about John Ellis. It's probably the reason we've got a photographer in hospital and a house burned out. For all I know, it triggered Ellis's suicide.'

'Bloody hell.'

'Yeah . . . Molyneux was shadowing Ellis, presumably hoping to be there at the arrest or something. His boss thinks Molyneux's source was a WDC.'

Jane Brinckley winced. 'You want me to find out who?'

'It'd be better coming from you than from me.'

CHAPTER 22

Conor Smith had known Jack Nelson for ten years. In that time he had developed — perhaps even nurtured — a profound dislike of the man. Nelson's son, Ian, had been admitted as a patient during Dr Smith's first week at Wesley Hospital. Since that time, Ian had returned, either as a voluntary patient or under a 'section' on scores of occasions. Nelson had refused to have anything to do with his son after he had reached sixteen, and so for Ian, Care in the Community had meant a series of hostels, bedsits and, latterly, doorways and dosses. He had disappeared for a few weeks, living rough, returning to the hospital some nights earlier because his voices were whispering to him to kill someone, and his only source of pride, the only sense of achievement Ian had, was in knowing that he had never harmed anyone but himself.

Smith searched Nelson's face for some glimmer of compassion or regret or guilt — any hint that the man was reachable, any sign of emotion that would make him despise Nelson less and perhaps help him to understand a little.

'I'd only make him worse,' Nelson said, staring back at him.

'He's *asking* for you.'

'You saw what he was like last time.'

'He needs you,' Smith insisted. 'He's afraid of you, but he needs you. Let him know he doesn't need to be afraid.'

'I never laid a finger on him.' A slight flare of indignation in those curious marmalade-orange eyes.

Smith wanted to tell Nelson that his total rejection of his son, the literal fact that he 'never laid a finger' on Ian unless to perform some unavoidable act of care, perfunctorily and without affection, had wrought up the young man's psychosis, that he was convinced Ian would be a normal, sane twenty year old if Nelson had responded to him and loved him, instead of depriving him of human contact and parental approval and affection from the day of his birth.

Nelson shrugged. 'The boy is worse when I'm around.'

He can't even give him his name.

'Ian needs you,' Smith said calmly. Ten years of psychiatric work had trained him in the art of hiding his true feelings so effectively that sometimes he had trouble analysing what he truly felt. 'If you don't speak to him, I can't vouch for his safety.'

'I'm no good to him,' Nelson said, stubbornly, but would not meet his eye, and Smith knew he was making headway.

'Ian has a knife in there. I think he'll use it if you don't talk to him.'

For a fleeting instant Nelson looked up and Smith saw in his eyes an icy crystal of hope that all of this would finally end. It melted in the heat of shame and anger that followed. *Now* Smith began to understand. What Nelson desired most was what he was constitutionally incapable of achieving: he was one of the breed which longs for peace and creates only strife. Was it, Smith wondered, his wife's death that had set up this irreconcilable conflict, or had Nelson always been like this? Had Nelson driven his wife to despair with his endless struggle against his own discontent — and blamed Ian rather than face his own part in her suicide?

* * *

'Aren't you going to get a warrant, Sarge?' DC Wright was anxious: he didn't like taking action without DI Nelson's say-so.

'We don't need a warrant to ask a few questions.'

'Yeah, but . . .'

'The Super's approved this course of action, in DI Nelson's absence,' Hackett said, shrewdly striking at the heart of Wright's objections.

Wright had worked with Nelson long enough to know that he liked to be in control of things. Long enough, also, to lose the imperative of working on initiative which had once been so important to him. He nodded. They'd have to wait a bit, anyway, if Hackett wanted to interview Dr Wilkinson at home. With a bit of luck, the boss would be back in time.

In the event, they waited until half past five, acting on a message from the surveillance team that had been placed outside Helen Wilkinson's house. When Wright came through with the message, Hackett had been dozing pleasantly in Nelson's chair.

'Still no sign of the boss, then, Sarge?' Wright said, remembering with spiteful glee something Nelson had said about Hackett reminding him of a ginger tom his wife had once owned.

Hackett narrowed his eyes. Smiling, he stood and turned his back to the constable. 'D'you see any boot marks on my backside?'

Jerked out of his ill-will by the shock of having his mind read a second time, Wright muttered, 'No, Sarge,' then blushed at the stupidity of the answer. When he mustered the courage to meet Hackett's eye, the sergeant chuckled.

'Just remember the boot is on *my* foot, at least for the moment, eh, Wright?'

'I'll get my coat,' Wright answered. He picked up the anorak he'd draped over his chair and met Hackett in the car park. He saw Hackett's disparaging look. The anorak was the nylon type, with a flimsy hood and a drawstring cord which tied under the chin, and taking in the sergeant's smart rain jacket, he felt scruffy, despite the good quality suit and silk tie he wore under his anorak.

'What d'you expect to find, Sarge?' Wright asked, breaking a silence which in the confines of the car was too uncomfortable to sustain, even on the short ride from headquarters to the Wilkinsons' house. Wright was sensitive to atmosphere.

Hackett leaned across Wright and pressed the release button of the glove compartment. 'Take a look at those pictures.'

Wright slid the two photographs onto his lap. Ellis checking the roadway before nipping down the side entry. Ellis with a white box in his hand. His own bloodier version of Dunkin' Donuts.

'So?'

Hackett tapped the first picture. 'The car.' A gleaming silver-grey Nissan stood outside the Wilkinsons' house. 'It's not hers. I checked.'

'Well if you checked, you must know whose it is, then.'

Hackett grinned. 'Oh, I do. And I'd be interested to know if she does. 'Course, it'd be even more instructive if we knew what that poor bugger Molyneux had photographed — aside from Ellis with his confectionery delights, that is.' He turned down the corners of his mouth. 'But they've had plenty of time to clear up since last night, so I'll settle for a chance to sniff around.' He frowned, his eyes on the road, but Wright could see he was distracted. 'Check the upstairs rooms, maybe . . . ?' he finished.

'Without a warrant?'

Hackett smiled. 'You're nothing if not dogged, I'll give you that.'

Wright squirmed in his seat.

'It's surprising what people will agree to,' Hackett said. 'After all, she is a grieving widow, isn't she? Surely a grieving widow would do anything to find her husband's murderer . . .'

Wright shrugged, unconvinced. 'D'you think someone's helping her?'

In answer to Hackett's quick, questioning look he went on, 'You said *they've* had chance to clear up. D'you reckon it's the gimp?'

Hackett shifted a little in his seat; the word offended his sensibilities. '*Doctor* Tuttle — possibly,' he said. 'Or even her friend, Dr Marks.'

At this time of the day, the Wilkinson's house was in deep shadow, while the other side of the street twinkled in sunshine after a shower. 'Dr Marks strikes me as the sort of woman who doesn't make affiliations, let alone friendships, lightly,' Hackett went on. 'But I should think she'd do a lot for someone she did like.'

'Pity you can't get them all together in the drawing room and sweat a confession out of them,' Wright said with heavy sarcasm.

Hackett surprised him by laughing. 'It worked for Poirot, eh, Wright?' He drew in to the kerb and stilled the engine. 'I'm not sure she's got a drawing room — d'you think the kitchen will do?'

Wright got out of the car scowling. Hackett had managed to turn the tables again, making it look like it was *him* who was making all these bloody daft suggestions. To make matters worse, Pete Unsworth strolled over from the surveillance car and giving Wright the once-over, said, 'What's up, Wrighty? Piles bothering you?'

Hackett laughed again. 'He's just feeling a bit *Hackett* off, eh, Wright?'

Unsworth raised his eyebrows at the pun and the sour look it elicited from Wright. 'She got here about twenty minutes ago,' he said. 'Arrived with Dr Marks.'

Hackett nodded. 'I see the press have made the connection between Molyneux and this lot.' Two sodden and rather sorry-looking journalists loitered outside the gate. 'If Tuttle arrives, make sure he doesn't leave until I've spoken to him.' Then, taking a deep breath of damp, grassy air, he walked, smiling, over to the journalists. Wright followed in bad humour.

Ruth Marks answered the front door when they rang. 'All on your own, Sergeant?'

She means Nelson's not with him, Wright thought.

Hackett didn't seem to mind. He said, 'I have DC Wright with me, Dr Marks.'

Wright had his warrant card ready. Dr Marks took it, making a careful comparison of the photograph with the real thing.

'Doesn't do you justice.' A smile twitched at the corner of Marks's mouth as she returned his card. 'But that's the British legal system for you. Come through.'

Dr Wilkinson was sitting at the kitchen table. Wright had seen her a few times during the investigation, and she seemed brighter, more alert. The room itself was neat, well ordered.

'How can I help you, Sergeant Hackett?' she asked, with no more than a dismissive glance at Wright.

'We've checked with the restaurant,' Hackett replied. 'They've confirmed you left at eleven o'clock, but we haven't found anyone who saw you between that time and twelve thirty, when we were called to your house.'

'It was a wild night. There weren't many people about.'

Hackett gave a non-committal grunt. He looked over at Wright. That was his cue: he fished in the inside pocket of his anorak for the photographs and placed them side by side on the kitchen table. Hackett took a step back and leaned against the sink unit. Helen gave him a furtive glance, and Wright thought, *If that isn't a guilty look, I'll hand in my resignation tomorrow.*

Ruth Marks picked up the shot of Ellis outside the house and peered at it. She laughed suddenly. 'Isaac Smolder!'

'What?' Dr Wilkinson turned her attention to the photographs.

'Look.' Ruth held up the picture for Helen to see. 'That's Isaac's car.' Snatching it back, she peered at it more closely. 'There doesn't seem to be anyone in it — I wonder where he was hiding. Jeez, Helen, you draw them like flies to shit!'

Helen gazed, startled, into her friend's face.

226

'Manner of speech,' Dr Marks said. 'Bees to a honey pot, wasps to a picnic, butterflies to a buddleia. Whatever.'

'Is there any reason you can think of, why Dr Smolder would be outside your house?' Hackett asked.

* * *

Helen Wilkinson shuddered. Smolder with his papery skin and his cold, analytical scrutiny. He seemed to like watching her, always positioning himself in the refectory or the coffee bar where he could see and be seen. She heard the whisper of his thumb against his forefinger as he carefully rubbed each tiny crumb of bread from his hands to his plate, an action so ritualistic she had half expected him to pick up the plate and wipe the crumbs into his glass — bread and wine, *Body and Blood*. The thought drew her eyes back to the sink unit, where Hackett stood.

'Dr Wilkinson?'

'Sorry? Oh, no. I can think of no earthly reason why he . . .' Her voice trailed off. It made her sick to think he had been outside her house, his unblinking eyes watching, watchful.

'You haven't had any other nasty surprises, Dr Wilkinson?'

Helen blanched, then recovered. 'No. Why do you ask?'

'It seems Ellis thought you had reported him to the Senate. Otherwise, why the rather crude attempt to shock you?'

'Not so crude,' Ruth said. She went to the kitchen unit and, having hustled the sergeant to one side, began rooting in the top drawer. Helen held her breath. 'There was a lot of blood,' she explained, 'which shows that he knew about Helen's previous research. Also,' she took out a teaspoon and slammed the drawer closed, 'in choosing a pregnant doe, he demonstrated a knowledge of *why* she's unable to perform that particular aspect of her research now.' She tilted her head on one side. 'I'd say brutal, rather than crude.'

Helen forced her attention from the set of drawers to Ruth, who was stirring heroic quantities of sugar into her coffee.

'You won't mind if we scout round and make sure he *didn't* leave anything else?' Hackett immediately turned and was on his way through the door into the hallway.

Helen jumped to her feet. 'Yes, I *do* mind.' She couldn't allow them to search the house. Not with the knife basking like a shark in the kitchen drawer.

He turned back.

'Why?'

'I don't have to give an explanation,' Helen said, trying to keep her voice steady, 'but I'll tell you anyway. I'm sick of the intrusion. My house doesn't seem like my own anymore. If you want to search it, you'll have to get a warrant.'

Hackett eyed her thoughtfully; could he know that her new-found confidence was a flimsy construct? He was about to push the point when Ruth Marks spoke:

'Helen! This is nice Sergeant Hackett. He's only trying to help.'

Helen stood her ground. 'I won't have them tramping through the house, prying.'

'Well, of course you are within your rights to refuse us permission to look around, but I *will* get a warrant, Dr Wilkinson, there's no question of that. You see we got notice today of a previous conviction. Assault, causing grievous bodily harm. That rather changes the complexion of things.'

Helen blinked. Staring out into the dimly lit hallway, she saw only the oily black night, a drizzle making a thousand pinpoints of light in the headlamp beams.

He's standing near a doorway, shuttered, as they all are against the vandals and the drug addicts. No shelter, but he doesn't need it; he can trade in broad daylight without fear of being caught. In the spotlight of the headlamps she sees something else — a quick movement, a flash of something silver, foil-wrapped. Sleight of hand: Now you see it, now you don't. Then he crosses the street, heading towards his own car.

She pulls out, anxious, the new driver, unsure of the acceleration, the power of her car. She needs to catch him before he gets to his car, to safety.

He turns, a casual look over his shoulder. He is handsome, young, convinced of his own immortality. An image comes unbidden, unwanted, of Robbie, grey, lifeless, already melting into a past she would give anything to be able to rewrite.

The pusher slows his pace, arrogant, daring her to sound her horn. Her foot presses heavily on the accelerator and the car slews a little to the left. Then she's moving forward, fast. She aims the car full at him and he turns again, smiling at first, but then alarmed. Terror strikes his features as they struck Robbie's. He tries to throw himself to one side, too late.

'What was it, Dr Wilkinson? Two years? It would have been a lot longer if he'd died, but you were lucky — that time.'

'Helen?' For the first time, Ruth seemed unsure of her. Uncertain how to react. Her cool cynicism seemed to have failed her entirely.

She reached to touch Helen's shoulder, but Helen shrugged her off. She went to the sink and ran a glass of water, taking a sip before looking Hackett in the eye.

'There was no luck in it,' she said. 'If I'd been *lucky*, my brother would be alive today.'

CHAPTER 23

Nelson seemed surprisingly philosophical about the usurping of his authority. He even congratulated Hackett on his success. Nobody mentioned his unexplained absence — Nelson was not the sort of man whose health and well-being were inquired after: he had, over the years, cultivated in his subordinates a healthy respect for his privacy. The Super had called him into office on his return, and he had gone without demur — another unusual occurrence.

When he came into the incident room, Hackett looked his boss over: Nelson had been with the Superintendent some thirty minutes, but he showed no signs of stress, nor even of annoyance. He was poker-faced, inscrutable.

Nelson's return gave DC Wright a new confidence; it made him belligerent. 'I don't get it, Sarge,' he said, suddenly heated, exasperated. 'We've got a confession from Clara Ainsley that she went to the professor's house just before he was killed. She admits she was pissed off with him — understatement — 'cos he was having it off with someone else. And you're not even interested.'

Nelson's eyes gleamed. 'Not *interested*, Sergeant?'

'Let's say the focus of my interest has shifted.'

'Well,' Nelson growled. 'Let's hear it.'

Hackett explained that he had found the report on Helen Wilkinson on his desk that afternoon. She had deliberately run down the drugs dealer who had supplied the E's that had killed her brother. He had survived, but she had been sent down for two years for causing grievous bodily harm; the prosecution would like to have charged her with attempted murder, but it was more difficult to prove, and she had a sympathetic and extremely persuasive barrister. Hackett recounted the details of their visit to Dr Wilkinson, her reaction to the news that Smolder's car had been parked outside her house and her refusal to let them conduct a search, all delivered in his usual, efficient, dispassionate manner, neither elaborating, nor offering his own interpretation, but sticking to reporting the plain facts.

He shot a look at Wright. 'Missed anything, have I?'

Wright looked at his shoes and muttered 'No, Sarge.'

Nelson thought for some time and Hackett left him to it.

'Have you applied for a warrant?' Nelson said at last.

Hackett nodded.

'There's a few unanswered questions, as yet,'

Wright gave an enthusiastic answer in the affirmative, but Nelson's withering look was not encouraging.

Nelson and Hackett renewed eye contact, and Hackett was astonished to see respect in the Inspector's eyes.

'*Shershay le fem,*' Nelson said, elliptically.

'Have been, sir,' Hackett said with a self-deprecating dip of his head. 'But Prof Wilkinson's MO was to be extremely discreet in his early liaisons with a new lover. It was only when he got bored, he got careless.'

'Clara Ainsley *invented* the other woman!' Wright said, heatedly. 'Why would he be seeing another woman when he'd got her all set up with a job as his secretary?'

'Last fling?' Hackett suggested.

'Couldn't help himself? One-night stand? Or afternoon delight, to be more precise,' Nelson added.

Wright looked from one to the other. 'This is crazy!'

'You could be right, lad,' Nelson agreed. 'But it never does any harm to examine all the facts and think through the possible scenarios.'

Astonished twice over by his boss's restraint, Hackett said, 'And whichever way you look at it, Clara Ainsley is in the clear for the attack on Molyneux. Her mother came up from Swindon to stay with her yesterday. Apparently, her husband has moved out, and the baby's driving her up the wall. She was with her the entire evening.'

'She's not in the clear for the murder, though, is she?' Wright said rather sulkily.

'No,' Nelson agreed, 'But it seems likely whoever murdered the professor, also attacked Molyneux.'

Hackett nodded.

'What about the husband?' Nelson asked.

'Dr Ainsley was moving his stuff into his new flat. A Dr Rutherford was with him until nearly midnight, and the neighbours went up to complain at about one o'clock, when he was still moving furniture around.'

Jane Brinckley appeared with a message for Hackett and he excused himself, stepping into the corridor.

'Found the leak,' she said, coming straight to the point. 'WPC Paula Jimson. What d'you want me to do about it?'

Hackett glanced at his watch. 'Can you administer a preliminary bollocking? The DI will want to speak to her when he's got a bit more time.'

'What about the Super?'

'See what Nelson has to say first,' he said. Jimson was new, and perhaps easily charmed by a bit of flattery from a journo; maybe Hackett, in his new-found tolerance, would let her off with a talking to.

Jane Brinckley relaxed visibly. 'Thanks, Terry.'

'It's like my daughter says — you can't have one rule for the lads and another for the lasses.'

'Where's Smolder now?' Nelson asked, as he stepped back into the office.

'At home, I should think.'

'Well, I hate to drag him from the warmth of his fireside on a night like this,' Nelson said, with an evil gleam in his eye, 'but I'm sure he won't mind assisting us in our inquiries.'

* * *

Smolder did mind. He made it clear that he minded a great deal. He minded so much, in fact, that he insisted on having his solicitor present at the interview.

Nelson, playing up the emphasis on correct procedure, was assiduous in his identification for the tape of those present. They were: Dr Isaac Smolder; his solicitor, Mr Julian Farrell, of Midhurst, Farrell and Binks, Detective Inspector Nelson and Detective Sergeant Hackett.

'Now, can you explain what you were doing at Dr Wilkinson's house yesterday evening, sir?'

'No.' Smolder folded his hands in front of him, on the desk and gazed levelly at Nelson.

Nelson's eyes sparked. 'No?'

'No,' repeated Smolder. 'I *cannot*, since I was not there.'

'Sure of that, are you?' Nelson's voice, normally a low growl, was almost a purr.

Mr Farrell, a small, balding man in a brown suit, tan shirt and brown woollen tie, leaned forward. 'My client has answered your question unequivocally, Inspector Nelson. Now, may we move on?'

Nelson smiled. He was enjoying this. He leaned back in his chair and casually assessed Dr Smolder's appearance. Fussy-looking. A bit overdone with the yellow bow tie and matching silk hankie. A bit yellow round the irises an' all. Still, we all enjoy a tipple once in a while, he conceded with a magnanimity born of recent suffering. Hackett, in his clear, factual presentation, had observed that Dr Wilkinson had shivered when she'd realized Smolder had been sat outside her house. Nelson saw nothing disgusting in the man. *But then*, he thought, *you're not a woman, are you, Jack?* His attention was drawn to the long, bony fingers of the academic. There was something prissy, too particular, in the way he neatly laced the fingers together, something creepy about the carefully manicured nails. It'd been so long since he'd taken an interest in such things that he hardly knew what a woman looked for in a man, these days. But he was fairly sure that Smolder didn't fit the bill.

'I repeated the question to give Dr Smolder a chance to correct himself,' he said, having finished his leisurely scrutiny of the man.

'I do not need to correct myself. I was not outside Dr Wilkinson's house.'

'Ah, but you were seen,' Nelson said in a soft, confidential tone.

Smolder straightened up — a slight movement, checked part way. 'By whom?'

Nelson did not answer at first but stared into Smolder's eyes. He saw something flutter there — guilt or fear. He raised one hand without looking away, and Hackett handed him the photograph of Ellis arriving at the house. Nelson identified the photograph for the tape with greater ostentation than was strictly necessary.

'This is your car, sir. The index number is quite clear, as you can see. Parked outside Dr Wilkinson's house, last night.' He saw the faintest flush of colour in the stretched skin over Smolder's cheekbones. 'What were you doing there?'

For a moment, he thought Smolder would not respond, then, in a thin, dry voice, he began: 'I was concerned for Helen. I called to see how she was.'

'At the front door, then, were you? The car's empty,' he added as an aside to the solicitor, who was ill-placed to see the picture. 'Only it seems odd that Mr Ellis here — who, you have to admit, looks more than a bit shifty — would check the street and then nip round the back if you were stood on the doorstep in broad daylight.' In fact, it was twilight, but Nelson felt justified in stretching the point.

The patches of colour on Smolder's cheeks grew, so that he looked like an ageing thespian wearing too much rouge.

'I don't believe it's a crime to visit a bereaved colleague,' he said.

'No,' Nelson agreed, raising his eyebrows in a fair enough gesture. 'No, *that's* not a crime. But let me put this into perspective for you, Dr Smolder. Hours after this photograph was taken, we had two serious incidents: John Ellis, found dead of a drugs overdose, and the lad who took this picture left for dead after a nasty arson attack,' he said, deliberately reversing the sequence of events. 'Now *that* puts you squarely in the frame.'

There was a rustle of concern from Smolder's solicitor, but Smolder waved one long-fingered hand to silence him.

'I wasn't at the front door,' he said stiffly. 'I saw Helen leave earlier and tried to follow her — just to ensure that she was quite safe,' he added hastily. 'But she evidently did not want anyone to follow her, and I'm afraid she lost me. I returned to the house. I don't know what I intended to do — I suppose I was curious. I went down the side passage and tried the gate. It was secure. I was about to leave when I heard that wretched boy Ellis. I didn't know it was him, but I'd heard footsteps. I tried the gate of the adjacent house. It was unlocked. I hid in there for a few minutes and then the damned photographer arrived. He climbed over the gate — I was sure he would see me, but he was looking the other way. I waited a few minutes more, then I left. I went home, had a large brandy and early night. That, gentlemen, is the truth.'

CHAPTER 24

'You were rude to Sergeant Hackett,' Ruth said, smiling.

'I had good reason.'

Helen and Ruth sat next to each other on the garden bench. Helen could not stand the proximity of the knife any longer and had escaped into the garden as soon as the police had left. She did not know how to tell Ruth about the knife, and the difficulty had made her uncommunicative.

'Personally, I find it more satisfying to be rude *without* good reason.'

'Yes,' Helen said, distractedly, looking up, away from the house, at the neighbouring properties, where she imagined uncomplicated, tranquil lives were being conducted in placid, unvarying rhythms. The evening was still and cold. Iron-grey clouds clustered in the west and the remaining light gleamed dull and flat on the slate roofs.

'What are you thinking about?' Ruth demanded.

'Ellis, and that poor boy — the photographer. He didn't deserve this. Neither of them did.'

'Who's to say what we deserve? And when did people ever get what they deserve?' Perhaps she saw a shadow flit across Helen's face, because she added, 'You're thinking Edward did, am I right?'

'I was thinking about my brother, Robbie,' Helen said. 'And the bastard who sold him E's.'

Ruth inhaled. Nodded. 'I must remember not to make assumptions about you anymore. Who'd've thought that little Helen was such a dark horse?'

'It's not something you go shouting about. And please don't patronize me.'

Ruth pulled a face. 'Sorry.'

After a silence, Ruth said, 'People don't get what they deserve unless someone takes it upon themselves to make sure they do.'

'Well,' Helen said. 'I failed pretty miserably on that score.'

'The dealer? You tried, that's the main thing.'

Helen's eyes raked her friend's face. 'I'm not proud of it, Ruth.'

'But you don't regret it, either — the trying, I mean. You took your destiny into your own hands, did your best to mete out justice where the legal system failed.'

Helen's pulse quickened. 'Are you saying that's what happened to Edward? That he *deserved* to die?'

Ruth's eyebrows quirked. 'He certainly didn't deserve to flourish.'

'I wish I had your single-minded sense of purpose,' Helen said bitterly.

Ruth laughed. 'But you do! How else d'you think you've survived all of this? Edward, his petty cruelty, the miscarriage, the death of your brother, the indifference of your parents — despite everything, and still you managed to make your mark in this male-dominated arsehole of academe?'

'I put up with Edward's infidelity,' Helen said, playing devil's advocate, 'I accepted his constant criticisms.'

'You wouldn't have for much longer. You'd been fantasizing about doing him in for months. It was only a matter of time.'

'They were just that — fantasies. I couldn't have killed him — at least I hope not. I might've left him . . .'

'Don't be so bloody wet, Helen! Left him! After what he did to you?'

'You meant it, didn't you?' Helen said, shivering in the cold, but unwilling to return to the house. 'When you said someone had done me a favour, getting rid of him. Do you really think the only fitting punishment for Ed was death?'

'Eye for an eye, life for a life. I can't help it, Helen, it's my Jewish upbringing,' Helen thought she was serious, at least in part. 'You should have some sympathy with that, being a good Catholic girl.'

Helen looked into Ruth's eyes and saw, for the first time in the blue irises, several shades lighter than her own, a cold, uncompromising venom. 'I'm an atheist,' she said, a little breathlessly. 'And anyway, Catholic teaching comes from the New Testament.'

'Turn the other cheek, all that bullshit? Spare me!' Ruth exclaimed. 'Accept that dishwater doctrine and you may as well go around with a "kick me" sign on your backside. That's your trouble, Helen. If a task is too unpalatable, you can't see it through to the end; it's a weakness that diseases every aspect of your life. Take your research — too *bloody* for you?' Her voice took on a whimpering, high-pitched, childish quaver. 'Let's use something innocuous and inoffensive, like nice, pink, agar jelly. What was it with the drugs pusher? Did you feel *sorry* for him at the last moment? His poor upbringing, his lack of a good male role model? Did you ease off the accelerator a millisecond before impact? Too much *blood*, Helen?'

Helen stared at her friend. Was this what Ruth really thought of her?

'Edward did everything in his power to destroy you,' Ruth went on, 'your confidence, your reputation, your academic standing within the department, even your identity as a woman — and yet you couldn't find it in you to do something about it.'

Helen's heartbeat matched the noise in her head — the insistent beat of Acid House music — the track that had been playing when she had heard Robbie's first screams and had run to find him squirming on the floor, grotesque, his head swollen, his face distorted with pain and retained fluid. The track ran on as she'd tried to revive him, called for an ambulance, rang her parents. One hundred and twenty beats per minute; the heartbeat of an infant.

Suddenly, everything made sense.

'Come into the kitchen,' Helen said. 'I want to show you something.'

* * *

'You might be interested in this, sir.' DC Tact had interrupted the continuing discussion between Hackett and Nelson.

'Well, will I or won't I?' Nelson snapped. 'Don't ponce about, lad!'

'Not for me to say, sir.'

Nelson sighed, heavily. Tact was another in the mould of Hackett. Said what he thought and remained impervious to criticism. He'd that dreamy, abstracted look on his face that he said he'd been pratting about with computers. 'All right,' he said. 'Let's have it.'

'Best if I demonstrate,' Tact said.

Nelson set his jaw and took a few deep breaths before slouching through to the main office with his hands in his pockets. Bits of cannibalized computer hardware had been tucked against the wall behind Tact's desk; among the detritus Nelson recognized the dented outer casing of Molyneux's PC.

'There was a lot of damage,' Tact explained, his voice taking on an authoritative air that only ever seemed to surface when he was talking about computers. 'Blown chips, mostly. But the hard drive was intact, apart from a few damaged sectors. I've fitted it into a similar PC, so we can run the programs and data stored on it.' His eyes were fixed on the monitor. 'Actually, it was a good idea of yours, sir, to check it over.'

'We aim to please.' Nelson replied, heavy on the sarcasm.

Tact did not notice. 'I'm going into the folder where Molyneux stored the images of Ellis before transmitting them. As you can see, there's four images stored. The first two are of Ellis — I've checked them. But this one . . .' There was a delay, while the computer loaded the file. A blurred image, shadowy behind the window of Helen's study. 'I think he was working on it, trying to enhance the focus before downloading it to the *Recorder*.'

'Not much help, is it, bar the fact you can see it's a woman.'

'The next image,' Tact said, clicking on icons and waiting while the drive loaded the second file, 'is much clearer.'

'Oh aye,' Nelson said, taking his hands from his pockets and leaning on the desk to get a closer look at the screen. 'You can see who that is, all right.'

* * *

The two women sat at opposite sides of Helen's kitchen table. Between them lay the blood-encrusted knife, still wrapped in its plastic food bag.

'How does it feel to be a fugitive from justice, Helen?' Ruth asked.

'Fugitive implies on the run,' she said. 'I don't intend to run.' Helen was shivering violently, but it wasn't from cold.

Ruth touched the corner of the bag, then withdrew her hand. 'What are you going to do about this? The police will be back soon, with their warrant.'

'I intend to give it to them.'

'They'll arrest you.'

'Yes, but they won't convict me.'

'You're certain you didn't kill Edward?'

Helen thought carefully about what she wanted to say, before answering that question. 'Someone killed Edward and kept the knife, and I can't imagine why anyone would do that. A woman might kill out of jealousy, or because Edward

240

was blackmailing her; a man — well, I suppose jealousy might be a motive there, too, but of a different kind. Almost anyone might have killed Ed in a rage against his vicious treatment of them during the interviews.'

'So, you do understand,' Ruth said quietly.

'I can understand the *motivation*, but not the hoarding of the knife, and I can't imagine what I did that so pissed them off that they planted the knife here, in my home.'

'Clara must be feeling fairly bruised — she's lost Ed and her husband,' Ruth suggested. 'She might blame you.'

'She may have a key, I suppose. Whoever it was must have had a key — there was no sign of break-in. But why would Clara blame me? And anyway, would she risk leaving the baby to come here and leave the knife, just to give me a scare?'

'Don't judge everyone by your own standards.'

Helen stared at Ruth. Her eyes seemed cold, wintry, bleak. 'That is a mistake I make, isn't it? For instance, when you concocted that story for the police about you and me being together most of the afternoon the day Edward was murdered. Were you my alibi, or was I yours?'

'Come on, Helen, there was a whole hour between three, when we said we split up, and the time you got home. What advantage could that give *me*?'

Helen wasn't ready to discuss that as yet. She said: 'He *was* seeing someone else.'

'Yes,' Ruth said, impatient. 'Clara. You knew that.'

'No. I mean other than Clara. I always knew when he'd found someone else, started a new affair. He was livelier. Jaunty. Never so alive as when he had a new lover.'

Ruth blinked. 'Who do you think that was?'

'I was hoping you'd tell me. You seem to know so much about everyone. We all confided in Ruth, didn't we? Reliable Ruth. Rational Ruth. Ruthless Ruth?'

'Nice alliteration,' Ruth smiled, uneasily.

'Did you want them to find it, Ruth? Did you *want* the police to arrest me? Why? I don't *understand*.'

'That makes two of us.' Ruth laughed. 'Look, why don't I pour us a drink and let's both calm down.'

'*Sit down.*' Helen stood, seizing the knife through the plastic and Ruth collapsed back in her chair. 'The police knew Ed had had sex before he was murdered — there's forensic evidence. Edward had a lot of failings — and believe me, I knew them all — but he wasn't a five-minute man. So, let's say, twenty minutes — that's how long it'd take me to walk home from the university. Time for a little foreplay, sex and murder, then enough leeway — another twenty minutes — for you to drive back to your office. It doesn't seem feasible.'

'You're bloody right it doesn't seem feasible.'

'Stop it, Ruth!' Helen begged. 'Please stop! Were you counting on the police thinking the same thing? That Edward's murder had been carefully planned and carried out — that it was unhurried, a precision job? With the alibi I gave you, how could they possibly suspect you?'

Ruth spread her hands. 'Helen, sweetheart, I really don't know what the hell you're talking about.'

'You put the knife in the cupboard upstairs. Why? Was it some kind of game? You always did like your games, didn't you Ruth?' She stopped, amazed she hadn't seen it before. 'You and Edward were so alike. Both supremely arrogant. Both feeding off control. Is that why you started seeing him? Because you had so much in *common*?'

'You bloody bitch!' Ruth snarled, suddenly furious. 'You've no idea, have you?'

'I know you had an affair with my husband while professing to loathe him, and all the while you let me believe that you were my friend.'

'Believe it,' Ruth said.

'I want an explanation.'

Ruth laughed, gently mocking, not without affection. 'I'm surprised you need one. And I'm not sure you deserve one. But for old times' sake . . . And do us both a favour — put down the knife — you know you're not going to use it.'

Until a few seconds ago, Helen had not been sure, but now she knew: she could not harm Ruth, no matter what she had done. She eased the knife onto the table.

Ruth stared at it for some time.

'I'm listening,' Helen said.

Ruth's gaze lifted slowly from the weapon to Helen's face. 'I did what you wanted, but couldn't do,' she said. 'You came up with the idea yourself. The fantasies. Killing him in bed, where he was at his most vulnerable, where he would least expect to be attacked. All I did was to act it out for you. It was the easiest thing in the world, persuading Edward I was infatuated with him. Narcissistic bastard! We had arranged to meet after he'd had a whole morning of humiliating his colleagues. He was horny as hell.'

She smiled at Helen's revulsion. 'Yes, I screwed him first. Just the once, to see what it was like. In a way, that's what all of this was about. Seeing what it was like. First encounters. New experiences. And, of course I knew I'd be helping you out.'

'I didn't ask for your help,' Helen said.

'Didn't you?' Ruth shrugged. 'Crossed wires, I suppose. Scrambled signals, but I took you at your word when you said you'd like to see him dead.'

'I never saw you as an altruist.'

'You know, Nelson said almost the same thing, only he didn't use that particular word.'

'You underestimate people, Ruth.' There was open hostility between them now.

Ruth shook her head, her mouth curved down. 'Nah. I know, for instance that you won't turn me in. You see, you really did want him dead. You hated Edward, and I haven't heard you lamenting his passing — no one has. Also, you'd tried to kill someone before — and failed, admittedly — but the will was there.'

She leaned forward suddenly. 'You understand it, Helen. Tell me you didn't enjoy the rush it gave you, seeing the look on his face.' She smiled. 'You can't, can you?'

Helen wouldn't lie, but she wouldn't answer the question, either.

'I've disappointed you, haven't I?' she said. 'What was it — the fact that I stopped acting like "poor little Helen", and started taking my own decisions? Did you disapprove of my independence, Ruth? Or was it the loss of control that infuriated you? I wasn't following the sub-routines you'd carefully tapped into my programming — you'll have to get to grips with that, Ruth. Neural Networks are *supposed* to develop minds of their own.'

She saw a flare of heat in Ruth's face and realized that she'd hit a nerve.

She couldn't know that for one brief fraction of time Ruth was a scabby-kneed child, crouched in the hot dirt on a spring day, screaming at a beetle, wanting to make it notice her, finally *making* it take notice.

Ruth's mouth twitched. 'Just thinking. The knife blade slipped between Edward's ribs easier than a blackthorn into the thorax of the beetle.'

* * *

'We *could* move in with the warrant and search the place,' Hackett suggested.

'And warn the other one we're on to her.' Nelson unwrapped the egg sandwich he had bought on the way to Helen Wilkinson's house. He'd parked with deliberate obtrusiveness directly outside her front gate.

'We both know it's got to be Ruth,' Hackett said. 'The picture's clear enough. Her going into the house shortly after Ellis left.'

'She's a friend of Helen's. She pops in and out all the time. Unless we can get confirmation from Molyneux that it was her who hit him over the head, we can't arrest her. Look, Hackett, I'm on your side. *We* know Ruth's done it, but what have we got? Bugger all's what we've got.'

'So we waste time freezing our arses outside an innocent woman's house,' Hackett said.

'Tetchy today, aren't we?' Nelson was feeling the kind of euphoria only experienced after the remission of a near-fatal hangover. 'Missed our beauty sleep, have we?' He sank his teeth into the egg sandwich, thinking with perverse satisfaction of the unsettling effect eggs invariably had on his digestion. 'Here,' He thrust a copy of the *Chester Recorder* in Hackett's lap. 'Have a squint at that, it'll take your mind off, make time pass.'

Hackett opened the paper and flicked the interior light on. The front-page headline read:

DON JUAN WIDOW IN NEW ATTACK PUZZLE

Below it, a picture of Helen Wilkinson gazing up at the house. Next to it, a column on Dermot Molyneux — *Ace photographer* . . . 'Bloody hell,' Hackett grumbled. '"Ace photographer." They're not serious, are they?' *Brought you the news as it happened* . . . He skimmed the rest. *Condition described as critical* . . . And a photograph. Molyneux with his tousled hair and disarming grin. Beneath that, a shorter piece on John Ellis:

SECOND TRAGEDY STRIKES JINXED COLLEGE

Hackett tilted the paper to Nelson. 'Yeah, really takes your mind off.'

Nelson found himself staring into the face of his son. He blinked, swallowed painfully, and the picture resolved into a bad passport photograph of Ellis. Hackett went back to reading the paper.

Nelson, who had never confided in a colleague, nor anyone else since Beth had died, suddenly felt the need to talk.

'You're a family man, aren't you?' If he'd he sensed a shift in attentiveness, if Hackett had given him one of his cat's eye once-overs, Nelson would have clammed up immediately, but he didn't.

'Teenage kids don't constitute a family,' Hackett said. 'They constitute trouble.'

Nelson glanced across.

'Don't ask,' Hackett said. 'You don't want to know.'

Nelson thought perhaps he did, which surprised him: he wasn't generally interested in the personal lives of his team. He thought he might even understand. Of course, the boy's psychiatrist wouldn't agree: Dr Smith acted like *he* was the one with the problem and not the boy. 'Rejection, isolation, they're very damaging,' Smith had said.

'I told my boy's shrink today that I'd hated my son ever since my wife died.' Had he really said that, and to a shrink?

'Why?' He sounded curious, rather than horrified.

'Christ knows. I suppose I'm just so bloody knackered I was off my guard.'

'No,' Hackett said. 'I meant, why do you hate him?'

Nelson realized belatedly that this was not something he wanted to discuss in detail. He had expected that he would say what he needed to say to unburden himself and that would be the end of it. He had not been prepared for this interest, even less for direct questions, however, since he had brought the subject up, he felt he had to say something aside from 'mind your own bloody business'.

'The shrink says it wasn't his fault.'

'Your wife's death?'

Nelson felt a shock like a physical blow. *Your wife's death.*

Just like that. Out in the open, like any normal topic of conversation. Like: did you watch the match on the telly last night? or I wish this sodding rain'd stop, or how're the kids — and by the way, *how do you feel about your wife's death?*

'Maybe it wasn't his fault,' Hackett said.

'What do you know?' Nelson demanded. Hackett sighed and went back to reading the paper, leaving Nelson to his thoughts.

It was the boy's fault. If he hadn't been born, she'd've been fine. She was okay until she had Ian. They had given him his name when Beth was seven months pregnant; they had waited until then because Beth didn't want to invite bad luck. And they had loved him, made plans for him, for the three of them. They had loved and wanted their son until he was born, then, because Beth had rejected him, Jack Nelson had no longer wanted the child, either.

'Christ!' he muttered. 'This bloody case is starting to get to me.' He threw the remains of the sandwich out of the window and stifled a belch.

Hackett grunted, distracted. He was poring over the article on Helen Wilkinson. 'This picture,' he said. 'Says here Molyneux took it.'

'So?'

'I've seen it somewhere else . . .'

'Well, where?' Nelson, always on a short fuse, was experiencing the stirrings of irritation.

Hackett's eyes darted right and left, and he seemed to be sifting through his memories like they were on a carousel. Suddenly he stopped. 'Bloody hell . . .' he murmured.

Nelson felt his eyes begin to bug with suppressed tension and readied himself to start yelling, but Hackett spoke just in time:

'There *was* a similar photo — not the same — but very like.' He peered at the newspaper under the car's interior light. 'A different angle, I think. Softer focus. Not so much of the house showing in the background.'

'*Where*, for God's sake?' Nelson exploded.

'It was in Ruth Marks's flat.'

Nelson frowned, running it through in his mind. Cluttered coffee table, steel shelves, coffee brewing to mask the smell of cannabis. Microscope on the table in the turret, mantelshelf a jumble of dusty postcards, wooden monkeys: *see no evil, hear no evil, speak no evil*. Behind them a photograph of Helen Wilkinson.

He shook his head, doubtful. 'Could be a copy from the *Recorder* photo. She could've ordered one.'

'Different picture. I'd swear to it. I think our Dr Marks likes to take mementoes. And if we can prove she got it from Molyneux's flat . . .'

* * *

'You know what it feels like to have that kind of power over someone else, Helen? The power to grant life or take it? It's God-like.' She closed her eyes and relived the moment:

She had slipped downstairs in Helen's dressing gown, to fetch Ed a drink, and had returned to the bedroom with a tall glass of icy beer in one hand and the knife in the other.

'What have you got behind your back?'
'A surprise. Do you want it?'
'That depends. Will I like it?'
'You may not like it, but it's just what you need. And I promise you, I'll be quick.'

'And I got away with it. I watched the police chasing in little circles — they even asked my advice! I tell you, Helen, it feels like I've fallen from a great height without so much as a bruise.'

'Was it revenge? Were you repaying the patronizing and the personal humiliations of a lifetime by killing the greatest chauvinist of all?'

Ruth laughed 'Spare me the psychobabble! I could have walked away — only I felt the need to help you out of the hole you'd dug for yourself.'

'And you wanted to see if you could do it.'

Ruth shrugged, a secret smile, a barely visible raising of her eyebrows.

'They were your keys, weren't they?' Helen said. 'How else could Ellis have got into the house?'

'Interesting choice wasn't it — the mouse, I mean. "The mouse that roared", and all that. I gave him his chance to make his point to you — he bottled out of that, too.'

'He didn't *bottle out*, Ruth, he killed himself.' Helen was shouting. 'Don't you care? Doesn't it matter at all to you?'

Ruth sighed. 'It's not my job to care about every inadequate who takes on more than he can handle. I warned him he was pissing in the wind with his ludicrous research into

Gaia. That's more than Mallory did for him.' She shot Helen a vicious look. 'Or you, for that matter. You were wallowing so deep in self-pity over the miscarriage, it's a wonder you didn't drown in it.'

Helen nodded. 'I was too engrossed in my own misery to see Ellis's; but what's your excuse?'

'Marriage/miscarriage. I wonder if poets ever use it as a rhyme?'

Ruth snapped to, sitting up and rapping the table with her knuckles. 'I don't need an excuse. I'm not sorry, or ashamed, of anything.'

'So is that really all this was?' Helen asked. 'An interesting experiment?'

'It was certainly that.'

'And what *did* I do that made you turn against me?'

Ruth smiled, but refused to answer.

'Is it Mick? Are you jealous of him?'

'Jealous? You replaced an emotional cripple with a physical cripple,' Ruth said. 'I might feel nauseated, but *jealous*?' She puffed air between her lips.

'You know they'll find you,' Helen said. 'The police aren't stupid, Ruth.'

'Perhaps, but they don't have any evidence. Here, look at this.' Ruth dipped into her jeans pocket and took out two fifty pence coins. She slapped them onto the table and looked up at Helen, triumphant. 'I've been walking around with those in my pocket ever since it happened.'

Helen glanced at the coins. 'You'll have to explain.'

Ruth picked up one coin between the thumb and forefinger of her right hand, the other in her left. She closed her eyes and carefully placed a coin on each eyelid. 'You did say his eyes had to be closed.'

Helen recoiled. 'Christ, Ruth, you're sick!'

Ruth tipped forward, catching the coins in the palm of her hand.

'My only sickness was allowing your pitiful defencelessness to affect me, letting myself be taken in by you.'

249

'I wasn't trying to fool anyone, Ruth. I was being what I am: human. I'm sorry if you thought my vulnerability was all of me. That was how I felt at the time. I was being honest with you.'

'Well, then, you're best off without Ed, and I did the right thing.'

'Don't you regret the photographer? And John Ellis?' Helen asked, desperate to find some remnant of humanity in her old friend.

'Ellis would've been turned in by Ed, if he'd lived. Or he'd've pointed the great fat finger of accusation at himself with his flimsy data and his botched results. No. I don't feel sorry for him — I did him a favour.'

'And the photographer — what about him?'

'I hadn't reckoned on the photographer. I don't even know him. Not really. Bit of a flirt, a ladies' man, no doubt, but that's hardly a capital offence. The problem is, when you act on someone else's behalf, there are complications. You have to look out for more than just yourself, and when you're looking out for someone else, sometimes things get by you. Like a photographer with a camera pointed right at you.'

Helen felt suddenly cold. 'What did he see?'

'Me at the window, I'd just put the knife in the bedside cabinet. Of course, he didn't have a shot of that, but he had me, on camera, where I wasn't supposed to be, at about the time a rather unpleasant package had been left in your fridge. If those pictures had been printed, you would have guessed.'

'I guessed anyway.'

Ruth smiled. 'Yes, you did — good for you. But the problem was, with the photographic evidence, the police might have guessed, too.'

'So you tried to kill him.'

'Molyneux took a chance. People in his profession measure risks and weigh them against the potential glory. If he'd pulled it off and got that crisp, clear picture of me, then I'd be the one in deep shit, and he'd be in clover.'

* * *

'It *must've* been taken at the same time as this one,' Hackett said. They were inside Ruth Marks's flat. Hackett held up the newspaper next to the photograph on the mantelshelf.

'It certainly looks like it,' Nelson agreed, peering at it. He glanced over his shoulder, giving the waiting SOCO the signal to get started.

'Is it enough?' Hackett asked.

'The *Recorder* haven't had any requests for that particular photograph from the public,' Nelson said. 'Where else would she get it, but from Molyneux's flat?'

'If we had the knife—'

'We'll search for it here, but I can't see her keeping it. She'd have chucked it by now, wouldn't she?'

Hackett shrugged. 'What about the forensic evidence from the bed? Could we do a match on the pubic hairs?' Hackett addressed this question to the SOCO who had just finished photographing the picture of Helen *in situ*, and was now lifting it with great care, into a flat cardboard box.

'If you get us something to match them with,' the SOCO said.

'That's just what we're about to do,' Nelson said, grinning.

* * *

'You're already up to your neck,' Helen said. 'I know everything. I even know *why*, God help me.'

'You're my friend,' Ruth said, with a smile. 'Friends look out for each other.'

The front doorbell rang and Ruth twitched. 'Hackett, with his warrant to search. What *are* they going to make of all this?' she asked, indicating the knife and the coins lying on the table.

Helen stared hard at her. 'My prints are on the knife. I expect yours aren't. I don't suppose the coins can be traced back to you, or to Edward's body—' Helen stopped.

Perhaps she had seen the shock in Ruth's face: she was thinking of the touching picture of Helen, very like the *House*

251

of Death photograph in the paper, but in this image, by some trick Molyneux had harnessed compassion. There was a softness in the shadows, a kindness in the light — it seemed to understand Helen's sadness. It must have affected the photographer, too, for he had kept it, tacked up on his wall.

'I had to have it,' she with a little groan, closing her eyes against the dazzling stupidity of her actions.

'Have what?' Helen said.

'Another memento, another trophy in the game. How*ever*—' Ruth added, brightening, ignoring Helen's confusion, 'When you analyse it, what exactly have the police got? A knife with Edward's blood and *your* fingerprints on it. A photographer with a fractured skull. His word would add weight to the argument if (if! Makes me breathless just thinking about it) he recovers. His fingerprints and mine on the portrait of you. Only Dermot knows I left him for dead. "Where there's life there's hope," my mother used to say.' She chuckled. 'Where there's life there's uncertainty, more like.'

'*I* know,' Helen said again, quietly. The hall echoed with the continuous ringing of the bell. 'I know you hit that poor man over the head and left him for dead.'

'Self-preservation, Helen.'

'Perhaps I would have protected you if it was only Edward to consider in the case,' Helen said. 'But there is Ellis's suicide. And Molyneux really didn't deserve this.'

'Life and death. It happens to us all,' Ruth said. 'I just decided when, and to whose advantage, that's all.'

Helen stared into Ruth's eyes. 'I wonder if I ever really knew you,' she murmured.

Ruth stared back, wondering how she could have so misjudged the situation. The doorbell kept up its persistent ringing — an alarm, a warning of imminent disaster. Then footsteps in the passage to the side of the house. Between them, a knife, two coins and a chasm of difference.

Ruth snatched up the knife, gripping it by the handle through the plastic bag.

Helen stood. Her chair clattered as it fell and the foot-steps, as if in sympathy, rattled like stones in the side passage of the house.

Helen backed into the hallway. 'Ruth—'

'You've been acting strangely,' Ruth said. 'You never really got over the miscarriage. But I couldn't believe it when you pulled the knife on me. I almost fainted with fright.'

She watched from the kitchen until Helen reached to the front door. It was almost funny seeing her to fumble ineffectively with the latch. 'It's on the mortise,' she said as Helen became frantic.

Helen turned, panting, like a trapped animal trying to find some route of escape.

'Of course, I tried to get out,' Ruth said. 'But you'd locked the doors. I was terrified. You came at me and I tried to grab the knife.' Ruth grasped the blade of the knife, still in the bag, with her left hand and then pulled back with her right. She shuddered slightly but did not take her eyes from Helen.

Helen eyes widened in horror, as fresh blood mingled with the old — Ruth's with Edward's — on the blade. Ruth listened to the blood drip with the regular ticking sound of a clock onto the faded strip of carpet in the hall. She felt suddenly faint and put her right hand against the wall to steady herself. The knife blade left a smear on the wall.

A hammering began at the back door. Ruth turned slightly, distracted by the noise, and by the pain in her left hand, turning back just in time to see Helen pluck a walking stick from the stand next to the front door. She swung, but Ruth ducked and it gouged a hole in the plaster of the wall. Helen ran to the stairs. She managed a few steps, but Ruth seized her ankle and dragged her back, slashing with the knife. The bag, now tattered, flapped like torn skin around the blade, and the handle, slick with blood, slipped in her hand. She tightened her grip and slashed again. It caught Helen's a grazing blow on the leg. Helen screamed, kicking out hard.

A crash of glass, followed by urgent shouts.

Hackett, Ruth thought. The knife fell from her hand and she found herself inexplicably face-down on the stairs. *That's not good.*

She tried to reach for the knife. Her fingers made small movements, but she couldn't seem to give them purpose. Helen was getting away. Get up!

No good. No strength . . .

She heard Helen whisper, Helen 'My God—'

A heavy footfall. Yells of, 'Police! Stay where you are!' Hackett's voice. He'd got in through the kitchen window.

Ruth coughed, turning on her back to greet the policeman, wanting to say something devastating. But she but couldn't make a sound.

She tried to raise her hands to her neck, and heard Helen say, 'No, no, don't—'

Sergeant Hackett was staring down at her with a look of almost comical horror on his face and Ruth knew, instantly, that when Helen lashed out, the knife blade must have slashed her throat.

A second later, Helen was by her side, cradling her head, trying to hold it steady. 'Call for an ambulance,' Helen shouted. 'And fetch some towels.'

Attagirl, Ruth thought, approving the tone of command in Helen's voice.

'The knife has gone deep,' she heard Helen say, as if talking to a child. 'So you need to keep quite still. Do you understand me? It's lodged between the third and fourth cervical vertebrae. Stay very, very still, Ruth.'

She saw tears in Helen's eyes.

Doesn't she know I won't go to prison?

As a neurobiologist, Ruth knew that the nerves located at C4 and C5 controlled the vocal cords. How about that? Helen getting the final word, for once. The same bundle of nerves also controlled breathing. Ruth looked into Helen's blue eyes, brimming with compassion, and smiled. Then with every inch of strength she had left, she gave a sudden convulsive movement which severed her spinal cord.

Helen screamed.

Ruth felt the flare of heat on her face once more: Spring sunshine melting the dusty tarmac of the pot-holed road near her childhood home. She had made the beetle notice — she must have — she could hear its screams — not in her imagination — these were real, high-pitched screams, like a woman's.

Simultaneously, she felt the blade of the knife slip sideways, and the screaming stopped. Everything stopped. And there was only silence.

THE END

ACKNOWLEDGEMENTS

I would like to thank Professor Jeff Parker, of Liverpool University, who sacrificed a sizeable chunk of his busy schedule to discuss Behavioural Ecology research methods with me, and who let me look around the Population Biology Research Group Lab and talk to his postgraduate researchers. For their insight into research techniques, I am grateful.

Any malpractice implied in the story is my own invention, and any errors of scientific procedure, I claim wholly for myself.

FREE KINDLE BOOKS

Made in the USA
Coppell, TX
10 November 2020